WHAT THE WORLD IS READING

Excerpts from a Selection of Bestselling
Paperback Titles from Penguin Group (USA)

PENGUIN

NEW
AMERICAN
LIBRARY

BERKLEY

RIVERHEAD
BOOKS

PLUME

Published by Penguin, Berkley, Riverhead, Plume, and NAL, divisions of
Penguin Group (USA) Inc., 375 Hudson Street,
New York, New York 10014, USA
Penguin Group (Canada), 90 Eglinton Avenue East, Suite 700, Toronto,
Ontario M4P 2Y3, Canada (a division of Pearson Penguin Canada Inc.)
Penguin Books Ltd., 80 Strand, London WC2R 0RL, England
Penguin Ireland, 25 St. Stephen's Green, Dublin 2,
Ireland (a division of Penguin Books Ltd.)
Penguin Group (Australia), 250 Camberwell Road, Camberwell, Victoria 3124,
Australia (a division of Pearson Australia Group Pty. Ltd.)
Penguin Books India Pvt. Ltd., 11 Community Centre, Panchsheel Park,
New Delhi - 110 017, India
Penguin Group (NZ), cnr Airborne and Rosedale Roads, Albany,
Auckland 1310, New Zealand (a division of Pearson New Zealand Ltd.)
Penguin Books (South Africa) (Pty.) Ltd., 24 Sturdee Avenue,
Rosebank, Johannesburg 2196, South Africa

Penguin Books Ltd., Registered Offices:
80 Strand, London WC2R 0RL, England

First published by Penguin and Berkley,
divisions of Penguin Group (USA) Inc.

First Printing, 2009
10 9 8 7 6 5 4 3 2 1

      REGISTERED TRADEMARKS—MARCA REGISTRADA

PENGUIN   NEW AMERICAN LIBRARY   BERKLEY   PLUME

Printed in the United States of America

WHAT THE WORLD IS READING

CONTENTS

from

The Cellist of Sarajevo

by

Steven Galloway

**"This gripping novel transcends time and place.
It is a universal story, and a testimony to the struggle
to find meaning, grace, and humanity, even amid
the most unimaginable horrors."**

—Khaled Hosseini, author of *The Kite Runner* and
A Thousand Splendid Suns

*The acclaimed and inspiring bestseller that is a tribute to the
human spirit.*

*In a city ravaged by war, a musician plays his cello for
twenty-two days at the site of a mortar attack, in memory of
the fallen. Among the strangers drawn into the orbit of his
music are a young father in search of water for his family,
an older man in search of the humanity he once knew, and
a young woman, a sniper, who will decide the fate of the
cellist—and the kind of person she wants to be.*

A novel of great intensity and power, The Cellist
of Sarajevo *is a testament to the subtle ways individuals
reclaim their humanity in a time of war.*

the cellist

It screamed downward, splitting air and sky without effort. A target expanded in size, brought into focus by time and velocity. There was a moment before impact that was the last instant of things as they were. Then the visible world exploded.

In 1945, an Italian musicologist found four bars of a sonata's bass line in the remnants of the firebombed Dresden Music Library. He believed these notes were the work of the seventeenth-century Venetian composer Tomaso Albinoni, and spent the next twelve years reconstructing a larger piece from the charred manuscript fragment. The resulting composition, known as Albinoni's Adagio, bears little resemblance to most of Albinoni's work and is considered fraudulent by most scholars. But even those who doubt its authenticity have difficulty denying the Adagio's beauty.

Nearly half a century later, it's this contradiction that appeals to the cellist. That something could be almost erased from existence in the landscape of a ruined city, and then rebuilt until it is new and worthwhile, gives him hope. A hope that, now, is one of a limited number of things remaining for the besieged citizens of Sarajevo and that, for many, dwindles each day.

And so today, like every other day in recent memory, the cellist sits beside the window of his second-floor apartment and plays until he feels his hope return. He rarely plays the Adagio. Most days he's able to feel the music rejuvenate him as simply as if he were filling a car with gasoline. But some days this isn't the case. If, after several hours, this hope doesn't return, he will pause to gather himself, and then he and his cello will coax Albinoni's Adagio out of the firebombed husk of Dresden and into the mortar-pocked, sniper-infested streets of Sarajevo. By the time the last few notes fade, his hope will be restored, but each time he's forced to resort to the Adagio it becomes harder, and he knows its effect is finite. There are only a certain number of Adagios left in him, and he will not recklessly spend this precious currency.

It wasn't always like this. Not long ago the promise of a happy life seemed almost inviolable. Five years ago, at his sister's wedding, he'd posed for a family photograph, his father's arm slung behind his neck, fingers grasping his shoulder. It was a firm grip, and to some it would have been painful, but to the cellist it was the opposite. The fingers on his flesh told him that he was loved, that he had always been loved, and that the world was a place where above all else the things that were good would find a way to burrow into you. Though he knew all of this then, he would give up nearly anything to be able to go back in time and slow down that moment, if only so he could more clearly recall it now. He would very much like to feel his father's hand on his shoulder again.

He can tell today won't be an Adagio day. It has been only a half hour since he sat down beside the window, but already he feels a little bit better. Outside, a line of people wait to buy bread. It's been over a week since the market's had any bread to buy, and he considers whether he might join them. Many of his friends and neighbors are in line. He decides against it, for now. There's still work to do.

It screamed downward, splitting air and sky without effort. A target expanded in size, brought into focus by time and velocity. There was a moment before impact that was the last instant of things as they were. Then the visible world exploded.

When the mortars destroyed the Sarajevo Opera Hall, the cellist felt as if he were inside the building, as if the bricks and glass that once bound the structure together had become projectiles that sliced and pounded into him, shredding him beyond recognition. He was the principal cellist of the Sarajevo Symphony Orchestra. That was what he knew how to be. He made the idea of music an actuality. When he stepped onstage in his tuxedo he was transformed into an instrument of deliverance. He gave to the people who came to listen what he loved most in the world. He was as solid as the vise of his father's hand.

Now he doesn't care whether anyone hears him play or not. His tuxedo hangs in the closet, untouched. The guns perched on the hills surrounding Sarajevo have dismantled him just as they have the Opera Hall, just as they have his family home in the night while his father and mother slept, just as they will, eventually, everything.

The geography of the siege is simple. Sarajevo is a long ribbon of flat land surrounded on all sides by hills. The men on the hills control all the high ground and one peninsula of level ground in the middle of the city, Grbavica. They fire bullets and mortars and tank shells and grenades into the rest of the city, which is being defended by one tank and small handheld weapons. The city is being destroyed.

The cellist doesn't know what is about to happen. Initially the impact of the shell won't even register. For a long time he'll stand at his window and stare. Through the carnage and confusion he'll notice a woman's handbag, soaked in blood and sparkled with broken glass. He won't be able to tell whom it belongs to. Then he'll look down and see he has dropped his bow on the floor, and somehow it will seem to him that there's a great connection between these two objects. He won't understand what the connection is, but the feeling that it exists will compel him to undress, walk to the closet, and pull the dry cleaner's plastic from his tuxedo.

He will stand at the window all night and all through the next day. Then, at four o'clock in the afternoon, twenty-four hours after the mortar fell on his friends and neighbors while they waited to buy bread, he will bend down and pick up his bow. He will carry his cello and stool down the narrow flight of stairs to the empty street. The war will go on around him as he sits in the small crater left at the mortar's point of impact. He'll play Albinoni's Adagio. He'll do this every day for twenty-two days, a day for each person killed. Or at least he'll try. He won't be sure he will survive. He won't be sure he has enough Adagios left.

The cellist doesn't know any of this now, as he sits at his window in the sun and plays. He isn't yet aware. But it's already on its way. It screams downward, splitting air and sky without effort. A target expands in size, brought into focus by time and velocity. There is a moment before impact that is the last instant of things as they are. Then the visible world explodes.

one

arrow

Arrow blinks. She has been waiting for a long time. Through the scope of her rifle she can see three soldiers standing beside a low wall on a hill above Sarajevo. One looks at the city as though he's remembering something. One holds out a lighter so another can light a cigarette. It's obvious they have no idea they're in her sights. Perhaps, she thinks, they believe they're too far from the front line. They're wrong. Perhaps they think no one could thread a bullet between the buildings that separate them from her. Again, they're wrong. She can kill any one of them, and maybe even two of them, whenever she chooses. And soon she'll make her choice.

The soldiers Arrow is watching have good reason to think they're safe. Were almost anyone else hunting them, they would be. They're almost a kilometer away, and the rifle she uses, the kind nearly all the defenders use, has a practical range of eight hundred meters. Beyond that, the chances of hitting a target are remote. This isn't the case for Arrow. She can make a bullet do things that others can't.

For most people, long-distance shooting is a question of the correct combination of observation and mathematics. Figure out the wind's speed and direction, and the target's distance. Measurements are calculated and factored into equations taking into account the velocity of the bullet, the drop over time, the magnification of the scope. It's no different from throwing a ball. A ball isn't thrown at a target, it's thrown in an arc calculated to intersect with a target. Arrow doesn't take measurements, she doesn't calculate formulas. She simply sends the bullet where she knows it needs to go. She has trouble understanding why other snipers can't do this.

She's hidden among the detritus of a burned-out office tower, a few meters back from a window with a view of the city's southern hills. Anyone looking would have a difficult if not impossible time spotting a slight young woman with shoulder-length black hair concealed within the smoking wreckage of workaday life. She lies with her stomach pressed to the floor, her legs partially covered by an old newspaper. Her eyes, large, blue, and bright, are the only sign of life.

Arrow believes she's different from the snipers on the hills. She shoots only soldiers. They shoot unarmed men, women, children. When they kill a person, they seek a result that is far greater than the elimination of that individual. They are trying to kill the city. Every death chips away at the Sarajevo of Arrow's youth with as much certainty as any mortar shell battering a building. Those left are robbed of not only a fellow citizen but the memory of what it was to be alive in a time before men on the hills shot at you while you tried to cross the street.

Ten years ago, when she was eighteen and was not called Arrow, she borrowed her father's car and drove to the countryside to visit friends. It was a bright, clear day, and the car felt alive to her, as though the way she and the car moved together was a sort of destiny, and everything was happening exactly as it ought to. As she rounded a corner one of her favorite songs came on the radio, and sunlight filtered through the trees the way it does with lace curtains, reminding her of her grandmother, and tears began to slide down her cheeks. Not for her grandmother, who was then still very much among the living, but because she felt an enveloping happiness to be alive, a joy made stronger by the certainty that someday it would all come to an end. It overwhelmed her, made her pull the car to the side of the road. Afterward she felt a little foolish, and never spoke to anyone about it.

Now, however, she knows she wasn't being foolish. She realizes that for no particular reason she stumbled into the core of what it is to be human. It's a rare gift to understand that your life is wondrous, and that it won't last forever.

So when Arrow pulls the trigger and ends the life of one of the soldiers in her sights, she'll do so not because she wants him dead, although she can't deny that she does, but because the soldiers have robbed her and almost everyone else in the city of this gift. That life will end has become so self-evident it's lost all meaning. But worse, for Arrow, is the damage done to the distance between what she knows and what she believes. For although she knows her tears that day were not the ridiculous sentimentality of a teenage girl, she doesn't really believe it.

From the elevated fortress of Vraca, above the occupied neighborhood of Grbavica, her targets bomb the city with assumed impunity. In the Second World War, Vraca was a place where the Nazis tortured and killed those who resisted them. The names of the dead are carved on the steps, but at the time few fighters used their real names. They took new names, names that said more about them than any boastful story told by drunks in a bar, names that defied the governments who later tried to twist their deeds into propaganda. It's said they took these new names so their families wouldn't be in danger, so they could slip in and out of two lives. But Arrow believes they took these names so they could separate themselves from what they had to do, so the person who fought and killed could someday be put away. To hate people because they hated her first, and then to hate them because of what they've done to her, has created a desire to separate the part of her that will fight back, that will enjoy fighting back, from the part that never wanted to fight in the first place. Using her real name would make her no different from the men she kills. It would be a death greater than the end of her life.

From the first time she picked up a rifle to kill she has called herself Arrow. There are some who continue to call her by her former name. She ignores them. If they persist, she tells them her name is Arrow now. No one argues. No one questions what she must do. Everyone does something to stay alive. But if they were to press her, she would say, "I am Arrow, because I hate them. The woman you knew hated nobody."

Arrow has chosen today's targets because she doesn't want the men at Vraca to feel safe. She will have to make an extremely difficult shot. Though she hides on the ninth floor of this depredated building, the fortress is an uphill run, and she must slip the bullet between a series of buildings that stand between her and her target. The soldiers must stay within a space of about three meters, and smoke from burning buildings periodically obscures her view. As soon as she lets off a shot, every sniper on the southern hill will begin to search for her. They'll quickly figure out where she is. At that point they'll shell the building, into the ground if necessary. And the reason this building is burned out is that it's an easy target. Her chances of escaping the repercussions of her own bullets are slim. But this isn't an unusual set of challenges. She has sent bullets through trickier air and faced swifter retaliation in the past.

Arrow knows exactly how long it will take them to locate her. She knows exactly where the snipers will look and exactly where the mortars will hit. By the time the shelling stops she'll be gone, though none will understand how, even those on her own side defending the city. If she told them they wouldn't understand. They wouldn't believe that she knows what a weapon will do because Arrow herself is a weapon. She possesses a particular kind of genius few would want to accept. If she could choose, she wouldn't believe in it either. But she knows it isn't up to her. You don't choose what to believe. Belief chooses you.

One of the three soldiers moves away from the other two. Arrow tenses, waiting to see if the two salute him. If they do she will fire. For a moment she's unsure, unable to read their gestures. Then the soldier steps out of the narrow corridor her bullet can travel through. He has, in an instant of seeming inconsequence, saved his life. A life is composed almost entirely of actions like this, Arrow knows.

She watches them a while longer, waiting for a detail to emerge that will dictate which one receives the first bullet. She wants to fire twice, to kill both of them, but she isn't confident there will be that opportunity, and if she must choose just one of the soldiers she would like to make the right choice, if there's a right choice to be made. Ultimately she doesn't believe it will make much difference. Perhaps one of them will live, but he'll never understand how slim the margin of his existence is. He will chalk it up to luck, or fate, or merit. He'll never know that an arbitrary fraction of a millimeter in her aim one way or another will make the difference between feeling the sun on his face ten minutes from now and looking down to see an unbelievable hole in his chest feeling all he was or could have become drain out of him, and then, in his final moments, inhaling more pain than he knew the world could hold.

One of the soldiers says something and laughs. The other one joins in, but from the tightness in his mouth it seems to Arrow that his laugh is perhaps only for his companion's benefit. She ponders this. Does she shoot the instigator or the collaborator? She's not sure. For the next few minutes she watches the two men smoke and talk. Their hands trace hard shapes through the air, physical punctuation, sometimes pausing, like knives poised in anticipation of a strike. They're both young, younger than she is, and if she wished herself into ignorance she could almost imagine they were discussing the outcome of a recent football match. Perhaps, she thinks, they are. It's possible, even likely, that they view this as some sort of game. Boys throwing bombs instead of balls.

Then they both turn their heads as though called by someone Arrow can't see, and she knows the time to fire has come. Nothing has made a decision for her, so Arrow simply chooses one. If there's a reason, if it's because one shot is easier, or one of them reminds her of someone she once knew and liked or didn't like, or one of them seems more dangerous than the other, she can't say. The only certainty is that she exhales and her finger goes from resting on the trigger to squeezing it, and a bullet breaks the sound barrier an instant before pulping fabric, skin, bone, flesh, and organ, beginning a short process that will turn motion into meat.

As Arrow readies her second shot, in the time between the tick of one second and another, she knows that something has gone wrong. The men on the hills know where she is. She abandons her shot and rolls to the side, aware of eyes upon her, that a sniper has been hunting her all along, and the instant she shot she was exposed. They have set a trap for her and she has fallen into it. A bullet hits the floor where she lay an instant before. As she scuttles toward the skeleton of a staircase that will lead her nine flights down and out of the building she hears a rifle fire, but doesn't hear the bullet strike. This means either the sniper has missed entirely or she has been hit. She doesn't feel any pain, though she's heard you don't at first. There isn't any need to check if she's hit. If a bullet has found her she'll know soon enough.

Arrow enters the stairwell and a mortar comes through the roof and explodes. She's two flights down when another lands, sending the ninth floor crumbling into the eighth. As she reaches the sixth floor the texture of the situation shifts in her mind, and she veers into a dark, narrow hallway and moves as quickly as she can away from the mortar she knows is about to penetrate the stairwell. She manages to make it far enough to avoid the steel and wood and concrete the explosion sends her, a multitude of bullets as interest paid on the loan of one. But then, as the last piece of shrapnel hits the ground, she turns and runs back toward the staircase. She has no choice. There's no other way out of this building, and if she stays she will collect on her loan. So she returns to the stairwell, not knowing what remains of it. The sixth floor has collapsed into the fifth, and when she jumps to the landing below she wonders if it will bear her. It does, and from there it's a matter of staying tight against the inner wall where the stairs meet the building, where the weight of the upper layers of the collapsed stairway has had less impact.

Arrow hears another mortar hit as she reaches the ground, and although the front entrance leading to the street is only steps away she continues to the basement, where she feels her way along a dim corridor until she finds a door. She shoulders it open. The immediate shift from darkness to light momentarily blinds her, but she emerges without hesitation into a low stairwell on the north side of the building, somewhat sheltered from the men on the southern hill. Before her eyes adjust to the world around her she begins to notice the percussion of mortars affecting her hearing, and it reminds her of being in a swimming pool, of a day when she and a friend took turns shouting each other's names underwater and laughing at how they came out, all garbled and distorted and foreign. When she turns east, away from the building, she feels a pain in her side, and she looks down, half expecting to see her stomach distended between splintered ribs. A quick inspection reveals only a slight cut, a small nothing that attached itself to her at some point during her exit.

As she walks toward her unit's headquarters in the city

center, she notices that the sky is beginning to darken. A few drops of rain hit her forehead, make her feel her own heat as they evaporate. When she touches her side, her hand comes away without any fresh blood on it, and Arrow wonders what it means that the insignificance of her injury does not bring her any particular sense of relief.

from

City of Thieves

by

David Benioff

"No recent novel I've read travels so quickly and surely between registers, from humor to devastation. . . . Benioff reminds us what a beautifully ambiguous world we live in."
—*The New York Times Book Review*

During the Nazis' brutal siege of Leningrad, Lev Beniov is arrested for looting and thrown into the same cell as a handsome deserter named Kolya. Instead of being executed, Lev and Kolya are given a shot at saving their own lives by complying with an outrageous directive: secure a dozen eggs for a powerful Soviet colonel to use in his daughter's wedding cake. In a city cut off from all supplies and suffering unbelievable deprivation, Lev and Kolya embark on a hunt through the dire lawlessness of Leningrad and behind enemy lines to find the impossible.

By turns insightful and funny, thrilling and terrifying, City of Thieves *is a gripping, cinematic World War II adventure and an intimate coming-of-age story with an utterly contemporary feel for how boys become men.*

You have never been so hungry; you have never been so cold. When we slept, if we slept, we dreamed of the feasts we had carelessly eaten seven months earlier—all that buttered bread, the potato dumplings, the sausages—eaten with disregard, swallowing without tasting, leaving great crumbs on our plates, scraps of fat. In June of 1941, before the Germans came, we thought we were poor. But June seemed like paradise by winter.

At night the wind blew so loud and long it startled you when it stopped; the shutter hinges of the burned-out café on the corner would quit creaking for a few ominous seconds, as if a predator neared and the smaller animals hushed in terror. The shutters themselves had been torn down for firewood in November. There was no more scrap wood in Leningrad. Every wood sign, the slats of the park benches, the floorboards of shattered buildings—all gone and burning in someone's stove. The pigeons were missing, too, caught and stewed in melted ice from the Neva. No one minded slaughtering pigeons. It was the dogs and cats that caused trouble. You would hear a rumor in October that someone had roasted the family mutt and split it four ways for supper; we'd laugh and shake our heads, not believing it, and also wondering if dog tasted good with enough salt—there was still plenty of salt, even when everything else ran out we had salt. By January the rumors had become plain fact. No one but the best connected could still feed a pet, so the pets fed us.

There were two theories on the fat versus the thin. Some said

those who were fat before the war stood a better chance of survival:
a week without food would not transform a plump man into a skeleton. Others said skinny people were more accustomed to eating
little and could better handle the shock of starvation. I stood in the
latter camp, purely out of self-interest. I was a runt from birth. Big
nosed, black haired, skin scribbled with acne—let's admit I was no
girl's idea of a catch. But war made me more attractive. Others
dwindled as the ration cards were cut and cut again, halving those
who looked like circus strongmen before the invasion. I had no
muscle to lose. Like the shrews that kept scavenging while the dino-
saurs toppled around them, I was built for deprivation.

On New Year's Eve I sat on the rooftop of the Kirov, the apartment building where I'd lived since I was five (though it had no
name until '34, when Kirov was shot and half the city was named
after him), watching the fat gray antiaircraft blimps swarm under
the clouds, waiting for the bombers. That time of year the sun lin-
gers in the sky for only six hours, scurrying from horizon to horizon
as if spooked. Every night four of us would sit on the roof for
a three-hour shift, armed with sand pails, iron tongs, and shovels,
bundled in all the shirts and sweaters and coats we could find,
watching the skies. We were the firefighters. The Germans had decided rushing the city would be too costly, so instead they encircled
us, intending to starve us out, bomb us out, burn us out.

Before the war began eleven hundred people lived in the Kirov.
By New Year's Eve the number was closer to four hundred. Most
of the small children were evacuated before the Germans closed
the circle in September. My mother and little sister, Taisya, went to
Vyazma to stay with my uncle. The night before they left I fought
with my mother, the only fight we'd ever had—or, more precisely,
the only time I ever fought back. She wanted me to go with them, of
course, far away from the invaders, deep into the heart of the country where the bombers couldn't find us. But I wasn't leaving Piter. I
was a man, I would defend my city, I would be a Nevsky for the
twentieth century. Perhaps I wasn't quite this ridiculous. I had a
real argument: if every able-bodied soul fled, Leningrad would fall

to the Fascists. And without Leningrad, without the City of Workers building tanks and rifles for the Red Army, what chance did Russia have?

My mother thought this was a stupid argument. I was barely seventeen. I didn't weld armor at the Works and I couldn't enlist in the army for close to a year. The defense of Leningrad had nothing to do with me; I was just another mouth to feed. I ignored these insults.

"I'm a firefighter," I told her, because it was true, the city council had ordered the creation of ten thousand firefighting units, and I was the proud commander of the Kirov Fifth-Floor Brigade.

My mother wasn't forty years old, but her hair was already gray. She sat across from me at the kitchen table, holding one of my hands in both of hers. She was a very small woman, barely five feet tall, and I had been afraid of her from birth.

"You are an idiot," she told me. Maybe this sounds insulting, but my mother always called me "her idiot" and by that point I thought of it as an affectionate nickname. "The city was here before you. It will be here after you. Taisya and I need you."

She was right. A better son would have gone with her, a better brother. Taisya adored me, jumped on me when I came home from school, read me the silly little poems she wrote as homework to honor martyrs of the revolution, drew caricatures of my big-nosed profile in her notebook. Generally, I wanted to strangle her. I had no desire to tramp across the country with my mother and kid sister. I was seventeen, flooded with a belief in my own heroic destiny. Molotov's declaration during his radio address on the first day of the war (OUR CAUSE IS JUST! THE ENEMY WILL BE BEATEN! WE SHALL TRIUMPH!) had been printed on thousands of posters and pasted on the city's walls. I believed in the cause; I would not flee the enemy; I would not miss out on the triumph.

Mother and Taisya left the next morning. They rode a bus part of the way, flagged down army trucks for rides, and walked endless miles on country roads in their split-soled boots. It took them three weeks to get there, but they made it, safe at last. She sent me a letter describing her journey, the terror and fatigue. Maybe she wanted me to feel guilty for abandoning them, and I did, but I also knew it was better with them gone. The great fight was coming and they did not belong on the front. On the seventh of October the Germans took Vyazma and her letters stopped coming.

I'd like to say I missed them when they were gone, and some nights I was lonely, and always I missed my mother's cooking, but I had fantasized about being on my own since I was little. My favorite folktales featured resourceful orphans who make their way through the dark forest, surviving all perils with clever problem solving, outwitting their enemies, finding their fortune in the midst of their wanderings. I wouldn't say I was happy—we were all too hungry to be happy—but I believed that here at last was the Meaning. If Leningrad fell, Russia would fall; if Russia fell, Fascism would conquer the world. All of us believed this. I still believe it.

So I was too young for the army but old enough to dig antitank ditches by day and guard the roofs by night. Manning my crew were my friends from the fifth floor—Vera Osipovna, a talented cellist, and the redheaded Antokolsky twins, whose only known talent was an ability to fart in harmony. In the early days of the war we had smoked cigarettes on the roof, posing as soldiers, brave and strong and square-chinned, scanning the skies for the enemy. By the end of December there were no cigarettes in Leningrad, at least none made with tobacco. A few desperate souls crushed fallen leaves, rolled them in paper, and called them Autumn Lights, claiming the right leaves provided a decent smoke, but in the Kirov, far from the nearest standing tree, this was never an option. We spent our spare minutes hunting rats, who must have thought the disappearance of the city's cats was the answer to all their ancient prayers, until they realized there was nothing left to eat in the garbage.

After months of bombing raids we could identify the various German planes by the pitch of their engines. That night it was the Junkers 88s, as it had been for weeks, replacing the Heinkels and Dorniers that our fighters had gotten good at gunning down. As wretched as our city had become in daylight, after dark there was a strange beauty in the siege. From the roof of the Kirov, if the moon was out, we could see all of Leningrad: the needlepoint of the Admiralty tower (splashed with gray paint to obscure it from the bombers); the Peter and Paul Fortress (spires draped with camouflage netting); the domes of Saint Isaac's and the Church on Spilled Blood. We could see the crews manning the antiaircraft guns on the rooftops of neighboring buildings. The Baltic Fleet had dropped anchor on the Neva; they floated there, giant gray sentries, firing their big guns at the Nazi artillery emplacements.

Most beautiful were the dogfights. The Ju88s and the Sukhois circled above the city, invisible from below unless they were caught in the eyes of the powerful searchlights. The Sukhois had large red stars painted on the undersides of their wings so our antiaircraft crews wouldn't shoot them down. Every few nights we'd see a battle spotlit as if for the stage, the heavier, slower German bombers banking hard to let their gunners get a bead on the darting Russian fighters. When a Junkers went down, the plane's burning carcass falling like an angel cast from heaven, a great shout of defiance rose up from rooftops all across the city, all the gunners and firefighters shaking their fists to salute the victorious pilot.

We had a little radio on the roof with us. On New Year's Eve we listened to the Spassky chimes in Moscow playing the *"Internationale."* Vera had found half an onion somewhere; she cut it into four pieces on a plate smeared with sunflower oil. When the onion was gone, we mopped up the remaining oil with our ration bread. Ration bread did not taste like bread. It did not taste like food. After the Germans bombed the Badayev grain warehouses, the city bakeries got creative. Everything that could be added to the recipe without poisoning people was added to the recipe. The entire city was starving, no one had enough to eat, and still, everyone cursed the bread, the sawdust flavor, how hard it got in the cold. People broke their teeth trying to chew it. Even today, even when I've forgotten the faces of people I loved, I can still remember the taste of that bread.

Half an onion and a 125-gram loaf of bread split four ways—this was a decent meal. We lay on our backs, wrapped in blankets, watching the air-raid blimps on their long tethers drifting in the wind, listening to the radio's metronome. When there was no music to play or news to report, the radio station transmitted the sound of a metronome, that endless tick-tick-tick letting us know the city was still unconquered, the Fascists still outside the gate. The broadcast metronome was Piter's beating heart and the Germans never stilled it.

It was Vera who spotted the man falling from the sky. She shouted and pointed and we all stood to get a better look. One of the searchlights shone on a parachutist descending toward the city, his silk canopy a white tulip bulb above him.

"A Fritz," said Oleg Antokolsky, and he was right; we could see the gray Luftwaffe uniform. Where had he come from? None of us had heard the sounds of aerial combat or the report of an AA gun. We hadn't heard a bomber passing overhead for close to an hour.

"Maybe it's started," said Vera. For weeks we'd been hearing rumors that the Germans were preparing a massive paratrooper drop, a final raid to pluck the miserable thorn of Leningrad from their advancing army's backside. At any minute we expected to look up and see thousands of Nazis drifting toward the city, a snowstorm of white parachutes blotting out the sky, but dozens of searchlights slashed through the darkness and found no more enemies. There was only this one, and judging from the limpness of the body suspended from the parachute harness, he was already dead.

We watched him drift down, frozen in the searchlight, low enough that we could see that one of his black boots was missing.

"He's coming our way," I said. The wind blew him toward Voinova Street. The twins looked at each other.

"Luger," said Oleg.

"Luftwaffe don't carry Lugers," said Grisha. He was five minutes older and the authority on Nazi weaponry. "Walther PPK."

Vera smiled at me. "German chocolate."

We ran for the stairway door, abandoning our firefighting tools, racing down the dark stairwell. We were fools, of course. A slip on one of those concrete steps, with no fat or muscle to cushion the fall, meant a broken bone, and a broken bone meant death. But none of us cared. We were very young and a dead German was falling onto Voinova Street carrying gifts from *das Vaterland*.

We sprinted through the courtyard and climbed over the locked gate. All the streetlamps were dark. The entire city was dark—partly to make the job tougher for the bombers and partly because most of the electricity was diverted to the munitions factories—but the moon was bright enough to see by. Voinova was wide open and deserted, six hours into curfew. No cars in sight. Only the military and government had access to gasoline, and all the civilian autos had been requisitioned during the first months of the war. Strips of paper crossed the shop windows, which the radio told us made them more resistant to shattering. Maybe this was true, though I had walked by many storefronts in Leningrad where nothing remained in the window frame but a dangling strip of paper.

Out on the street we looked into the sky but could not find our man.

"Where'd he go?"

"You think he landed on a roof?"

The searchlights were tracking the sky, but they were all mounted on top of tall buildings and none of them had an angle to shine down Voinova Street. Vera tugged on the collar of my greatcoat, a vast old navy coat inherited from my father and still too big for me, but warmer than anything else I owned.

I turned and saw him gliding down the street, our German, his single black boot skidding over the frozen pavement, the great canopy of his white parachute still swollen in the wind, blowing him toward the gates of the Kirov, his chin slumped against his chest, his dark hair flecked with crystals of ice, his face bloodless in the moonlight. We stood very still and watched him sail closer. We had seen things that winter no eyes should ever see, we thought we were beyond surprise, but we were wrong, and if the German had drawn his Walther and begun shooting, none of us would have been able to get our feet moving in time. But the dead man stayed dead and at last the wind gave out, the parachute deflated, and he slumped to the pavement, dragged another few meters facedown in final humiliation.

We gathered around the pilot. He was a tall man, well built, and if we had seen him walking around Piter in street clothes, we would have known him at once for an infiltrator—he had the body of a man who ate meat every day.

Grisha knelt and unholstered the German's sidearm. "Walther PPK. Told you."

We rolled the German onto his back. His pale face was scuffed, the skin scraped on the asphalt, the abrasions as colorless as the intact skin. The dead don't bruise. I couldn't tell if he had died frightened or defiant or peaceful. There was no trace of life or personality in his face—he looked like a corpse who had been born a corpse.

Oleg stripped off the black leather gloves while Vera went for the scarf and goggles. I found a sheath strapped to the pilot's ankle and pulled out a beautifully weighted knife with a silver finger guard and a fifteen-centimeter single-edge blade etched with words I could not read in the moonlight. I resheathed the blade and strapped it to my own ankle, feeling for the first time in months that my warrior destiny was at last coming true.

Oleg found the dead man's wallet and grinned as he counted out the deutsche marks. Vera pocketed a chronometer, twice as big as a wristwatch, that the German had worn around the sleeve of his flight jacket. Grisha found a pair of folded binoculars in a leather case, two extra magazines for the Walther, and a slim hip flask. He unscrewed the cap, sniffed, and passed me the flask.

"Cognac?"

I took a sip and nodded. "Cognac."

"When did you ever taste cognac?" asked Vera.

"I've had it before."

"When?"

"Let me see," said Oleg, and the bottle went around the circle, the four of us squatting on our haunches around the fallen pilot, sipping the liquor that might have been cognac or brandy or Armagnac. None of us knew the difference. Whatever it was, the stuff was warmth in the belly.

Vera stared at the German's face. Her expression held no pity, no fear, only curiosity and contempt—the invader had come to drop his bombs on our city and instead had dropped himself. We hadn't shot him down, but we felt triumphant anyway. No one else in the Kirov had come across an enemy's corpse. We would be the talk of the apartment bloc in the morning.

"How do you think he died?" she asked. No bullet wounds blemished the body, no singed hair or leather, no sign of any violence at all. His skin was far too white for the living, but nothing had pierced it.

"He froze to death," I told them. I said it with authority because I knew it was true and I had no way to prove it. The pilot had bailed out thousands of meters above nighttime Leningrad. The air at ground level was too cold for the clothes he was wearing—up in the clouds, outside of his warm cockpit, he never had a chance.

Grisha raised the flask in salute. "Here's to the cold."

The flask began to circle again. It never got to me. We should have heard the car's engine from two blocks away, the city after curfew was quiet as the moon, but we were busy drinking our German liquor, making our toasts. Only when the GAZ turned onto Voinova Street, heavy tires rattling on the asphalt, headlights stabbing toward us, did we realize the danger. The punishment for violating curfew without a permit was summary execution. The punishment for abandoning a firefighting detail was summary execution. The punishment for looting was summary execution. The courts no longer operated; the police officers were on the front lines, the prisons half full and dwindling fast. Who had food for an enemy of the state? If you broke the law and you were caught, you were dead. There wasn't time for any legal niceties.

So we ran. We knew the Kirov better than anyone. Once we got inside the courtyard gates and into the chilled darkness of the sprawling building, no one could find us if they had three months to search. We could hear the soldiers shouting at us to stop, but that didn't matter; voices didn't frighten us, only bullets made a difference and no one had pulled a trigger yet. Grisha made it to the gate first—he was the closest thing to an athlete among us—he leaped onto the iron bars and hoisted himself upward. Oleg was right behind him and I was behind Oleg. Our bodies were weak, muscles shrunken from lack of protein, but fear helped us scale the gate as quickly as we ever had.

Near the top of the gate I looked back and saw that Vera had slipped on a patch of ice. She stared up at me, her eyes round and fearful, on her hands and knees as the GAZ braked beside the body of the German pilot and four soldiers stepped out. They were ten meters away, their rifles in their hands, but I still had time to pull myself over the gate and disappear into the Kirov.

I wish I could tell you that the thought of deserting Vera never entered my mind, that my friend was in danger and I went to her rescue without hesitation. Truly, though, at that moment I hated her. I hated her for being clumsy at the worst possible time, for staring up at me with her panicked brown eyes, electing me to be her savior even though Grisha was the only one she had ever kissed. I knew that I could not live with the memory of those eyes pleading for me, and she knew it, too, and I hated her even as I jumped down from the gate, lifted her to her feet, and hauled her to the iron bars. I was weak, but Vera couldn't have weighed forty kilos. I boosted her onto the gate as the soldiers shouted and their boot heels slapped on the pavement and the bolts of their rifles snapped into place.

Vera went over the top and I scrambled up behind her, ignoring the soldiers. If I stopped, they would gather around me, tell me I was an enemy of the state, force me to kneel, and shoot me in the back of the head. I was an easy target now, but maybe they were drunk, maybe they were city boys like me who had never fired a shot before in their lives; maybe they would miss on purpose because they knew I was a patriot and a defender of the city and I had snuck out of the Kirov only because a German had fallen five thousand meters onto my street, and what seventeen-year-old Russian boy would not sneak outside to peek at a dead Fascist?

My chin was level with the top of the gate when I felt the gloved hands wrap around my ankles. Strong hands, the hands of army men who ate two meals every day. I saw Vera run inside the Kirov, never looking back. I tried to cling to the iron bars, but the soldiers dragged me down, tossed me to the sidewalk, and stood above me, the muzzles of their Tokarevs jabbing at my cheeks. None of the soldiers looked older than nineteen and none seemed reluctant to splatter the street with my brains.

"Looks ready to shit himself, this one."

"You having a party here, son? Found yourself some schnapps?"

"He's a good one for the colonel. He can ride with the Fritz."

Two of them bent down, grabbed me under the armpits, yanked me to my feet, guided me to the still-idling GAZ, and shoved me into the backseat. The other two soldiers lifted the German by his hands and boots and swung him into the car beside me.

"Keep him warm," one of them said, and they all laughed as if it were the funniest joke ever told. They squeezed into the car and slammed the doors.

I decided I was still alive because they wanted to execute me in public, as a warning to other looters. A few minutes before, I had felt far more powerful than the dead pilot. Now, as we sped down the dark street, swerving to avoid bomb craters and sprays of rubble, he seemed to be smirking at me, his white lips a scar splitting his frozen face. We were going the same way.

f you grew up in Piter, you grew up fearing the Crosses, that gloomy redbrick stain on the Neva, a brutish, brooding warehouse of the lost. Six thousand convicts lived there in peacetime. I doubt a thousand were left by January. Hundreds imprisoned for petty crimes were released into Red Army units, released into the meat grinder of the German Blitzkrieg. Hundreds more starved in their cells. Each day the guards dragged the skin-draped skeletons out of the Crosses and onto sledges where the dead were stacked eight high.

When I was small, it was the silence of the prison that frightened me most. You walked by expecting to hear the shouts of rough men or the clamor of a brawl, but no noise escaped the thick walls, as if the prisoners inside—most of them awaiting trial or a trip to the gulag or a bullet in the head—hacked out their own tongues to protest their fate. The place was an antifortress, designed to keep the enemies inside, and every boy in Leningrad had heard the phrase a hundred times: "You keep on with that and you'll end up in the Crosses."

I had seen my cell only for a second when the guards shoved me inside, their lamps shining on the rough stone walls, a cell two meters wide and four meters long, with bunk beds for four and all of them empty. I was relieved at that, I didn't want to share the darkness with a stranger with tattooed knuckles, but after a time—

minutes? hours?—the black silence began to feel tangible, something that could get into your lungs and drown you.

Darkness and solitude generally didn't frighten me. Electricity was as rare as bacon in Piter those days, and my apartment in the Kirov was empty now that Mother and Taisya had fled. The long nights were dark and quiet, but there was always noise somewhere. Mortars fired from the Germans lines; an army truck motoring down the boulevard; the dying old woman upstairs moaning in her bed. Awful sounds, really, but *sounds*—something to let you know you were still in this world. That cell in the Crosses was the only truly silent place I'd ever entered. I could hear nothing at all; I could see nothing. They had locked me in death's waiting room.

As siege-hardened as I believed I was before my arrest, the truth was that I had no more courage in January than I had in June— contrary to popular belief, the experience of terror does not make you braver. Perhaps, though, it is easier to hide your fear when you're afraid all the time.

I tried to think of a song to sing, a poem to recite, but all the words were stuck inside my head like salt in a caked shaker. I lay on one of the top bunks, hoping whatever heat existed within the Crosses would rise and find me. Morning promised nothing but a bullet in the brain and yet I longed for daylight to seep inside. When they dumped me in the cell, I thought I had seen a sliver of barred window near the ceiling, but now I couldn't remember. I tried counting to a thousand to pass some time but always got lost around four hundred, hearing phantom rats that turned out to be my own fingers scratching the torn mattress.

The night was never going to end. The Germans had shot down the fucking sun, they could do it, why not, their scientists were the best in the world, they could figure it out. They had learned how to stop time. I was blind and deaf. Only the cold and my thirst re- minded me that I was alive. You get so lonely you start longing for the sentries, just to hear their footsteps, smell the vodka on their breath.

So many great Russians endured long stretches in prison. That night I learned I would never be a great Russian. A few hours alone in a cell, suffering no torture other than the darkness and the silence and the absolute cold, a few hours of that and I was already half broken. The fierce souls who survived winter after winter in Siberia possessed something I did not, great faith in some splendid destiny, whether God's kingdom or justice or the distant promise of revenge. Or maybe they were so beaten down they became nothing more than animals on their hind legs, working at their masters' command, eating whatever slop he threw down for them, sleeping when ordered and dreaming of nothing but the end.

At last there was noise, footsteps, several sets of heavy boots clomping in the corridor. A key turned in the lock. I sat up in bed and cracked my skull against the ceiling, hard enough that I bit through my lip.

Two guards—one of them holding an oil lamp, the prettiest light I ever saw, better than any sunrise—escorted a new prisoner, a young, uniformed soldier who glanced around the cell like a man viewing an apartment he's considering for rent. The soldier was tall and stood very straight; he towered over the guards, and though they had pistols in their holsters and the soldier was unarmed, he seemed ready to give orders. He held his Astrakhan fur hat in one hand and his leather gloves in the other.

He looked at me just as the guards left, shutting the cell door and bolting it from the outside, taking their light with them. His face was the last thing I saw before the darkness resumed, so it stuck in my mind: the high Cossack cheekbones, the amused twist of the lips, the hay-blond hair, the eyes blue enough to please any Aryan bride.

I sat on the bed and he stood on the stone floor and from the perfect silence I knew neither of us had shifted position—we were still staring at each other in the darkness.

"Are you a Jew?" he asked.

"What?"

"A Jew. You look like a Jew."

"You look like a Nazi."

"I know. *Ich spreche ein bisschen Deutsch,* too. I volunteered to be a spy, but nobody listened to me. So, you are a Jew?"

"Why do you care?"

"Don't be ashamed of it. I don't have a problem with Jews. Emanuel Lasker is my second-favorite chess player. Just a rung under Capablanca. . . . Capablanca is Mozart, pure genius; you can't love chess and not love Capablanca. But Lasker, nobody's better in the endgame. You have any food?"

"No."

"Put out your hand."

This seemed like some sort of trap, a game children played to snare morons. He would slap my palm or just let it hang there till I realized my stupidity. But no offer of food could be refused, even the least likely, so I stretched my hand into the darkness and waited. A moment later a sliver of something cold and greasy sat on my palm. I don't know how he found my hand, but he did, without any fumbling.

"Sausage," he said. And then, after a pause, "Don't worry. It's not pork."

"I eat pork." I sniffed at the sausage and then nibbled off a bit. It was as far from real meat as ration bread from real bread, but there was fat in it, and fat was life. I chewed on the sliver as slowly as I could, trying to make it last.

"You chew loudly," he told me, a reprimand from the dark. I heard the creak of bedsprings as he sat on one of the lower bunk beds. "And you're supposed to say thank you."

"Thank you."

"You're welcome. What's your name?"

"Lev."

"Lev what?"

"What do you care?"

"It's just manners," he said. "For instance, if I introduce myself, I say, 'Good evening, my name is Nikolai Alexandrovich Vlasov, my friends call me Kolya.'"

"You just want to know if I have a Jewish name."

"Do you?"

"Yes."

"Ah." He sighed happily, pleased to hear his instincts confirmed. "Thank you. Don't know why you're so afraid of telling people."

I didn't answer. If he didn't know why, there was no point explaining it.

"So why are you here?" he asked.

"They caught me looting a dead German on Voinova Street."

This alarmed him. "The Germans are already on Voinova? So it's begun?"

"Nothing's begun. He was a bomber pilot. He ejected."

"The AA boys got him?"

"The cold got him. Why are you here?"

"Sheer idiocy. They think I'm a deserter."

"So why didn't they shoot you?"

"Why didn't they shoot *you*?"

"Don't know," I admitted. "They said I was a good one for the colonel."

"I'm not a deserter. I'm a student. I was defending my thesis."

"Really? Your thesis?" It sounded like the dumbest excuse in the history of desertion.

"An interpretation of Ushakovo's *The Courtyard Hound*, through the lens of contemporary sociological analysis." He waited for me to say something, but I had nothing to say to that. "You know the book?"

"No. Ushakovo?"

"Miserable how bad the schools have gotten. They should have you memorizing passages." He sounded like a crotchety old professor, though from my one look at him I would have guessed he was twenty. " '*In the slaughterhouse where we first kissed, the air still stank from the blood of the lambs.*' First line. Some say it's the greatest Russian novel. And you've never heard of it."

He sighed extravagantly. A moment later I heard a strange

scratching sound, as if a rat were sharpening its claws on the mattress ticking.

"What is that?" I asked.

"Hm?"

"You don't hear that noise?"

"I'm writing in my journal."

I could see no farther with my eyes open than with them closed and this one was writing in his journal. Now I could tell the scratching was a pencil on paper. After a few minutes the journal slapped closed and I heard him stuff the book into his pocket.

"I can write in the dark," he said, punctuating the sentence with a light burp. "One of my talents."

"Notes on *The Courtyard Hound*?"

"Exactly. How's this for strange? Chapter six: Radchenko spends a month in the Crosses because his former best friend . . . Well, I don't want to give it away. But I have to say, it seemed like fate when they brought me here. I've been every other place Radchenko visited—every restaurant and theater and graveyard, the ones that are still around, anyway—but I've never been inside here. A critic could argue that until you spend a night in the Crosses, you can't understand Radchenko."

"Pretty lucky for you."

"Mm."

"So you think they'll shoot us in the morning?"

"I doubt it. They're not preserving us for the night just to shoot us tomorrow." He sounded quite jaunty about it, as if we were discussing a sporting event, as if the outcome wasn't particularly momentous no matter which way it went.

"I haven't had a shit in eight days," he confided. "I'm not saying a good shit—it's been months since I've had a good shit—I mean no shit at all for eight days."

We were quiet for a moment, considering these words.

"How long do you think a man can last without shitting?"

It was an interesting question and I was curious to know the answer myself, but I didn't have one for him. I heard him lie down, heard him yawn happily, relaxed and content, his piss-stained straw mattress as comfortable as a feather bed. The silence lingered for a minute and I thought my cell mate had fallen asleep.

"These walls must be a meter thick," he said at last. "This is probably the safest place in Piter to spend a night." And then he did fall asleep, shifting from speech into snores so quickly that at first I thought he was faking.

I've always envied people who sleep easily. Their brains must be cleaner, the floorboards of the skull well swept, all the little monsters closed up in a steamer trunk at the foot of the bed. I was born an insomniac and that's the way I'll die, wasting thousands of hours along the way longing for unconsciousness, longing for a rubber mallet to crack me in the head, not so hard, not hard enough to do any damage, just a good whack to put me down for the night. But that night I didn't have a chance. I stared into the blackness until the blackness blurred into gray, until the ceiling above me began to take form and the light from the east dribbled in through the narrow barred window that existed after all. Only then did I realize that I still had a German knife strapped to my calf.

3

An hour after dawn two new guards opened the cell door, rousted us from bed, and clamped handcuffs on our wrists. They ignored my questions but seemed amused when Kolya asked for a cup of tea and an omelet. Jokes must have been rare in the Crosses, because it wasn't such a good joke, but the guards grinned as they shoved us down the hallway. Somewhere someone was moaning, a low and endless moan, a ship's horn heard from a great distance.

I didn't know if we were heading for the gallows or an interrogation chamber. The night had passed without sleep; save for a swig from the German's flask, there hadn't been a sip to drink since the rooftop of the Kirov; a lump the size of an infant's fist had swelled where my forehead had cracked the ceiling—it was a bad morning, really; among my worst—but I wanted to live. I wanted to live and I knew I could not face my execution with grace. I would kneel before the hangman or the firing squad and plead my youth, detail my many hours served on the rooftop waiting for the bombs, all the barricades I had helped to build, the ditches I had dug. All of us had done it, we were all serving the cause, but I was one of Piter's true sons and I didn't deserve to die. What harm had been done? We drank a dead German's cognac—for this you want to end me? You want to tie rough hemp around my skinny neck and shut down my brain forever because I stole a knife? Don't do this, comrade. I don't think there is greatness in me, but there is something better than this.

The guards led us down a stone staircase, the steps beaten smooth by hundreds of thousands of boot heels. An old man with a heavy gray scarf wrapped twice around his throat sat on the far side of the iron bars that blocked the bottom of the staircase. He gave us a gummy grin and unlocked the gate. A moment later we walked through a heavy wooden door into the sunlight, emerging from the Crosses intact and alive.

Kolya, unimpressed by our apparent reprieve, scooped up a palmful of clean snow with his shackled hands and licked it. The boldness of the maneuver made me jealous, as did the thought of cold water on my tongue. But I didn't want to do anything to anger the guards. Our escape from the Crosses seemed like an odd mistake and I expected to be shoved inside again if I did something wrong.

The guards escorted us to a waiting GAZ, its big engine grumbling, exhaust pipes spewing dirty vapor, two soldiers sitting in the front seat watching us with zero curiosity, their fur-lined hats pulled down low on their foreheads.

Kolya hopped into the backseat without waiting for an order.

"Gentlemen, to the opera!"

The guards, standards diminished by years of working the Crosses, gave Kolya another good laugh. The soldiers did not. One of them turned and inspected Kolya.

"You say another word and I'll break your fucking arm. It were up to me, you'd already have a bullet in your head. Fucking deserter. You"—and this was addressed to me—"get in."

Kolya's mouth was already open and I knew violence was on the way; the soldier did not look like a bluffer and Kolya, clearly, was incapable of heeding a simple threat.

"I'm not a deserter," he said. With his manacled hands he managed to push up the left sleeve of his greatcoat, the left sleeve of his army sweater, the left sleeves of the two shirts beneath it, and offered his forearm to the soldier in the front seat. "You want to break the arm, break it, but I'm not a deserter."

For a long count nobody spoke—Kolya stared at the soldier, the soldier stared back, and the rest of us watched and waited, impressed by this match of wills and curious to see who would win. Finally, the soldier conceded defeat by turning away from Kolya and barking at me.

"Get in the car, you little cunt."

The guards grinned. This was their morning's entertainment. They had no torture scheduled, no teeth to wrench, no nails to pluck from a screaming man's nail beds, so they got their fun watching me, the little cunt, scurry into the backseat next to Kolya.

The soldier drove very fast, caring not at all about the slicks of ice on the road. We sped along the banks of the frozen Neva. I had my collar upturned so I could hide my face from the wind that blasted in beneath the canvas roof. Kolya didn't seem bothered by the cold. He stared at the spire of the Church of John the Baptist across the river and said nothing.

We turned onto the Kamennoostrovsky Bridge, the old steel of its arches rimed with frost, the lampposts bearded with icicles. Onto Kamenny Island, slowing only a bit to circle around a bomb crater that had shattered the center of the road, pulling into a long driveway lined with the stumps of lime trees, and parking in front of a magnificent wooden mansion with a white-columned portico. Kolya studied the house.

"The Dolgorukovs lived here," he said, as we stepped out of the car. "I suppose none of you have heard of the Dolgorukovs."

"A bunch of aristocrats who got their necks snapped," said one of the soldiers, gesturing with the barrel of his rifle for us to walk toward the front door.

"Some of them," admitted Kolya. "And some of them slept with emperors."

In the daylight Kolya looked like he could have stepped out of one of the propaganda posters pasted on walls throughout the city; the angles of his face were heroic—the strong chin, the straight nose, the blond hair that fell across his forehead. He was a finelooking deserter.

The soldiers escorted us onto the porch, where sandbags had

been piled high to form a machine-gun nest. Two soldiers sat near their gun, passing a cigarette between them. Kolya sniffed the air and stared longingly at the hand-rolled butt.

"Real tobacco," he said, before our armed guides pushed open the front door and herded us inside.

I had never been inside a mansion before, had only read about them in the novels: the dances on the parquet floors, the servants ladling soup from silver tureens, the stern patriarch in his book-lined study warning his weeping daughter to stay away from the lowborn boy. But while the old Dolgorukov home still looked magnificent on the outside, the revolution had come to the interior. The marble floor was tracked with a thousand muddy boot prints, unwashed for months. The smoke-stained wallpaper curled away from the baseboards. None of the original furniture had survived, none of the oil paintings and Chinese vases that must have lined the walls and rested on teak shelves.

Dozens of uniformed officers hurried from one room to the next, hustled up a curving double staircase missing its balustrade and all the balusters, probably torn down for firewood weeks ago. The uniforms were not Red Army. Kolya noticed me staring.

"NKVD. Maybe they think we're spies."

I didn't need Kolya to tell me the men were NKVD. Since I was little I had known what their uniforms looked like, with their peaked blue-and-maroon caps and their holstered Tokarevs. I had learned to dread the sight of their Packards idling outside the gates of the Kirov, the Black Ravens, waiting to carry some unlucky citizen away from his home. The NKVD arrested at least fifteen men from the building while I lived there. Sometimes those taken returned after a few weeks, their heads shaved and their faces pale and lifeless, avoiding my eyes in the stairwell as they limped up to their apartments. The broken men who came home must have known how rare and lucky they were, but they took no apparent joy in their survival. They knew what happened to my father and they could not meet my eyes.

The soldiers kept prodding us forward till we entered a sunroom at the very rear of the house, the tall French windows offering a fine vantage of the Neva and the grim, stolid apartment buildings of the Vyborg section on the far side of the river. An older man sat alone at a simple wood desk set down in the middle of the sunroom. He had a telephone receiver nestled between his face and his shoulder so he could scribble with a pen on a pad of paper as he listened.

He glanced at us as we waited at the entryway. He looked like an ex-boxer with his thick neck and crooked, flattened nose. The shadows below his hooded eyes were deep, as were the furrows that crossed his forehead. His gray hair was shaved very close to the scalp. He might have been fifty years old, but he looked like he could rise from his chair and beat us all down without mussing his uniform. Three metal stars shone on the collar tabs of his jacket. I didn't know precisely what three stars signified, but they were three stars more than anyone else in the mansion.

He tossed his pad of paper on the desk and I could see that he hadn't been taking notes, as I'd thought, but simply drawing X's, over and over again, till the entire sheet of paper was covered with them. For some reason this frightened me more than his uniform or his brawler's face. A man who drew pictures of tits or dogs seemed like a man I could understand. But a man who drew nothing but X's?

He was watching us, Kolya and me, and I knew that he was judging us, condemning us for our crimes and sentencing us to death, all while listening to a voice traveling across wires.

"Good," he said at last, "I want it done by noon. No exceptions."

He hung up the phone and smiled at us, and the smile was as incongruous on his face as the man and his plain wood desk were in the gorgeous sunroom of the old noble house. The colonel (for I assumed now that this was the colonel the soldiers had spoken of the night before) had a beautiful smile, his teeth surprisingly white, his brutal face shifting instantly from menace to welcome.

"The deserter and the looter! Come, come closer, we don't need the cuffs. I don't think these boys will cause any trouble." He gestured to the soldiers, who reluctantly pulled out their keys and removed our manacles.

"I'm not a deserter," said Kolya.

"No? Go," he ordered the soldiers, not bothering to look at them. The soldiers obeyed, leaving us alone with the colonel. He stood and walked toward us, the pistol on his waist holster slapping against his hip. Kolya stood very straight, at attention for the officer's inspection, and I, not knowing what to do, followed his lead. The colonel kept coming until his battered face nearly touched Kolya's.

"You're not a deserter and yet your unit reported you missing and you were picked up forty kilometers from where you were supposed to be."

"Well, there's a simple explanation—"

"And you," he continued, turning to me. "A German paratrooper falls on your block and you don't notify the authorities. You decide to enrich yourself at the city's expense. Is there a simple explanation for that, too?"

I needed water. My mouth was so dry it felt scaly, like the skin of a lizard, and I had begun to see bright little sparks of light swimming in the peripheries of my vision.

"Well?"

"I'm sorry," I said.

"You're sorry?" He looked at me a moment longer and laughed. "Ah, well, you're sorry, all right then, that's fine. As long as you're sorry, that's the important thing. Listen, boy, do you know how many people I've executed? I don't mean on my orders, I mean done it myself, with this Tokarev—" Here he slapped the holstered pistol. "Do you want to guess? No? Good, because I don't know. I've lost count. And I'm the kind of man who likes to know. I keep track of things. I know exactly how many women I've fucked, and it's quite a few, believe me. You're a handsome boy," he said to Kolya, "but trust me, you won't catch up with me, even if you live to a hundred, and that seems doubtful."

I glanced at Kolya, expecting him to say something stupid and get us both killed, but Kolya, for once, had nothing to say.

"Sorry is what you say to the schoolmaster when you break a piece of chalk," the colonel continued. "Sorry doesn't work for looters and deserters."

"We thought he might have a little food on him."

The colonel stared at me for a long moment.

"Did he?"

"Just some cognac. Or brandy . . . schnapps, maybe."

"We shoot a dozen people every day for forging ration cards. You know what they tell us, before we put bullets in their brains? They were hungry. Of course they were hungry! Everyone is hungry. That won't stop us from shooting thieves."

"I wasn't stealing from Russians—"

"You stole state property. Did you take anything from the body?"

I hesitated as long as I dared.

"A knife."

"Ah. The honest thief."

I knelt, unstrapped the sheath from my ankle, and handed it to the colonel. He stared at the German leather.

"You had this on you all night? No one searched you?" He exhaled with a soft curse, weary of the incompetence. "No wonder we're losing the war." He pulled out the blade and studied the inscription. "BLOOD AND HONOR. Ha. May God fuck those whoresons in the ass. You know how to use it?"

"What?"

"The knife. Slashing," he said, slashing the air with the steel blade, "is better than stabbing. Harder to block. Go for the throat, and if that's not working, go for the eyes or the belly. Thigh's good, too, big veins in the thighs." All this instruction was accompanied by vigorous demonstration. "And never stop," he said, dancing closer, the steel flashing, "never let up; keep the knife moving, keep him on the defensive."

He sheathed the blade and tossed it to me.

"Keep it. You'll need it."

I stared at Kolya, who shrugged. All of this was too strange to understand so there was no point straining the mind, trying to sort out where we stood. I got back on one knee and strapped the knife to my ankle again.

The colonel had moved to the French windows, where he watched yesterday's snow blowing across the frozen Neva.

"Your father was the poet."

"Yes," I admitted, standing straight and staring at the back of the colonel's head. No one outside my family had mentioned my father in four years. I mean this literally. Not a word.

"He could write. What happened was . . . unfortunate."

What could I say to that? I stared at my boots and knew that Kolya was squinting at me, trying to figure out which unfortunate poet sired me.

"Neither of you has eaten today," said the colonel, not asking a question. "Black tea and toast, how does that sound? Maybe we can find some fish soup somewhere. Borya!"

An aide stepped into the sunroom, a pencil tucked behind his ear.

"Get these boys some breakfast."

Borya nodded and disappeared as quickly as he'd appeared.

Fish soup. I hadn't had fish soup since summer. The idea of it was wild and exotic, like a naked girl on a Pacific island.

"Come over here," said the colonel. He opened one of the French doors and stepped into the cold. Kolya and I followed him along a gravel path that led through a frost-blasted garden, down to the banks of the river.

A girl in a fox fur coat skated on the Neva. In a normal winter you'd see hundreds of girls skating on a weekend afternoon, but this wasn't a normal winter. The ice was solid and had been for weeks, but who had the strength for figure eights? Standing on the frozen mud at the river's edge, Kolya and I stared at her the way you'd stare at a monkey riding a unicycle down the street. She was freakishly lovely, her dark hair parted in the middle and tied up in a loose bun, her wind-whipped cheeks flushed and full and healthy. It took me a few seconds to realize why she looked so strange, and then it was obvious—even at a distance you could tell that the girl was well fed. There was nothing pinched and desperate about her face. She had an athlete's casual grace; her pirouettes were tight and fast; she never got winded. Her thighs must have been magnificent—long, pale, and strong—and I could feel my prick hardening for the first time in days.

"She's getting married next Friday," said the colonel. "A piece of meat she's marrying, I say, but all right. He's a Party man, he can afford her."

"That's your daughter?" asked Kolya.

The colonel grinned, his white teeth splitting his brawler's face.

"You don't think she looks like me? No, no, she got lucky there. She got her mother's face and her father's temper—this one will conquer the world."

Only then did I realize that the colonel's teeth were false, a bridge that seemed to encompass the entire upper row. And I knew, suddenly but surely, that the man had been tortured. They had brought him in during one purge or another, called him a Trotskyite or a White or a Fascist sympathizer, pried the teeth from his mouth, and beaten him till his eyes bled, till he pissed blood and shat blood, till the order came from whatever Moscow office: we have rehabilitated the man, let him alone now, he is one of us again.

I could picture it because I had pictured it often, whenever I wondered about my father's last days. He had the misfortune of being a Jew and a poet and mildly famous, friends once with Maya-kovsky and Mandelstam, bitter enemies with Obranovich and the others he considered tongues of the bureaucracy, the slingers of revolutionary verse who labeled my father an agitator and a para-site because he wrote about the Leningrad underworld, though—officially—there was no Leningrad underworld. More than this, he had the temerity to title his book *Piter*, the city's nickname, the name every native used, but banned from all Soviet text because "Saint

Petersburg" was a czar's arrogance, named for the old tyrant's pa-
tron saint.

One summer afternoon in 1937 they took my father from the offices of the literary magazine where he worked. They never gave
him back. The call from the Moscow office never came for him; re-
habilitation was not an option. An intelligence officer might hold
future value for the state, but a decadent poet did not. He might
have died in the Crosses or in Siberia or somewhere in between, we
never learned. If he was buried, there is no marker; if he was burned,
there is no urn.

For a long time I was angry with my father for writing such dangerous words; it seemed stupid that a book was more important
than sticking around and slapping the back of my head when I picked
my nose. But later I decided he hadn't chosen to insult the Party, not
consciously, not the way Mandelstam had (Mandelstam with his
crazy bravery, writing that Stalin had fat fingers like slugs, a mus-
tache like two cockroaches). My father didn't know that *Piter* was
dangerous until the official reviews were written. He thought he
was writing a book five hundred people would read, and maybe
he was right, but at least one of those five hundred denounced him
and that was that.

The colonel had survived, though, and looking at him I wondered if he found it strange that he had been so close to the shark's
jaws and somehow fought his way back to shore, that he who had
waited for another's mercy could now decide for himself whether
to grant it. He didn't seem troubled at the moment; he watched
his daughter skate, he clapped his busted-knuckled hands as she
spun.

"So, the wedding is Friday. Even now, even in the middle of all
of this—" said the colonel, gesturing with his hands to indicate Leningrad, the famine, the war, "—she wants a real wedding, a *proper*
wedding. This is good, life must continue, we're fighting barbarians
but we must remain human, *Russian*. So we will have music, dancing . . . a cake."

He looked at us each in turn as if there were something momentous about the word *cake* and he needed us both to understand.

"This is the tradition, says my wife, we need a cake. It is terrible luck, a wedding with no cake. Now, I've been fighting all my life against these peasant superstitions, the priests used them to keep people stupid and afraid, but my wife . . . she wants the cake. Fine, fine, make the cake. For months she's been hoarding her sugar, her honey, flour, all the rest."

I thought about this, the sacks of sugar, the jars of honey, the flour that must have been real flour, not moldy salvage from a torpedoed barge. Half the Kirov could probably survive two weeks on her batter alone.

"She has everything she needs, all except the eggs." Again the portentous look. "Eggs," said the colonel, "are hard to find."

For several seconds we all stood silently, watching the colonel's daughter twirl.

"The fleet might have some," said Kolya.

"No. They don't."

"They have tinned beef. I traded a pack of playing cards for some tinned beef from one of the sailors—"

"They don't have eggs."

I don't think I'm stupid, but it was taking me a very long time to understand what the colonel was asking, and a longer time to fire up my courage to ask him.

"You want us to find eggs?"

"A dozen," he said. "She only needs ten, but I figure, one might break, a couple might be rotten." He saw our confusion and he smiled his wonderful smile, gripping our shoulders hard enough to make me stand straighter. "My men say there are no eggs in Leningrad, but I believe there is everything in Leningrad, even now, and I just need the right fellows to find it. A pair of thieves."

"We're not thieves," said Kolya, very righteous, staring into the colonel's eyes. I wanted to punch him. By all rights we should have been dead and frozen, piled onto a sledge with the rest of the day's corpses. We had our reprieve. Our lives had been returned in ex-change for a simple task. A strange task, perhaps, but simple enough. And now he was going to ruin it—he was asking for his bullet, which was bad, but he was asking for my bullet, too, which was far worse.

"You're not thieves? You abandoned your unit—no, no, shut up, don't say anything. You abandoned your unit and the moment you did that you forfeited your rights as a soldier in the Red Army—your right to carry your rifle, to wear that coat, those boots. You're a thief. And you, Big Nose, you looted a corpse. It was a German corpse so it doesn't personally offend me, but looting is theft. Let's not play games. You're both thieves. Bad thieves, that's true, incom-petent thieves, absolutely, but you're in luck. The good thieves haven't been caught."

He turned and walked back toward the house. Kolya and I lin-gered, watching the colonel's daughter, her fox fur flashing in the sun. She must have seen us by now, but she never acknowledged us, never glanced our way. We were two of her father's lackeys and therefore entirely boring. We watched her as long as we could, try-ing to etch the image into our brains for future masturbation, until the colonel barked at us and we hurried after him.

"You have your ration cards?" he asked, taking long strides, his respite finished, ready again for the long day's work. "Hand them over."

I kept mine pinned to the inside pocket of my coat. I unpinned it and saw Kolya pull his from his folded sock. The colonel took them from us.

"You bring me the eggs by sunrise Thursday, you get them back. You don't, well, you've got all of January to eat snow, and there won't be any cards waiting for you in February, either. That's as-suming one of my men doesn't find you and kill you before then, and my men are very good at that."

"They just can't find eggs," said Kolya.

The colonel smiled. "I like you, boy. You won't live a long life, but I like you."

We stepped inside the sunroom. The colonel sat down at his desk and stared at the black telephone. He raised his eyebrows, remembering something, opened the desk drawer, and pulled out a folded letter. He held it out for Kolya.

"That's a curfew waiver for the two of you. Anyone gives you trouble, show them that, you'll be on your way. And here, this, too. . . ."

He pulled four 100-ruble notes from his wallet and gave them to Kolya, who glanced at the letter and the rubles and slipped them into his pocket.

"That would have bought me a thousand eggs in June," said the colonel.

"And it will again next June," said Kolya. "Fritz won't last the winter."

"With soldiers like you," said the colonel, "we'll be paying for eggs with deutsche marks soon."

Kolya opened his mouth to defend himself, but the colonel shook his head.

"You understand this is a gift? You bring me a dozen eggs by Thursday, I give you your lives back. You understand the rareness of this gift?"

"What day is today?"

"Today is Saturday. You deserted your unit on a Friday. When the sun rises tomorrow it is Sunday. Can you keep track from this point forward? Yes? Good."

Borya returned with four slices of toast on a blue plate. The toast had been slathered with something oily, lard maybe, glistening and fatty and luscious. Another aide stepped into the sunroom behind him, carrying two cups of steaming tea. I waited for a third aide carrying bowls of fish soup, but he never came.

"Eat quick, boys," said the colonel. "You've got a lot of walking to do."

from

In Defense of Food
An Eater's Manifesto

by

Michael Pollan

"A tough, witty, cogent rebuttal to the proposition that food can be reduced to its nutritional components without the loss of something essential . . . [a] lively, invaluable book."
—Janet Maslin, *The New York Times*

Because in the so-called Western diet, food has been replaced by nutrients, and common sense by confusion—most of what we're consuming today is no longer the product of nature but of food science. The result is what Michael Pollan calls the American Paradox: The more we worry about nutrition, the less healthy we seem to become. With In Defense of Food, *Pollan proposes a new (and very old) answer to the question of what we should eat that comes down to seven simple but liberating words: Eat food. Not too much. Mostly plants.*

Pollan's bracing and eloquent manifesto shows us how we can start making thoughtful choices that will enrich our lives, enlarge our sense of what it means to be healthy, and bring pleasure back to eating.

ONE ᧥ FROM FOODS
TO NUTRIENTS

If you spent any time at all in a supermarket in the 1980s, you might have noticed something peculiar going on. The food was gradually disappearing from the shelves. Not literally vanishing—I'm not talking about Soviet-style shortages. No, the shelves and refrigerated cases still groaned with packages and boxes and bags of various edibles, more of them landing every year in fact, but a great many of the traditional supermarket foods were steadily being replaced by "nutrients," which are not the same thing. Where once the familiar names of recognizable comestibles—things like eggs or breakfast cereals or snack foods—claimed pride of place on the brightly colored packages crowding the aisles, now new, scientific-sounding terms like "cholesterol" and "fiber" and "saturated fat" began rising to large-type prominence. More important than mere foods, the presence or absence of these invisible substances was now generally believed to confer health benefits on their eaters. The implicit message was that foods, by comparison, were coarse, old-fashioned, and decidedly unscientific things—who could say *what* was in them really? But nutrients—those chemical compounds and minerals in foods that scientists have identified as important to our health—gleamed with the promise of scientific certainty. Eat more of the right ones, fewer of the wrong, and you would live longer, avoid chronic diseases, and lose weight.

Nutrients themselves had been around as a concept and a set of words since early in the nineteenth century. That was when William Prout, an English doctor and chemist, identified the three principal constituents of food—protein, fat, and carbohydrates—that would come to be known as macronutrients. Building on Prout's discovery, Justus von Liebig, the great German scientist credited as one of the founders of organic chemistry, added a couple of minerals to the big three and declared that the mystery of animal nutrition—how food turns into flesh and energy—had been solved. This is the very same Liebig who identified the macronutrients in soil—nitrogen, phosphorus, and potassium (known to farmers and gardeners by their periodic table initials, N, P, and K). Liebig claimed that all that plants need to live and grow are these three chemicals, period. As with the plant, so with the person: In 1842, Liebig proposed a theory of metabolism that explained life strictly in terms of a small handful of chemical nutrients, without recourse to metaphysical forces such as "vitalism."

Having cracked the mystery of human nutrition, Liebig went on to develop a meat extract—Liebig's Extractum Carnis—that has come down to us as bouillon and concocted the first baby formula, consisting of cow's milk, wheat flour, malted flour, and potassium bicarbonate.

Liebig, the father of modern nutritional science, had driven food into a corner and forced it to yield its chemical secrets. But the post–Liebig consensus that science now pretty much knew what was going on in food didn't last long. Doctors began to notice that many of the babies fed exclusively on Liebig's formula failed to thrive. (Not surprising, given that his preparation lacked any vitamins or several essential fats and amino acids.) That Liebig might have overlooked a few little things in food also began to occur to doctors who observed that sailors on long ocean voyages often got sick, even when they had adequate supplies of protein, carbohydrates, and fat. Clearly the chemists were missing something—some essential ingredients present in the fresh plant foods (like oranges and potatoes) that miraculously cured the sailors. This observation led to the discovery early in the twentieth century of the first set of micronutrients, which the Polish biochemist Casimir Funk, harkening back to older vitalist ideas of food, christened "vitamines" in 1912 ("vita-" for life and "-amines" for organic compounds organized around nitrogen).

Vitamins did a lot for the prestige of nutritional science. These special molecules, which at first were isolated from foods and then later synthesized in a laboratory, could cure people of nutritional deficiencies such as scurvy or beriberi almost overnight in a convincing demonstration of reductive chemistry's power. Beginning in the 1920s, vitamins enjoyed a vogue among the middle class, a group not notably afflicted by beriberi or scurvy. But the belief took hold that these magic molecules also promoted growth in children, long life in adults, and, in a phrase of the time, "positive health" in everyone. (And what would "negative health" be exactly?) Vitamins had brought a kind of glamour to the science of nutrition, and though certain elite segments of the population now began to eat by its expert lights, it really wasn't until late in the twentieth century that nutrients began to push food aside in the popular imagination of what it means to eat.

No single event marked the shift from eating food to eating nutrients, although in retrospect a little-noticed political dustup in Washington in 1977 seems to have helped propel American culture down this unfortunate and dimly lighted path. Responding to reports of an alarming increase in chronic diseases linked to diet—including heart disease, cancer, obesity, and diabetes—the Senate Select Committee on Nutrition and Human Needs chaired by South Dakota Senator George McGovern held hearings on the problem. The committee had been formed in 1968 with a mandate to eliminate malnutrition, and its work had led to the establishment of several important food-assistance programs. Endeavoring now to resolve the question of diet and chronic disease in the general population represented a certain amount of mission creep, but all in a good cause to which no one could possibly object.

After taking two days of testimony on diet and killer diseases, the committee's staff—comprised not of scientists or doctors but of lawyers and (ahem) journalists—set to work preparing what it had every reason to assume would be an uncontroversial document called *Dietary Goals for the United States*. The committee learned that while rates of coronary heart disease had soared in America since World War II, certain other cultures that consumed traditional diets based mostly on plants had strikingly low rates of chronic diseases. Epidemiologists had also observed that in America during the war years, when meat and dairy products were strictly rationed, the rate of heart disease had temporarily plummeted, only to leap upward once the war was over.

Beginning in the 1950s, a growing body of scientific opinion held that the consumption of fat and dietary cholesterol, much of which came from meat and dairy products, was responsible for rising rates of heart disease during the twentieth century. The "lipid hypothesis," as it was called, had already been embraced by the American Heart Association, which in 1961 had begun recommending a "prudent diet" low in saturated fat and cholesterol from animal products. True, actual proof for the lipid hypothesis was remarkably thin in 1977—it was still very much a hypothesis, but one well on its way to general acceptance.

In January 1977, the committee issued a fairly straightforward set of dietary guidelines, calling on Americans to cut down on their consumption of red meat and dairy products. Within weeks a firestorm of criticism, emanating chiefly from the red meat and dairy industries, engulfed the committee, and Senator McGovern (who had a great many cattle ranchers among his South Dakota constituents) was forced to beat a retreat. The committee's recommendations were hastily rewritten. Plain talk about actual foodstuffs—the committee had advised Americans to "reduce consumption of meat"—was replaced by artful compromise: "choose meats, poultry, and fish that will reduce saturated fat intake."

Leave aside for now the virtues, if any, of a low-meat and/or low-fat diet, questions to which I will return, and focus for a moment on language. For with these subtle changes in wording a whole way of thinking about food and health underwent a momentous shift. First, notice that the stark message to "eat less" of a particular food—in this case meat—had been deep-sixed; don't look for it ever again in any official U.S. government dietary pronouncement. Say what you will about this or that food, you are not allowed officially to tell people to eat less of it or the industry in question will have you for lunch. But there is a path around this immovable obstacle, and it was McGovern's staffers who blazed it: *Speak no more of foods, only nutrients.* Notice how in the revised guidelines, distinctions between entities as different as beef and chicken and fish have collapsed. These three venerable foods, each representing not just a different species but an entirely different taxonomic class, are now lumped together as mere delivery systems for a single nutrient. Notice too how the new language exonerates the foods themselves. Now the culprit is an obscure, invisible, tasteless—and politically unconnected—substance that may or may not lurk in them called saturated fat.

The linguistic capitulation did nothing to rescue McGovern from his blunder. In the very next election, in 1980, the beef lobby succeeded in rusticating the three-term senator, sending an unmistakable warning to anyone who would challenge the American diet, and in particular the big chunk of animal protein squatting in the middle of its plate. Henceforth, government dietary guidelines would shun plain talk about whole foods, each of which has its trade association on Capitol Hill, but would instead arrive dressed in scientific euphemism and speaking of nutrients, entities that few Americans (including, as we would find out, American nutrition scientists) really understood but that, with the notable exception of sucrose, lack powerful lobbies in Washington.*

The lesson of the McGovern fiasco was quickly absorbed by all who would pronounce on the American diet. When a few years later the National Academy of Sciences looked into the question of diet and cancer, it was careful to frame its recommendations nutrient by nutrient rather than food by food, to avoid offending any powerful interests. We now know the academy's panel of thirteen scientists adopted this approach over the objections of at least two of its members who argued that most of the available science pointed toward conclusions about foods, not nutrients. According to T. Colin Campbell, a Cornell nutritional biochemist who served on the panel, all of the human population studies linking dietary fat to cancer actually showed that the groups with higher cancer rates consumed not just more fats, but also more animal foods and fewer plant foods as well. "This meant that these cancers could

---

*Sucrose is the exception that proves the rule. Only the power of the sugar lobby in Washington can explain the fact that the official U.S. recommendation for the maximum permissible level of free sugars in the diet is an eye-popping 25 percent of daily calories. To give you some idea just how permissive that is, the World Health Organization recommends that no more than 10 percent of daily calories come from added sugars, a benchmark that the U.S. sugar lobby has worked furiously to dismantle. In 2004 it enlisted the Bush State Department in a campaign to get the recommendation changed and has threatened to lobby Congress to cut WHO funding unless the organization recants. Perhaps we should be grateful that the saturated fat interests have as yet organized no such lobby.

just as easily be caused by animal protein, dietary cholesterol, something else exclusively found in animal-based foods, or a lack of plant-based foods," Campbell wrote years later. The argument fell on deaf ears.

In the case of the "good foods" too, nutrients also carried the day: The language of the final report highlighted the benefits of the antioxidants in vegetables rather than the vegetables themselves. Joan Gussow, a Columbia University nutritionist who served on the panel, argued against the focus on nutrients rather than whole foods. "The really important message in the epidemiology, which is all we had to go on, was that some vegetables and citrus fruits seemed to be protective against cancer. But those sections of the report were written as though it was the vitamin C in the citrus or the beta-carotene in the vegetables that was responsible for the effect. I kept changing the language to talk about 'foods that contain vitamin C' and 'foods that contain carotenes.' Because how do you know it's not one of the other things in the carrots or the broccoli? There are hundreds of carotenes. But the biochemists had their answer: 'You can't do a trial on broccoli.' "

So the nutrients won out over the foods. The panel's resort to scientific reductionism had the considerable virtue of being both politically expedient (in the case of meat and dairy) and, to these scientific heirs of Justus von Liebig, intellectually sympathetic. With each of its chapters focused on a single nutrient, the final draft of the National Academy of Sciences report, *Diet, Nutrition and Cancer*, framed its recommendations in terms of saturated fats and antioxidants rather than beef and broccoli.

In doing so, the 1982 National Academy of Sciences report

helped codify the official new dietary language, the one we all still speak. Industry and media soon followed suit, and terms like polyunsaturated, cholesterol, monounsaturated, carbohydrate, fiber, polyphenols, amino acids, flavonols, carotenoids, antioxidants, probiotics, and phytochemicals soon colonized much of the cultural space previously occupied by the tangible material formerly known as food.

The Age of Nutritionism had arrived.

TWO ✑ NUTRITIONISM DEFINED

The term isn't mine. It was coined by an Australian sociologist of science by the name of Gyorgy Scrinis, and as near as I can determine first appeared in a 2002 essay titled "Sorry Marge" published in an Australian quarterly called Meanjin. "Sorry Marge" looked at margarine as the ultimate nutritionist product, able to shift its identity (no cholesterol! one year, no trans fats! the next) depending on the prevailing winds of dietary opinion. But Scrinis had bigger game in his sights than spreadable vegetable oil. He suggested that we look past the various nutritional claims swirling around margarine and butter and consider the underlying message of the debate itself: "namely, that we should understand and engage with food and our bodies in terms of their nutritional and chemical constituents and requirements—the assumption being that this is all we need to understand." This reductionist way of thinking about food had been pointed out and criticized before (notably by the Canadian historian Harvey Levenstein, the British nutritionist Geoffrey Cannon, and the American nutritionists Joan Gussow and Marion Nestle), but it had never before been given a proper name: "nutritionism." Proper names have a way of making visible things we don't easily see or simply take for granted.

The first thing to understand about nutritionism is that it is not the same thing as nutrition. As the "-ism" suggests, it is not a scientific subject but an ideology. Ideologies are ways of organizing large swaths of life and experience under a set of shared but unexamined assumptions. This quality makes an ideology particularly hard to see, at least while it's still exerting its hold on your culture. A reigning ideology is a little like the weather—all pervasive and so virtually impossible to escape. Still, we can try.

In the case of nutritionism, the widely shared but unexamined assumption is that the key to understanding food is indeed the nutrient. Put another way: Foods are essentially the sum of their nutrient parts. From this basic premise flow several others.

Since nutrients, as compared with foods, are invisible and therefore slightly mysterious, it falls to the scientists (and to the journalists through whom the scientists reach the public) to explain the hidden reality of foods to us. In form this is a quasireligious idea, suggesting the visible world is not the one that really matters, which implies the need for a priesthood. For to enter a world where your dietary salvation depends on unseen nutrients, you need plenty of expert help.

But expert help to do what exactly? This brings us to another unexamined assumption of nutritionism: that the whole point of eating is to maintain and promote bodily health. Hippocrates' famous injunction to "let food be thy medicine" is ritually invoked to support this notion. I'll leave the premise alone for now, except to point out that it is not shared by all cultures and, further, that the experience of these other cultures suggests that, paradoxically, regarding food as being about things other than bodily health—like pleasure, say, or sociality or identity—makes people no less healthy; indeed, there's some reason to believe it may make them more healthy. This is what we usually have in mind when we speak of the French paradox. So there is at least a question as to whether the ideology of nutritionism is actually any good for you.

It follows from the premise that food is foremost about promoting physical health that the nutrients in food should be divided into the healthy ones and the unhealthy ones—good nutrients and bad. This has been a hallmark of nutritionist thinking from the days of Liebig, for whom it wasn't enough to identify the nutrients; he also had to pick favorites, and nutritionists have been doing so ever since. Liebig claimed that protein was the "master nutrient" in animal nutrition, because he believed it drove growth. Indeed, he likened the role of protein in animals to that of nitrogen in plants: Protein (which contains nitrogen) comprised the essential human fertilizer. Liebig's elevation of protein dominated nutritionist thinking for decades as public health authorities worked to expand access to and production of the master nutrient (especially in the form of animal protein), with the goal of growing bigger, and therefore (it was assumed) healthier, people. (A high priority for Western governments fighting imperial wars.) To a considerable extent we still have a food system organized around the promotion of protein as the master nutrient. It has given us, among other things, vast amounts of cheap meat and milk, which have in turn given us much, much bigger people. Whether they are healthier too is another question.

It seems to be a rule of nutritionism that for every good nutrient, there must be a bad nutrient to serve as its foil, the latter a focus for our food fears and the former for our enthusiasms. A backlash against protein arose in America at the turn of the last century as diet gurus like John Harvey Kellogg and Horace Fletcher (about whom more later) railed against the deleterious effects of protein on digestion (it supposedly led to the proliferation of toxic bacteria in the gut) and promoted the cleaner, more wholesome carbohydrate in its place. The legacy of that revaluation is the breakfast cereal, the strategic objective of which was to dethrone animal protein at the morning meal.

Ever since, the history of modern nutritionism has been a history of macronutrients at war: protein against carbs; carbs against proteins, and then fats; fats against carbs. Beginning with Liebig, in each age nutritionism has organized most of its energies around an imperial nutrient: protein in the nineteenth century, fat in the twentieth, and, it stands to reason, carbohydrates will occupy our attention in the twenty-first. Meanwhile, in the shadow of these titanic struggles, smaller civil wars have raged within the sprawling empires of the big three: refined carbohydrates versus fiber; animal protein versus plant protein;

saturated fats versus polyunsaturated fats; and then, deep down within the province of the polyunsaturates, omega-3 fatty acids versus omega-6s. Like so many ideologies, nutritionism at bottom hinges on a form of dualism, so that at all times there must be an evil nutrient for adherents to excoriate and a savior nutrient for them to sanctify. At the moment, trans fats are performing admirably in the former role, omega-3 fatty acids in the latter. It goes without saying that such a Manichaean view of nutrition is bound to promote food fads and phobias and large abrupt swings of the nutritional pendulum.

Another potentially serious weakness of nutritionist ideology is that, focused so relentlessly as it is on the nutrients it can measure, it has trouble discerning qualitative distinctions among foods. So fish, beef, and chicken through the nutritionist's lens become mere delivery systems for varying quantities of different fats and proteins and whatever other nutrients happen to be on their scope. Milk through this lens is reduced to a suspension of protein, lactose, fats, and calcium in water, when it is entirely possible that the benefits, or for that matter the hazards, of drinking milk owe to entirely other factors (growth hormones?) or relationships between factors (fat-soluble vitamins and saturated fat?) that have been overlooked. Milk remains a food of humbling complexity, to judge by the long, sorry saga of efforts to simulate it. The entire history of baby formula has been the history of one overlooked nutrient after another: Liebig missed the vitamins and amino acids, and his successors missed the omega-3s, and still to this day babies fed on the most "nutritionally complete" formula fail to do as well as babies fed human milk. Even more than margarine, infant formula stands as the ultimate test product of nutritionism and a fair index of its hubris.

This brings us to one of the most troubling features of nutritionism, though it is a feature certainly not troubling to all. When the emphasis is on quantifying the nutrients contained in foods (or, to be precise, the *recognized* nutrients in foods), any qualitative distinction between whole foods and processed foods is apt to disappear. "[If] foods are understood only in terms of the various quantities of nutrients they contain," Gyorgy Scrinis wrote, then "even processed foods may be considered to be 'healthier' for you than whole foods if they contain the appropriate quantities of some nutrients."

How convenient.

THREE ∽ NUTRITIONISM COMES TO MARKET

No idea could be more sympathetic to manufacturers of processed foods, which surely explains why they have been so happy to jump on the nutritionism bandwagon. Indeed, nutritionism supplies the ultimate justification for processing food by implying that with a judicious application of food science, fake foods can be made even more nutritious than the real thing. This of course is the story of margarine, the first important synthetic food to slip into our diet. Margarine started out in the nineteenth century as a cheap and inferior substitute for butter, but with the emergence of the lipid hypothesis in the 1950s, manufacturers quickly figured out that their product, with some tinkering, could be marketed as better—smarter!—than butter: butter with the bad nutrients removed (cholesterol and saturated fats) and replaced with good nutrients (polyunsaturated fats and then vitamins). Every time margarine was found wanting, the wanted nutrient could simply be added (Vitamin D? Got it now. Vitamin A? Sure, no problem). But of course margarine, being the product not of nature but of human ingenuity, could never be any smarter than the nutritionists dictating its recipe, and the nutritionists turned out to be not nearly as smart as they thought. The food scientists' ingenious method for making healthy vegetable oil solid at room temperature—by blasting it with hydrogen—turned out to produce unhealthy trans fats, fats that we now know are more dangerous than the saturated fats they were designed to replace. Yet the beauty of a processed food like margarine is that it can be endlessly reengineered to overcome even the most embarrassing about-face in nutritional thinking—including the real wincer that its main ingredient might cause heart attacks and cancer. So now the trans fats are gone, and margarine marches on, unfazed and apparently unkillable. Too bad the same cannot be said of an unknown number of margarine eaters.

By now we have become so inured to fake foods that we forget what a difficult trail margarine had to blaze before it and other synthetic food products could win government and consumer acceptance. At least since the 1906 publication of

Upton Sinclair's *The Jungle*, the "adulteration" of common foods has been a serious concern of the eating public and the target of numerous federal laws and Food and Drug Administration regulations. Many consumers regarded "oleomargarine" as just such an adulteration, and in the late 1800s five states passed laws requiring that all butter imitations be dyed pink so no one would be fooled. The Supreme Court struck down the laws in 1898. In retrospect, had the practice survived, it might have saved some lives.

The 1938 Food, Drug and Cosmetic Act imposed strict rules requiring that the word "imitation" appear on any food product that was, well, an imitation. Read today, the official rationale behind the imitation rule seems at once commonsensical and quaint: ". . . there are certain traditional foods that everyone knows, such as bread, milk and cheese, and that when consumers buy these foods, they should get the foods they are expecting . . . [and] if a food resembles a standardized food but does not comply with the standard, that food must be labeled as an 'imitation.' "

Hard to argue with that . . . but the food industry did, strenuously for decades, and in 1973 it finally succeeded in getting the imitation rule tossed out, a little-noticed but momentous step that helped speed America down the path to nutritionism.

Industry hated the imitation rule. There had been such a tawdry history of adulterated foods and related forms of snake oil in American commerce that slapping the word "imitation" on a food product was the kiss of death—an admission of adulteration and inferiority. By the 1960s and 1970s, the requirement that such a pejorative term appear on fake food packages stood in the way of innovation, indeed of the wholesale refor-mulation of the American food supply—a project that, in the wake of rising concerns about dietary fat and cholesterol, was coming to be seen as a good thing. What had been regarded as hucksterism and fraud in 1906 had begun to look like sound public health policy by 1973. The American Heart Association, eager to get Americans off saturated fats and onto vegetable oils (including hydrogenated vegetable oils), was actively en-couraging the food industry to "modify" various foods to get the saturated fats and cholesterol out of them, and in the early seventies the association urged that "any existing and regula-tory barriers to the marketing of such foods be removed."

And so they were when, in 1973, the FDA (not, note, the Congress that wrote the law) simply repealed the 1938 rule concerning imitation foods. It buried the change in a set of new, seemingly consumer-friendly rules about nutrient label-ing so that news of the imitation rule's repeal did not appear until the twenty-seventh paragraph of *The New York Times*' account, published under the headline F.D.A. PROPOSES SWEEPING CHANGE IN FOOD LABELING: NEW RULES DESIGNED TO GIVE CONSUMERS A BETTER IDEA OF NUTRITIONAL VALUE. (The second deck of the headline gave away the game: PROCESSORS BACK MOVE.) The revised imitation rule held that as long as an imitation product was not "nutritionally infe-rior" to the natural food it sought to impersonate—as long as it had the same quantities of recognized nutrients—the imita-tion could be marketed without using the dreaded "i" word.

With that, the regulatory door was thrown open to all man-ner of faked low-fat products: Fats in things like sour cream and yogurt could now be replaced with hydrogenated oils or guar gum or carrageenan, bacon bits could be replaced with soy protein, the cream in "whipped cream" and "coffee creamer" could be replaced with corn starch, and the yolks of liquefied eggs could be replaced with, well, whatever the food scientists could dream up, because the sky was now the limit. As long as the new fake foods were engineered to be nutritionally equivalent to the real article, they could no longer be considered fake. Of course the operative nutritionist assumption here is that we know enough to determine nutritional equivalence—something that the checkered history of baby formula suggests has never been the case.

Nutritionism had become the official ideology of the Food and Drug Administration; for all practical purposes the government had redefined foods as nothing more than the sum of their recognized nutrients. Adulteration had been repositioned as food science. All it would take now was a push from McGovern's *Dietary Goals* for hundreds of "traditional foods that everyone knows" to begin their long retreat from the supermarket shelves and for our eating to become more "scientific."

from

In the Woods

by

Tana French

In the summer of 1984, three children leave their small Dublin neighborhood to play in the surrounding woods. Hours later, their mothers' calls go unanswered. When the police arrive, they find only one of the children, gripping a tree trunk in terror, wearing blood-filled sneakers, and unable to recall a single detail of the previous hours.

Twenty years later, Detective Rob Ryan—the found boy, who has kept his past a secret—and his partner Cassie Maddox investigate the murder of a twelve-year-old girl in the same woods. Now, with only snippets of long-buried memories to guide him, Ryan has the chance to uncover both the mystery of the case before him, and that of his own shadowy past.

Prologue

Picture a summer stolen whole from some coming-of-age film set in small-town 1950s. This is none of Ireland's subtle seasons mixed for a connoisseur's palate, watercolor nuances within a pinch-sized range of cloud and soft rain; this is summer full-throated and extravagant in a hot pure silkscreen blue. This summer explodes on your tongue tasting of chewed blades of long grass, your own clean sweat, Marie biscuits with butter squirting through the holes and shaken bottles of red lemonade picnicked in tree houses. It tingles on your skin with BMX wind in your face, ladybug feet up your arm; it packs every breath full of mown grass and billowing wash lines; it chimes and fountains with birdcalls, bees, leaves and football-bounces and skipping-chants, *One! two! three!* This summer will never end. It starts every day with a shower of Mr. Whippy notes and your best friend's knock at the door, finishes it with long slow twilight and mothers silhouetted in doorways calling you to come in, through the bats shrilling among the black lace trees. This is Everysummer decked in all its best glory.

Picture an orderly little maze of houses on a hill, only a few miles from Dublin. Someday, the government declared, this will be a buzzing marvel of suburban vitality, a plan-perfect solution to overcrowding and poverty and every urban ill; for now it is a few handfuls of cloned semi-detacheds, still new enough to look startled and gauche on their hillside. While the government rhapsodized about McDonald's and multiscreens, a few young families—escaping from the tenements and outdoor toilets that went unmentioned in 1970s Ireland, or dreaming big back gardens and hopscotch roads for their children, or just buying as close to home as a teacher's or bus driver's salary would let them—packed rubbish bags and bumped along a two-track path, grass and daisies growing down the middle, to their mint-new start.

That was ten years ago, and the vague strobe-light dazzle of chain stores and community centers conjured up under "infrastructure" has so far failed to materialize (minor politicians occasionally bellow in the Dáil, unreported, about shady land deals). Farmers still pasture cows across the road, and night flicks on only a sparse constellation of lights on the neighboring hillsides; behind the estate, where the someday plans show the shopping center and the neat little park, spreads a square mile and who knows how many centuries of wood.

Move closer, follow the three children scrambling over the thin membrane of brick and mortar that holds the wood back from the semi-ds. Their bodies have the perfect economy of latency; they are streamlined and unselfconscious, pared to light flying machines. White tattoos—lightning bolt, star, A—flash where they cut Band-Aids into shapes and let the sun brown around them. A flag of white-blond hair flies out: toehold, knee on the wall, up and over and gone.

The wood is all flicker and murmur and illusion. Its silence is a pointillist conspiracy of a million tiny noises—rustles, flurries, nameless truncated shrieks; its emptiness teems with secret life, scurrying just beyond the corner of your eye. Careful: bees zip in and out of cracks in the leaning oak; stop to turn any stone and strange larvae will wriggle irritably, while an earnest thread of ants twines up your ankle. In the ruined tower, someone's abandoned stronghold, nettles thick as your wrist seize between the stones, and at dawn rabbits bring their kittens out from the foundations to play on ancient graves.

These three children own the summer. They know the wood as surely as they know the microlandscapes of their own grazed knees; put them down blindfolded in any dell or clearing and they could find their way out without putting a foot wrong. This is their territory, and they rule it wild and lordly as young animals; they scramble through its trees and hide-and-seek in its hollows all the endless day long, and all night in their dreams.

They are running into legend, into sleepover stories and nightmares parents never hear. Down the faint lost paths you would never find alone, skidding round the tumbled stone walls, they stream calls and shoelaces behind them like comet-trails. And who is it waiting on the riverbank with his hands in the willow branches, whose laughter tumbles swaying from a branch high above, whose is the face in the undergrowth in the corner of your eye, built of light and leaf-shadow, there and gone in a blink?

These children will not be coming of age, this or any other summer. This August will not ask them to find hidden reserves of strength and courage as they confront the complexity of the adult world and come away sadder and wiser and bonded for life. This summer has other requirements for them.

1

What I warn you to remember is that I am a detective. Our relationship with truth is fundamental but cracked, refracting confusingly like fragmented glass. It is the core of our careers, the endgame of every move we make, and we pursue it with strategies painstakingly constructed of lies and concealment and every variation on deception. The truth is the most desirable woman in the world and we are the most jealous lovers, reflexively denying anyone else the slightest glimpse of her. We betray her routinely, spending hours and days stupor-deep in lies, and then turn back to her holding out the lover's ultimate Möbius strip: *But I only did it because I love you so much.*

I have a pretty knack for imagery, especially the cheap, facile kind. Don't let me fool you into seeing us as a bunch of parfit gentil knights galloping off in doublets after Lady Truth on her white palfrey. What we do is crude, crass and nasty. A girl gives her boyfriend an alibi for the evening when we suspect him of robbing a north-side Centra and stabbing the clerk. I flirt with her at first, telling her I can see why he would want to stay home when he's got her; she is peroxided and greasy, with the flat, stunted features of generations of malnutrition, and privately I am thinking that if I were her boyfriend I would be relieved to trade her even for a hairy cellmate named Razor. Then I tell her we've found marked bills from the till in his classy white tracksuit bottoms, and he's claiming that she went out that evening and gave them to him when she got back.

I do it so convincingly, with such delicate crosshatching of discomfort and compassion at her man's betrayal, that finally her faith in four shared years disintegrates like a sand castle and through tears and snot, while her man sits with my partner in the next interview room saying nothing except "Fuck off, I was home with Jackie," she tells me everything from the time he left the house to the details of his sexual shortcomings. Then I pat her gently on the shoulder and give her a tissue and a cup of tea, and a statement sheet.

This is my job, and you don't go into it—or, if you do, you don't last—without some natural affinity for its priorities and demands. What I am telling you, before you begin my story, is this—two things: I crave truth. And I lie.

This is what I read in the file, the day after I made detective. I will come back to this story again and again, in any number of different ways. A poor thing, possibly, but mine own: this is the only story in the world that nobody but me will ever be able to tell.

On the afternoon of Tuesday, August 14, 1984, three children—Germaine ("Jamie") Elinor Rowan, Adam Robert Ryan and Peter Joseph Savage, all aged twelve—were playing in the road where their houses stood, in the small County Dublin town of Knocknaree. As it was a hot, clear day, many residents were in their gardens, and numerous witnesses saw the children at various times during the afternoon, balancing along the wall at the end of the road, riding their bicycles and swinging on a tire swing.

Knocknaree was at that time very sparsely developed, and a sizable wood adjoined the estate, separated from it by a five-foot wall. Around 3:00 p.m., the three children left their bicycles in the Savages' front garden, telling Mrs. Angela Savage—who was in the garden hanging washing on the line—that they were going to play in the wood. They did this often and knew that part of the wood well, so Mrs. Savage was not worried that they would become lost. Peter had a wristwatch, and she told him to be home by 6:30 for his tea. This conversation was confirmed by her next-door neighbor, Mrs. Mary Therese Corry, and several witnesses saw the children climbing over the wall at the end of the road and going into the wood.

When Peter Savage had not returned by 6:45 his mother called around to the mothers of the other two children, assuming he had gone to one of their houses. None of the children had returned. Peter Savage was normally reliable, but the parents did not at that point become worried; they assumed that the children had become absorbed in a game and forgotten to check the time. At approximately five minutes to seven, Mrs. Savage went around to the wood by the road, walked a little way in and called the children. She heard no answer and neither saw nor heard anything to indicate any person was present in the wood.

She returned home to serve tea to her husband, Mr. Joseph Savage, and their four younger children. After tea, Mr. Savage and Mr. John Ryan, Adam Ryan's father, went a little further into the wood, called the children and again received no response. At 8:25, when it was beginning to grow dark, the parents became seriously worried that the children might have become lost, and Miss Alicia Rowan (Germaine's mother, a single parent), who had a telephone, rang the police.

A search of the wood began. There was at this point some fear that the children might have run away. Miss Rowan had decided that Germaine was to go to boarding school in Dublin, remaining there during the week and returning to Knocknaree at weekends; she had been scheduled to leave two weeks later, and all three children had been very upset at the thought of being separated. However, a preliminary search of the children's rooms revealed that no clothing, money or personal items appeared to be missing. Germaine's piggy bank, in the form of a Russian doll, contained £5.85 and was intact.

At 10:20 p.m. a policeman with a torch found Adam Ryan in a densely wooded area near the center of the wood, standing with his back and palms pressed against a large oak tree. His fingernails were digging into the trunk so deeply that they had broken off in the bark. He appeared to have been there for some time but had not responded to the searchers' calling. He was taken to hospital. The Dog Unit was called in and tracked the two missing children to a point not far from where Adam Ryan had been found; there the dogs became confused and lost the scent.

When I was found I was wearing blue denim shorts, a white cotton T-shirt, white cotton socks and white lace-up running shoes. The shoes were heavily bloodstained, the socks less heavily. Later analysis of the staining patterns showed that the blood had soaked through the shoes from the inside outwards; it had soaked through the socks, in lesser concentrations, from the outside in. The implication was that the shoes had been removed and blood had spilled into them; some time later, when it had begun to coagulate, the shoes had been replaced on my feet, thus transferring blood to the socks. The T-shirt showed four parallel tears, between three and five inches in length, running diagonally across the back from the mid-left shoulder blade to the right back ribs.

I was uninjured except for some minor scratches on my calves, splinters (later found to be consistent with the wood of the oak tree) under my fingernails, and a deep abrasion on each kneecap, both beginning to form scabs. There was some uncertainty as to whether the grazes had been made in the wood or not, as a younger child (Aideen Watkins, aged five) who had been playing in the road stated that she had seen me fall from a wall earlier that day, landing on my knees. However, her statement varied with retelling and was not considered reliable. I was also near-catatonic: I made no voluntary movement for almost thirty-six hours and did not speak for a further two weeks. When I did, I had no memory of anything between leaving home that afternoon and being examined in the hospital.

The blood on my shoes and socks was tested for ABO type—DNA analysis was not a possibility in Ireland in 1984—and found to be type A positive. My blood was also found to be type A positive; however, it was judged to be unlikely that the abrasions on my knees, although deep, could have drawn enough blood to cause the heavy soaking in the running shoes. Germaine Rowan's blood had been tested prior to an appendectomy two years earlier, and her records showed that she was also A positive. Peter Savage, though no blood type was on record for him, was eliminated as the source of the stains: both his parents were found to be type O, making it impossible that he could be anything else. In the absence of conclusive identification, investigators could not eliminate the possibility that the blood had come from a fourth individual, nor the possibility that it originated from multiple sources.

The search continued throughout the night of August 14 and for weeks thereafter—teams of volunteers combed the nearby fields and hills, every known bog hole and bog drain in the area was explored, divers searched the river that ran through the wood—with no result. Fourteen months later, Mr. Andrew Raftery, a local resident walking his dog in the wood, spotted a wristwatch in the undergrowth about two hundred feet from the tree where I had been found. The watch was distinctive—the face showed a cartoon of a footballer in action, and the second-hand was tipped with a football—and Mr. and Mrs. Savage identified it as having belonged to their son Peter. Mrs. Savage confirmed that he had been wearing it on the afternoon of his disappearance. The watch's plastic strap appeared to have been torn from the metal face with some force, possibly by catching on a low branch when Peter was running. The Technical Bureau identified a number of partial fingerprints on the strap and face; all were consistent with prints found on Peter Savage's belongings.

Despite numerous police appeals and a high-profile media campaign, no other trace of Peter Savage and Germaine Rowan was ever found.

I became a policeman because I wanted to be a Murder detective. My time in training and in uniform—Templemore College, endless complicated physical exercises, wandering around small towns in a cartoonish Day-Glo jacket, investigating which of the three unintelligible local delinquents had broken Mrs. McSweeney's garden-shed window—all felt like an embarrassing daze scripted by Ionesco, a trial by tedium I had to endure, for some dislocated bureaucratic reason, in order to earn my actual job. I never think about those years and cannot remember them with any clarity. I made no friends; to me my detachment from the whole process felt involuntary and inevitable, like the side effect of a sedative drug, but the other cops read it as deliberate superciliousness, a studied sneer at their solid rural backgrounds and solid rural ambitions. Possibly it was. I recently found a diary entry from college in which I described my classmates as "a herd of mouth-breathing fucktard yokels who wade around in a miasma of cliché so thick you can practically smell the bacon and cabbage and cow shite and altar candles." Even assuming I was having a bad day, I think this shows a certain lack of respect for cultural differences.

When I made the Murder squad, I had already had my new work clothes—beautifully cut suits in materials so fine they felt alive to your fingers, shirts with the subtlest of blue or green pinstripes, rabbit-soft cashmere scarves—hanging in my wardrobe for almost a year. I love the unspoken dress code. It was one of the things that first fascinated me about the job—that and the private, functional, elliptical shorthand: latents, trace, Forensics. One of the Stephen King small towns where I was posted after Templemore had a murder: a routine domestic-violence incident that had escalated beyond even the perpetrator's expectations, but, because the man's previous girlfriend had died in suspicious circumstances, the Murder squad sent down a pair of detectives. All the week they were there, I had one eye on the coffee machine whenever I was at my desk, so I could get my coffee when the detectives got theirs, take my time adding milk and eavesdrop on the streamlined, brutal rhythms of their conversation: when the Bureau comes back on the tox, once the lab IDs the serrations. I started smoking again so I could follow them out to the car park and smoke a few feet from them, staring blindly at the sky and listening. They would give me brief unfocused smiles, sometimes a flick of a tarnished Zippo, before dismissing me with the slightest angle of a shoulder and going back to their subtle, multidimensional strategies. *Pull in the ma first, then give him an hour or two to sit at home worrying about what she's saying, then get him back in. Set up a scene room but just walk him through it, don't give him time for a good look.*

Contrary to what you might assume, I did not become a detective on some quixotic quest to solve my childhood mystery. I read the file once, that first day, late on my own in the squad room with my desk lamp the only pool of light (forgotten names setting echoes flicking like bats around my head as they testified in faded Biro that Jamie had kicked her mother because she didn't want to go to boarding school, that "dangerous-looking" teenage boys spent evenings hanging around at the edge of the wood, that Peter's mother once had a bruise on her cheekbone), and then never looked at it again. It was these arcana I craved, these near-invisible textures like a Braille legible only to the initiated. They were like thoroughbreds, those two Murder detectives passing through Ballygobackwards; like trapeze artists honed to a sizzling shine. They played for the highest stakes, and they were experts at their game.

I knew that what they did was cruel. Humans are feral and ruthless; this, this watching through cool intent eyes and delicately adjusting one factor or another till a man's fundamental instinct for self-preservation cracks, is savagery in its most pure, most polished and most highly evolved form.

We heard about Cassie days before she joined the squad, probably before she even got the offer. Our grapevine is ridiculously, old-ladyishly efficient. Murder is a high-pressure squad and a small one, only twenty permanent members, and under any added strain (anyone leaving, anyone new, too much work, too little work), it tends to develop a tinge of cabin-fevery hysteria, full of complicated alliances and frantic rumors. I am usually well out of the loop, but the Cassie Maddox buzz was loud enough that even I picked up on it.

For one thing she was a woman, which caused a certain amount of poorly sublimated outrage. We are all well trained to be horrified by the evils of prejudice, but there are deep stubborn veins of nostalgia for the 1950s (even among people my age; in much of Ireland the fifties didn't end until 1995, when we skipped straight to Thatcher's eighties), when you could scare a suspect into confession by threatening to tell his mammy and the only foreigners in the country were med students and work was the one place where you were safe from nagging females. Cassie was only the fourth woman Murder had taken on, and at least one of the others had been a huge mistake (a deliberate one, according to some people) who had entered squad lore when she nearly got herself and her partner killed by freaking out and throwing her gun at a cornered suspect's head.

Also, Cassie was only twenty-eight and only a few years out of Templemore. Murder is one of the elite squads, and nobody under thirty gets taken on unless his father is a politician. Generally you have to spend a couple of years as a floater, helping out wherever someone is needed for legwork, and then work your way up through at least one or two other squads. Cassie had less than a year in Drugs under her belt. The grapevine claimed, inevitably, that she was sleeping with someone important, or alternatively that she was someone's illegitimate daughter, or—with a touch more originality—that she had caught someone important buying drugs and this job was a payoff for keeping her mouth shut.

I had no problem with the idea of Cassie Maddox. I had been in Murder only a few months, but I disliked the New Neanderthal locker-room overtones, competing cars and competing aftershaves and subtly bigoted jokes justified as "ironic," which always made me want to go into a long pedantic lecture on the definition of irony. On the whole I prefer women to men. I also had complicated private insecurities to do with my own place on the squad. I was almost thirty-one and had two years as a floater and two in Domestic Violence, so my appointment was less sketchy than Cassie's, but I sometimes thought the brass assumed I was a good detective in the mindless preprogrammed way that some men will assume a tall, slim, blond woman is beautiful even if she has a face like a hyperthyroid turkey: because I have all the accessories. I have a perfect BBC accent, picked up at boarding school as protective camouflage, and all that colonization takes awhile to wear off: even though the Irish will cheer for absolutely any team playing against England, and I know a number of pubs where I couldn't order a drink without risking a glass to the back of the head, they still assume that anyone with a stiff upper lip is more intelligent, better educated and generally more likely to be right. On top of this I am tall, with a bony, rangy build that can look lean and elegant if my suit is cut just right, and fairly good-looking in an offbeat way. Central Casting would definitely think I was a good detective, probably the brilliant maverick loner who risks his neck fearlessly and always gets his man.

I have practically nothing in common with that guy, but I wasn't sure anyone else had noticed. Sometimes, after too much solitary vodka, I came up with vivid paranoid scenarios in which the superintendent found out I was actually a civil servant's son from Knocknaree and I got transferred to Intellectual Property Rights. With Cassie Maddox around, I figured, people were much less likely to spend time having suspicions about me.

When she finally arrived, she was actually sort of an anticlimax. The lavishness of the rumors had left me with a mental picture of someone on the same TV-drama scale, with legs up to here and shampoo-ad hair and possibly a catsuit. Our superintendent, O'Kelly, introduced her at Monday-morning parade, and she stood up and said something standard about being delighted to join the squad and hoping she'd live up to its high standards; she was barely medium height, with a cap of dark curls and a boyish, slim, square-shouldered build. She wasn't my type—I have always liked girlie girls, sweet, tiny bird-boned girls I can pick up and whirl around in a one-armed hug—but there was something about her: maybe the way she stood, weight on one hip, straight and easy as a gymnast; maybe just the mystery.

"I heard her family are Masons and they threatened to have the squad dissolved if we didn't take her on," said Sam O'Neill, behind me. Sam is a stocky, cheerful, unflappable guy from Galway. I hadn't had him down as one of the people who would get swept up in the rumor tsunami.

"Oh for God's sake," I said, falling for it. Sam grinned and shook his head at me, and slid past me to a seat. I went back to looking at Cassie, who had sat down and propped one foot against the chair in front of her, leaning her notebook on her thigh.

She wasn't dressed like a Murder detective. You learn by osmosis, as soon as you set your sights on the job, that you are expected to look professional, educated, discreetly expensive with just a soupçon of originality. We give the taxpayers their money's worth of comforting cliché. We mostly shop at Brown Thomas, during the sales, and occasionally come into work wearing embarrassingly identical soupçons. Up until then, the wackiest our squad had got was this cretin called Quigley, who sounded like Daffy Duck with a Donegal accent and wore slogan T-shirts (MAD BASTARD) under his suits because he thought he was being daring. When he eventually realized that none of us were shocked, or even remotely interested, he got his mammy to come up for the day and take him shopping at BT.

That first day I put Cassie in the same category. She was wearing combat trousers and a wine-colored woollen sweater with sleeves that came down past her wrists, and clunky runners, and I put this down as affectation: *Look, I'm too cool for your conventions.* The spark of animosity this ignited increased my attraction to her. There is a side of me that is most intensely attracted to women who annoy me.

I didn't register her very much over the next couple of weeks, except in the general way that you do register any decent-looking woman when you're surrounded by men. She was being shown the ropes by Tom Costello, our resident grizzled veteran, and I was working on a homeless man found battered to death in an alleyway. Some of the depressing, inexorable flavor of his life had leaked over into his death, and it was one of those cases that are hopeless from the start—no leads, nobody saw anything, nobody heard anything, whoever killed him was probably so drunk or high he didn't even remember doing it—so my gung-ho newbie sparkle was starting to look a little patchy. I was also partnered with Quigley, which wasn't working out; his idea of humor was to reenact large segments of *Wallace & Gromit* and then do a Woody Woodpecker laugh to show you they were funny, and it was dawning on me that I'd been teamed up with him not because he would be friendly to the new boy but because nobody else wanted him. I didn't have the time or the energy to get to know Cassie. Sometimes I wonder how long we might have gone on like that. Even in a small squad, there are always people with whom you never get beyond nods and smiles in corridors, simply because your paths never happen to cross anywhere else.

We became friends because of her moped, a cream 1981 Vespa that somehow, in spite of its classic status, reminds me of a happy mutt with some border collie in its pedigree. I call it the Golf Cart to annoy Cassie; she calls my battered white Land Rover the Compensation Wagon, with the odd compassionate remark about my girlfriends, or the Ecomobile when she is feeling bolshie. The Golf Cart chose a viciously wet, windy day in September to break down outside work. I was on my way out of the car park and saw this little dripping girl in a red rain jacket, looking like Kenny out of *South Park,* standing beside this little dripping bike and yelling after a bus that had just drenched her. I pulled over and called out the window, "Could you use a hand?"

She looked at me and shouted back, "What makes you think that?" and then, taking me completely by surprise, started to laugh.

For about five minutes, as I tried to get the Vespa to start, I fell in love with her. The oversized raincoat made her look about eight, as though she should have had matching Wellies with ladybugs on them, and inside the red hood were huge brown eyes and rain-spiked lashes and a face like a kitten's. I wanted to dry her gently with a big fluffy towel, in front of a roaring fire. But then she said, "Here, let me—you have to know how to twist the thingy," and I raised an eyebrow and said, "The *thingy*? Honestly, *girls*."

I immediately regretted it—I have never been talented at banter, and you never know, she could have been some earnest droning feminist extremist who would lecture me in the rain about Amelia Earhart. But Cassie gave me a deliberate, sideways look, and then clasped her hands with a wet spat and said in a breathy Marilyn voice, "Ohhh, I've always *dreamed* of a knight in shining armor coming along and rescuing little me! Only in my dreams he was good-looking."

What I saw transformed with a click like a shaken kaleidoscope. I stopped falling in love with her and started to like her immensely. I looked at her hoodie jacket and said, "Oh my God, they're about to kill Kenny." Then I loaded the Golf Cart into the back of my Land Rover and drove her home.

She had a studio flat, which is what landlords call a bedsit where there is room to have a friend over, on the top floor of a semi-dilapidated Georgian house in Sandymount. The road was quiet; the wide sash window looked out over rooftops to Sandymount beach. There were wooden bookshelves crammed with old paperbacks, a low Victorian sofa upholstered in a virulent shade of turquoise, a big futon with a patchwork duvet, no ornaments or posters, a handful of shells and rocks and chestnuts on the windowsill.

I don't remember very many specifics about that evening, and according to Cassie neither does she. I can remember some of the things we talked about, a few piercingly clear images, but I could give you almost none of the actual words. This strikes me as odd and, in certain moods, as very magical, linking the evening to those fugue states that over the centuries have been blamed on fairies or witches or aliens, and from which no one returns unchanged. But those lost, liminal pockets of time are usually solitary; there is something about the idea of a shared one that makes me think of twins, reaching out slow blind hands in a gravity-free and wordless space.

I know I stayed for dinner—a studenty dinner, fresh pasta and sauce from a jar, hot whiskey in china mugs. I remember Cassie opening a huge wardrobe that took up most of one wall, to pull out a towel for me to dry my hair. Someone, presumably her, had slotted bookshelves inside the wardrobe. The shelves were set at odd, off-kilter heights and packed with a wild variety of objects: I didn't get a proper look, but there were chipped enamel saucepans, marbled notebooks, soft jewel-colored sweaters, tumbles of scribbled paper. It was like something in the background of one of those old illustrations of fairy-tale cottages.

I do remember finally asking, "So how did you end up in the squad?" We had been talking about how she was settling in, and I thought I had dropped it in pretty casually, but she gave me a tiny, mischievous smile, as though we were playing checkers and she had caught me trying to distract her from a clumsy move.

"Being a girl, you mean?"

"Actually, I meant being so young," I said, although of course I had been thinking of both.

"Costello called me 'son' yesterday," Cassie said. " 'Fair play to you, son.' Then he got all flustered and stammery. I think he was afraid I'd sue."

"It was probably a compliment, in its own way," I said.

"That's how I took it. He's quite sweet, really." She tucked a cigarette in her mouth and held out her hand; I threw her my lighter.

"Someone told me you were undercover as a hooker and ran into one of the brass," I said, but Cassie just tossed the lighter back to me and grinned.

"Quigley, right? He told me you were an MI6 mole."

"What?" I said, outraged and falling straight into my own trap. "Quigley is a cretin."

"Gee, you think?" she said, and started to laugh. After a moment I joined in. The mole thing bothered me—if anyone actually believed it, they would never tell me anything again—and being taken for English infuriates me to an irrational degree, but I sort of enjoyed the absurd idea of me as James Bond.

"I'm from *Dublin*," I said. "I got the accent at boarding school in England. And that lobotomized bogger knows it." Which he did; in my first weeks on the squad he had pestered me so monotonously about what an English guy was doing in the Irish police force, like a child poking you in the arm and droning "Why? Why? Why?" that I had finally broken my need-to-know rule and explained the accent. Apparently I should have used smaller words.

"What are you doing working with him?" Cassie asked.

"Quietly losing my mind," I said.

Something, I'm still not sure what, had made up Cassie's mind. She leaned sideways, switching her mug to the other hand (she swears we were drinking coffee by that stage and claims that I only think it was hot whiskey because we drank it so often that winter, but I know, I remember the sharp prongs of a clove on my tongue, the heady steam), and pulled up her top to just under her breast. I was so startled that it took me a moment to realize what she was showing me: a long scar, still red and raised and spidered with stitch marks, curving along the line of a rib. "I got stabbed," she said.

It was so obvious that I was embarrassed nobody had thought of it. A detective wounded on duty gets his or her choice of assignment. I suppose we had overlooked this possibility because normally a stabbing would have practically shorted out the grapevine; we had heard nothing about this.

"Jesus," I said. "What happened?"

"I was undercover in UCD," Cassie said. This explained both the clothes and the information gap—undercover are serious about secrecy. "That's how I made detective so fast: there was a ring dealing on campus, and Drugs wanted to find out who was behind it, so they needed people who could pass for students. I went in as a psychology postgrad. I did a few years of psychology at Trinity before Templemore, so I could talk the talk, and I look young."

She did. There was a specific clarity about her face that I've never seen in anyone else; her skin was poreless as a child's, and her features—wide mouth, high round cheekbones, tilted nose, long curves of eyebrow—made other people's look smudged and blurry. As far as I could tell she never wore makeup, except for a red-tinted lip balm that smelled of cinnamon and made her seem even younger. Few people would have considered her beautiful, but my tastes have always leaned toward bespoke rather than brand name, and I took far more pleasure in looking at her than at any of the busty blond clones whom magazines, insultingly, tell me I should desire.

"And your cover got blown?"

"No," she said, indignant. "I found out who the main dealer was—this brain-dead rich boy from Blackrock, studying business, of course—and I spent months making friends with him, laughing at his crap jokes, proofreading his essays. Then I suggested maybe I could deal to the girls, they'd be less nervous about buying drugs from another woman, right? He liked the idea, everything was going great, I was dropping hints that maybe it would be simpler if I met the supplier myself instead of getting the stuff through him. Only then Dealer Boy started snorting a little too much of his own speed—this was in May, he had exams coming up. He got paranoid, decided I was trying to take over his business and stabbed me." She took a sip of her drink. "Don't tell Quigley, though. The operation's still going on, so I'm not supposed to talk about it. Let the poor little fucker enjoy his illusions."

I was secretly terribly impressed, not only by the stabbing (after all, I told myself, it wasn't as though she had done something outstandingly brave or intelligent; she had just failed to dodge fast enough), but by the dark, adrenaline-paced thought of undercover work and by the utter casualness with which she told the story. Having worked hard to perfect an air of easy indifference, I recognize the real thing when I see it.

"Jesus," I said again. "I bet he got a good going-over when they brought him in." I've never hit a suspect—I find there's no need to, as long as you make them think you might—but there are guys who do, and anyone who stabs a cop is likely to pick up a few bruises en route to the station.

She cocked an eyebrow at me, amused. "They didn't. That would've wrecked the whole operation. They need him to get to the supplier; they just started over with a new undercover."

"But don't you want him taken down?" I said, frustrated by her calm and by my own creeping sense of naïveté. "He *stabbed* you."

Cassie shrugged. "After all, if you think about it, he had a point: I *was* only pretending to be his friend to screw him over. And he was a strung-out drug dealer. That's what strung-out drug dealers do."

After that my memory grows hazy again. I know that, determined to impress her in my turn, and never having been stabbed or involved in a shootout or anything, I told her a long and rambling and mostly true story about talking down a guy who was threatening to jump off the roof of a block of flats with his baby, back when I was in Domestic Violence (really, I think I must have been a little drunk: another reason I'm so sure we had hot whiskey). I remember a passionate conversation about Dylan Thomas, I think, Cassie kneeling up on the sofa and gesturing, her cigarette burning away forgotten in the ashtray. Bantering, smart but tentative as shy circling children, both of us checking covertly after each riposte to make sure we hadn't crossed any line or hurt any feelings. Firelight and the Cowboy Junkies, Cassie singing along in a sweet rough undertone.

"The drugs you got from Dealer Boy," I said, later. "Did you actually sell them to students?"

Cassie got up to put on the kettle. "Occasionally," she said.

"Didn't that bother you?"

"Everything about undercover bothered me," Cassie said. "Everything."

When we went into work the next morning we were friends. It really was as simple as that: we planted seeds without thinking, and woke up to our own private beanstalk. At break time I caught Cassie's eye and mimed a cigarette, and we went outside to sit cross-legged at either end of a bench, like bookends. At the end of the shift she waited for me, bitching to the air about how long I took to get my things together ("It's like hanging out with Sarah Jessica Parker. Don't forget your lip liner, sweetie, we don't want the chauffeur to have to go back for it again"), and said "Pint?" on the way down the stairs. I can't explain the alchemy that transmuted one evening into the equivalent of years held lightly in common. The only way I can put it is that we recognized, too surely even for surprise, that we shared the same currency.

As soon as she finished learning the ropes with Costello, we partnered up. O'Kelly put up a bit of a fight—he didn't like the idea of two shiny new rookies working together, and it meant he would have to find something else to do with Quigley—but I had, by sheer luck rather than shrewd detection, found someone who had heard someone bragging about killing the homeless guy, so I was in O'Kelly's good books, and I took full advantage of it. He warned us that he would give us only the simplest cases and the no-hopers, "nothing that needs real detective work," and we nodded meekly and thanked him again, aware that murderers aren't considerate enough to ensure that the complex cases come up in strict rotation. Cassie moved her stuff to the desk beside mine, and Costello got stuck with Quigley and gave us sad reproachful looks for weeks, like a martyred Labrador.

Over the next couple of years we developed, I think, a good reputation within the squad. We pulled in the suspect from the alley beating and interrogated him for six hours—although, if you deleted every recurrence of "Ah, fuck, man" from the tape, I doubt it would run over forty minutes—

until he confessed. He was a junkie called Wayne (*"Wayne,"* I said to Cassie, while we were getting him a Sprite and watching him pick his acne in the one-way glass. "Why didn't his parents just tattoo 'Nobody in my family has ever finished secondary school' on his forehead at birth?") and he had beaten up the homeless guy, who was known as Beardy Eddie, for stealing his blanket. After he signed his statement, Wayne wanted to know if he could have his blanket back. We handed him over to the uniforms and told him they would look into it, and then we went back to Cassie's with a bottle of champagne and stayed up talking till six in the morning, and came in to work late and sheepish and still a little giggly.

We went through the predictable process where Quigley and a few of the others spent awhile asking me whether I was shagging her and whether, if so, she was any good; once it dawned on them that I genuinely wasn't, they moved on to her probable dykehood (I have always considered Cassie to be very clearly feminine, but I could see how, to a certain kind of mind, the haircut and the lack of makeup and the boys'-department corduroys would add up to Sapphic tendencies). Cassie eventually got bored of this and tidied things up by appearing at the Christmas party with a strapless black velvet cocktail dress and a bullishly handsome rugby player named Gerry. He was actually her second cousin and happily married, but he was heartily protective of Cassie and had no objection to gazing adoringly at her for an evening if it would smooth her career path.

After that, the rumors faded and people more or less left us to our own devices, which suited us both. Contrary to appearances, Cassie is not a particularly social person, any more than I am; she is vivacious and quick with banter and can talk to anyone, but given the choice, she preferred my company to that of a big group. I slept on her sofa a lot. Our solve rate was good and rising; O'Kelly stopped threatening to split us up every time we were late turning in paperwork. We were in the courtroom to see Wayne found guilty of manslaughter ("Ah, *fuck,* man"). Sam O'Neill drew a deft little caricature of the two of us as Mulder and Scully (I still have it, somewhere) and Cassie stuck it to the side of her computer, next to a bumper sticker that said BAD COP! NO DOUGHNUT!

In retrospect, I think Cassie came along at just the right time for me. My dazzling, irresistible outsider's vision of the Murder squad had not included things like Quigley, or gossip, or interminable circular interrogations of junkies with six-word vocabularies and dentist's-drill accents. I had pictured

97

a tensile, heightened mode of existence, everything small and petty bush-fired away by a readiness so charged it snapped sparks, and the reality had left me bewildered and let down, like a child opening a glittering Christmas present and finding woolly socks inside. If it hadn't been for Cassie, I think I might have ended up turning into that detective on *Law & Order,* the one who has ulcers and thinks everything is a government conspiracy.

2

We caught the Devlin case on a Wednesday morning in August. It was, according to my notes, 11:48, so everyone else was out getting coffee. Cassie and I were playing Worms on my computer.

"Ha," said Cassie, sending one of her worms bopping over to mine with a baseball bat and thwacking him off a cliff. My worm, Groundsweeper Willy, yelled, "Och, ye big mammy's boy!" at me on his way down towards the ocean.

"I let you do that," I told her.

"Course you did," said Cassie. "No real man could actually be beaten by a little girl. Even the worm knows it: only a raisin-balled, testosterone-free cream puff could—"

"Fortunately I'm secure enough in my masculinity that I don't feel remotely threatened by—"

"Shh," said Cassie, turning my face back towards the monitor. "Nice boy. Shush, look pretty and play with your worm. God knows nobody else is going to."

"I think I'll transfer somewhere nice and peaceful, like ERU," I said.

"ERU needs fast response times, sweetie," Cassie said. "If it takes you half an hour to decide what to do with an imaginary worm, they're not gonna want you in charge of hostages."

At that point O'Kelly banged into the squad room and demanded, "Where is everyone?" Cassie hit Alt-Tab fast; one of her worms was named O'Smelly and she had been purposefully sending him into hopeless situations, to watch him get blown up by exploding sheep.

"Break," I said.

"Bunch of archaeologists found a body. Who's up?"

"We'll have it," said Cassie, shoving her foot off my chair so that hers shot back to her own desk.

"Why us?" I said. "Can't the pathologist deal with it?"

Archaeologists are required by law to call the police if they find human remains at a depth of less than nine feet below ground level. This is in case some genius gets the idea of concealing a murder by burying the corpse in a fourteenth-century graveyard and hoping it gets marked down as medieval. I suppose they figure that anyone who has the enterprise to dig down more than nine feet without getting spotted deserves a little leeway for sheer dedication. Uniforms and pathologists get called out fairly regularly, when subsidence and erosion have brought a skeleton close to the surface, but usually this is only a formality; it's relatively simple to distinguish between modern and ancient remains. Detectives are called only in exceptional circumstances, usually when a peat bog has preserved flesh and bone so perfectly that the body has all the clamoring immediacy of a fresh corpse.

"Not this time," said O'Kelly. "It's modern. Young female, looks like murder. Uniforms asked for us. They're only in Knocknaree, so you won't need to stay out there."

Something strange happened to my breath. Cassie stopped shoving things into her satchel and I felt her eyes flick to me for a split second. "Sir, I'm sorry, we really can't take on another full murder investigation right now. We're bang in the middle of the McLoughlin case and—"

"That didn't bother you when you thought this was just an afternoon off, Maddox," said O'Kelly. He dislikes Cassie for a series of mind-numbingly predictable reasons—her sex, her clothes, her age, her semiheroic record—and the predictability bothers her far more than the dislike. "If you had time for a day out down the country, you have time for a serious murder investigation. The Tech Bureau are already on their way." And he left.

"Oh, shit," said Cassie. "Oh, shit, the little wanker. Ryan, I'm so sorry. I just didn't think—"

"It's fine, Cass," I said. One of the best things about Cassie is that she knows when to shut up and leave you alone. It was her turn to drive, but she picked out my favorite unmarked—a '98 Saab that handles like a dream—and threw me the keys. In the car, she dug her CD holder out of her satchel and passed it to me; driver chooses the music, but I tend to forget to bring any. I picked the first thing that looked as if it had a hard pounding bass, and turned it up loud.

I hadn't been to Knocknaree since that summer. I went to boarding school a few weeks after Jamie should have gone—not the same school; one in Wiltshire, as far away as my parents could afford—and when I came back at Christmas we lived in Leixlip, out on the other side of Dublin. Once we hit the highway, Cassie had to dig out the map and find the exit, then navigate us down potholed side roads edged with long grass, hedges grown wild and scraping at the windows.

Obviously, I have always wished I could remember what happened in that wood. The very few people who know about the whole Knocknaree thing invariably suggest, sooner or later, that I should try hypnotic regression, but for some reason I find the idea distasteful. I'm deeply suspicious of anything with a whiff of the New Age about it—not because of the practices themselves, which as far as I can tell from a safe distance may well have a lot to them, but because of the people who get involved, who always seem to be the kind who corner you at parties to explain how they discovered that they are survivors and deserve to be happy. I worry that I might come out of hypnosis with that sugar-high glaze of self-satisfied enlightenment, like a seventeen-year-old who's just discovered Kerouac, and start proselytizing strangers in pubs.

The Knocknaree site was a huge field set on a shallow slope, down the side of a hill. It was stripped to bare earth, churned up by purposeful, indecipherable archaeological scribblings—trenches, giant anthills of soil, Portakabins, scattered fragments of rough stone wall like outlines for some lunatic maze—that made it surreal, postnuclear. It was bordered on one side by a thick stand of trees, on another by a wall, tidy gables peeking over it, that ran from the trees to the road. Towards the top of the slope, near the wall, techs were clustered around something cordoned off by blue-and-white crime-scene tape. I probably knew every one of them, but the context translated them—white coveralls, busy gloved hands, nameless delicate instruments—into something alien and sinister and possibly CIA-related. The one or two identifiable objects looked picture-book solid and comforting: a low whitewashed cottage just off the road, with a black-and-white sheepdog stretched in front of it, paws twitching; a stone tower covered in ivy that rippled like water in the breeze. Light fluttered off the dark slice of a river cutting across one corner of the field.

runner heels dug into the earth of the bank, leaf-shadows dappling a red T-shirt, fishing-rods of branches and string, slapping at midges: Shut up! You'll scare the fish!—

This field was where the wood had been, twenty years ago. The strip of trees was what was left of it. I had lived in one of the houses beyond the wall.

I had not expected this. I don't watch Irish news; it always morphs into a migraine blur of identical sociopath-eyed politicians mouthing meaningless white noise, like the gibber you get when you play a 33-rpm record at 45. I stick to foreign news, where distance gives enough simplification for the comforting illusion that there is some difference between the various players. I had known, by vague osmosis, that there was an archaeological site somewhere around Knocknaree and that there was some controversy about it, but I hadn't picked up the details, or the exact location. I had not been expecting this.

I parked on the shoulder across the road from the Portakabin cluster, between the bureau van and a big black Merc—Cooper, the forensic pathologist. We got out of the car and I stopped to check my gun: clean, loaded, safety on. I wear a shoulder holster; anywhere more obvious feels gauche, a legal equivalent of flashing. Cassie says fuck gauche, when you are five foot five and young and female a little blatant authority isn't a bad thing, and wears a belt. Often the discrepancy works for us: people don't know who to worry about, the little girl with the gun or the big guy apparently without, and the distraction of deciding keeps them off balance.

Cassie leaned against the car and dug her smokes out of her satchel. "Want one?"

"No, thanks," I said. I went over my harness, tightened the straps, made sure none of them were twisted. My fingers seemed thick and clumsy, detached from my body. I did not want Cassie to point out that, whoever this girl was and whenever she had been killed, it was unlikely that the murderer was skulking behind a Portakabin needing to be taken at gunpoint. She tipped her head back and blew smoke up into the branches overhead. It was your basic Irish summer day, irritatingly coy, all sun and skidding clouds and jackknifing breeze, ready at any second to make an effortless leap into bucketing rain or blazing sun or both.

"Come on," I said. "Let's get into character." Cassie put out her smoke on the sole of her shoe and tucked the butt back into the packet, and we headed across the road.

A middle-aged guy in an unraveling sweater was hovering between the Portakabins, looking lost. He perked up when he saw us.

"Detectives," he said. "You must be the detectives, yes? Dr. Hunt . . . I mean, Ian Hunt. Site director. Where would you like to—well, the office or the body or . . . ? I'm not sure, you know. Protocol and things like that." He was one of those people whom your mind instantly starts turning into a cartoon: scribbled wings and beak and ta-da, Road Runner.

"Detective Maddox, and this is Detective Ryan," Cassie said. "If it's all right, Dr. Hunt, maybe one of your colleagues could give Detective Ryan an overview of the whole site, while you show me the remains?"

Little bitch, I thought. I felt jittery and dazed at the same time, as if I had a massive stone-over and had tried to clear it with way too much caffeine; the light jinking off fragments of mica in the rutted ground looked too bright, tricky and fevered. I was in no mood to be protected. But one of Cassie's and my unspoken rules is that, in public at least, we do not contradict each other. Sometimes one of us takes advantage of it.

"Um . . . yes," said Hunt, blinking at us through his glasses. He somehow gave the impression of constantly dropping things—lined yellow pages, chewed-looking tissues, half-wrapped throat lozenges—even though he wasn't holding anything. "Yes, of course. They're all . . . Well, Mark and Damien usually do the tours, but you see Damien's . . . Mark!" He aimed it in the general direction of the open door of a Portakabin, and I had a fleeting glimpse of a bunch of people crowded around a bare table: army jackets, sandwiches and steaming mugs, clods of earth on the floor. One of the guys tossed down a hand of cards and started disentangling himself from the plastic chairs.

"I told them all, stay in there," said Hunt. "I wasn't sure. . . . Evidence. Footprints and . . . fibers."

"That's perfect, Dr. Hunt," Cassie said. "We'll try to clear the scene and let you get back to work as soon as possible."

"We've only got a few weeks left," said the guy at the Portakabin door. He was short and wiry, with a build that would have looked almost childishly slight under a heavy sweater; he was wearing a T-shirt, though, with muddy combats and Doc Martens, and below the sleeves his muscles were complex and corded as a featherweight's.

"Then you'd better get a move on and show my colleague around," Cassie told him.

"Mark," said Hunt. "Mark, this detective needs a tour. The usual, you know, around the site."

Mark eyed Cassie for another moment, then gave her a nod; she had apparently passed some private test. He moved on to me. He was somewhere in his mid-twenties, with a long fair ponytail and a narrow, foxy face with very green, very intense eyes. Men like him—men who are obviously interested purely in what they think of other people, not in what other people think of them—have always made me violently insecure. They have a kind of gyroscopic certainty that makes me feel bumbling, affected, spineless, in the wrong place in the wrong clothes.

"You'll want wellies," he told me, giving my shoes a sardonic look: QED. His accent had a hard border-country edge. "Spares in the tools shed."

"I'll be fine as I am," I said. I had an idea that archaeological digs involved trenches several feet deep in mud, but I was damned if I was going to spend the morning clumping around after this guy with my suit trailing off ludicrously into someone's discarded wellies. I wanted something—a cup of tea, a smoke, anything that would give me an excuse to sit still for five minutes and figure out how to do this.

Mark raised one eyebrow. "Fair enough. Over this way."

He headed off between the Portakabins without checking whether I was behind him. Cassie, unexpectedly, grinned at me as I followed him—a mischievous *Gotcha!* grin, which made me feel a little better. I scratched my cheek at her, with my middle finger.

Mark took me across the site, along a narrow path between mysterious earthworks and clumps of stones. He walked like a martial artist or a poacher, a long, easy, balanced lope. "Medieval drainage ditch," he said, pointing. A couple of crows shot up from an abandoned wheelbarrow full of dirt, decided we were harmless and went back to picking through the earth. "And that's a Neolithic settlement. This site's been inhabited more or less nonstop since the Stone Age. Still is. See the cottage, that's eighteenth-century. It was one of the places where they planned the 1798 Rebellion." He glanced over his shoulder at me, and I had an absurd impulse to explain my accent and inform him that I was not only Irish but from just around the corner, so there. "The guy who lives there now is descended from the guy who built it."

We had reached the stone tower in the middle of the site. Arrow slits showed through gaps in the ivy, and a section of broken wall sloped down from one side. It looked vaguely, frustratingly familiar, but I couldn't tell whether this was because I actually remembered it or because I knew I should.

Mark pulled a packet of tobacco out of his combats and started rolling a cigarette. There was masking tape wrapped around both his hands, at the base of the fingers. "The Walsh clan built this keep in the fourteenth century, added a castle over the next couple of hundred years," he said. "This was all their territory, from those hills over there"—he jerked his head at the horizon, high overlapping hills furred with dark trees—"to a bend in the river down beyond that gray farmhouse. They were rebels, raiders. In the seventeenth century they used to ride into Dublin, all the way to the British barracks in Rathmines, grab a few guns, whack the heads off any soldiers they saw, and then leg it. By the time the British got organized to go after them, they'd be halfway back here."

He was the right person to tell the story. I thought of rearing hooves, torchlight and dangerous laughter, the rising pulse of war drums. Over his shoulder I could see Cassie, up by the crime-scene tape, talking to Cooper and taking notes.

"I hate to interrupt you," I said, "but I'm afraid I won't have time for the full tour. I just need a very basic overview of the site."

Mark licked the cigarette paper, sealed his rollie and found a lighter. "Fair enough," he said, and started pointing. "Neolithic settlement, Bronze Age ceremonial stone, Iron Age roundhouse, Viking dwellings, fourteenth-century keep, sixteenth-century castle, eighteenth-century cottage." "Bronze Age ceremonial stone" was where Cassie and the techs were.

"Is the site guarded at night?" I asked.

He laughed. "Nah. We lock the finds shed, obviously, and the office, but anything really valuable goes back to head office right away. And we started locking the tools shed a month or two ago—some of our tools went missing, and we found out the farmers had been using our hoses to water their fields in dry weather. That's it. What's the point of guarding it? In a month it'll all be gone anyway, except for this." He slapped the wall of the tower; something scuttled in the ivy above our heads.

"Why's that?" I asked.

He stared at me, giving it an impressive level of incredulous disgust. "In a month's time," he said, enunciating clearly for me, "the fucking government is going to bulldoze this whole site and build a fucking motorway over it. They graciously agreed to leave a fucking traffic island for the keep, so they can wank off about how much they've done to preserve our heritage."

I remembered the motorway now, from some news report: a bland politician being shocked at the archaeologists who wanted the taxpayer to pay millions to redesign the plans. I had probably changed the channel at that point. "We'll try not to delay you for too long," I said. "The dog at the cottage: does he bark when people come to the site?"

Mark shrugged and went back to his cigarette. "Not at us, but he knows us. We feed him scraps and all. He might if someone went too near the cottage, specially at night, but probably not for someone up by the wall. Off his territory."

"What about cars—does he bark at them?"

"Did he bark at yours? He's a sheepdog, not a guard dog." He sent out a narrow ribbon of smoke between his teeth.

So the killer could have come to the site from any direction: by road, from the estate, even along the river if he liked making things difficult. "That's all I need for now," I said. "Thanks for your time. If you'll wait with the others, we'll come and update you in just a few minutes."

"Don't walk on anything that looks like archaeology," Mark said, and loped off back to the Portakabins. I headed up the slope towards the body.

The Bronze Age ceremonial stone was a flat, massive block, maybe seven feet long by three wide by three high, chipped from a single boulder. The field around it had been crudely bulldozed away—not too long ago, judging by the way the ground gave under my shoes—but a cushion around the stone had been left untouched, so that it rode high like an island amid the churned earth. On top of it, something flashed blue and white between the nettles and long grass.

It wasn't Jamie. I had more or less known this already—if there had been a chance it might be, Cassie would have come to tell me—but it still blew my mind empty. This girl had long dark hair, one plait thrown across her face. That was all I noticed, at first, the dark hair. It didn't even occur to me that Jamie's body wouldn't have been in this condition.

I had missed Cooper: he was picking his way back towards the road, shaking his foot like a cat on every step. A tech was taking photos, another was dusting the table for prints; a handful of local uniforms were fidgeting and chatting with the morgue guys, over by their stretcher. The grass was scattered with triangular numbered markers. Cassie and Sophie Miller were crouching beside the stone table, looking at something on the edge. I knew it was Sophie right away; that backboard-straight posture cuts through the anonymous coveralls. Sophie is my favorite crime-scene tech. She is slim and dark and demure, and on her the white shower cap looks like she should be bending over wounded soldiers' beds with cannon fire in the background, murmuring something soothing and giving out sips of water from a canteen. In actual fact, she is quick and impatient and can put anyone from superintendents to prosecutors in their place with a few crisp words. I like incongruity.

"Which way?" I called, at the tape. You don't walk on a crime scene until the Bureau guys say you can.

"Hi, Rob," Sophie shouted, straightening up and pulling down her mask. "Hang on."

Cassie reached me first. "Only been dead a day or so," she said quietly, before Sophie caught up. She looked a little pale around the mouth; kids do that to most of us.

"Thanks, Cass," I said. "Hi, Sophie."

"Hey, Rob. You two still owe me a drink." We had promised to buy her cocktails if she got the lab to fast-track some blood analysis for us, a couple of months before. Since then we'd all been saying, "We have to meet up for that drink," on a regular basis, and never getting around to it.

"Come through for us on this one and we'll buy you dinner as well," I said. "What've we got?"

"White female, ten to thirteen," Cassie said. "No ID. There's a key in her pocket, looks like a house key, but that's it. Her head's smashed in, but Cooper found petechial hemorrhaging and some possible ligature marks on her neck, too, so we'll have to wait for the post for cause of death. She's fully dressed, but it looks like she was probably raped. This one's weird all round, Rob. Cooper says she's been dead somewhere around thirty-six hours, but there's been practically no insect activity, and I don't see how the archaeologists could have missed her if she'd been there all yesterday."

"This isn't the primary scene?"

"No way," Sophie said. "There's no spatter on the rock, not even any blood from the head wound. She was killed somewhere else, probably kept for a day or so and then dumped."

"Find anything?"

"Plenty," she said. "Too much. It looks like the local kids hang out here. Cigarette butts, beer cans, a couple of Coke cans, gum, the ends of three joints. Two used condoms. Once you find a suspect, the lab can try matching him to all this stuff—which will be a nightmare—but to be honest I think it's just your basic teenage debris. Footprints all over the place. A hair clip. I don't think it was hers—it was shoved right down into the dirt at the base of the stone, and I'd bet it's been there a good while—but you might want to check. It doesn't look like it belonged to some teenager; it's the all-plastic kind, with a plastic strawberry on the end, and you'd usually see them on younger kids."

blond wing lifting

I felt as though I had tilted sharply backwards; I had to stop myself jerking for balance. I heard Cassie say quickly, somewhere on the other side of Sophie, "Probably not hers. Everything she's wearing is blue and white, right down to the hair elastics. This kid coordinated. We'll check it out, though."

"Are you OK?" Sophie asked me.

"I'm fine," I said. "I just need coffee." The joy of the new, hip, happening, double-espresso Dublin is that you can blame any strange mood on coffee deprivation. This never worked in the era of tea, at least not at the same level of street cred.

"I'm going to get him an IV caffeine drip for his birthday," said Cassie. She likes Sophie, too. "He's even more useless without his fix. Tell him about the rock."

"Yeah, we found two interesting things," said Sophie. "There's a rock about this size"—she cupped her hands: about eight inches wide—"that I'm pretty sure is one of the weapons. It was in the grass by the wall. Hair and blood and bone fragments all over one end of it."

"Any prints?" I asked.

"No. A couple of smudges, but they look like they came from gloves. The interesting parts are where it was—up by the wall; could mean he came over it, from the estate, although that could be what we're meant to think— and the fact that he bothered dumping it. You'd think he'd just rinse it and stick it in his garden, rather than carrying it as well as a body."

"Couldn't it have been in the grass already?" I asked. "He might have dropped the body on it, maybe getting her over the wall."

"I don't think so," said Sophie. She was shifting her feet delicately, trying to nudge me towards the stone table; she wanted to get back to work. I looked away. I am not squeamish about bodies, and I was pretty sure I had seen even worse than this one—a toddler, the year before, whose father kicked him until he basically broke in half—but I still felt weird, light-headed, as though my eyes weren't focusing clearly enough to take in the image. *Maybe I really do need coffee,* I thought. "It was blood-side down. And the grass underneath it is fresh, still alive; the rock hadn't been there long."

"Plus, she wasn't bleeding any more by the time she was brought here," Cassie said.

"Oh, yeah—the other interesting thing," Sophie said. "Come look at this."

I bowed to the inevitable and ducked under the tape. The other techs glanced up and moved back from the stone to give us room. They were both very young, barely more than trainees, and suddenly I thought of how we must look to them: how much older, how aloof, how much more confident in the little arts and negotiations of adulthood. It steadied me somehow, the image of two Murder detectives with their practiced faces giving away nothing, walking shoulder to shoulder and in step towards this dead child.

She was lying curled on her left side, as though she had fallen asleep on the sofa under the peaceful murmurs of adult conversation. Her left arm was flung out over the edge of the rock; her right fell across her chest, the hand bent under at an awkward angle. She was wearing smoke-blue combats, the kind with tags and zippers in peculiar places, and a white T-shirt with a line of stylized cornflowers printed on the front, and white runners. Cassie was right, she had taken trouble: the thick plait trailing across her cheek was secured with a blue silk cornflower. She was small and very slight, but her calf showed taut and muscular where one leg of the combats was rucked up. Ten to thirteen sounded about right: her breasts were just beginning, barely denting the folds of the T-shirt. Blood was caked on her nose and mouth and the tips of her front teeth. The breeze whirled the soft, curling fronds at her hairline.

Her hands were covered in clear plastic bags, tied at the wrists. "Looks like she fought," Sophie said. "A couple of nails were broken off. I wouldn't bet on finding DNA under the others—they look pretty clean—but we should get fibers and trace off her clothes."

For a moment I was dizzied by the impulse to leave her there: shove the techs' hands away, shout at the hovering morgue men to get the hell out. We had taken enough toll on her. All she had left was her death and I wanted to leave her that, that at least. I wanted to wrap her up in soft blankets, stroke back her clotted hair, pull up a duvet of falling leaves and little animals' rustles. Leave her to sleep, sliding away forever down her secret underground river, while breathing seasons spun dandelion seeds and moon phases and snowflakes above her head. She had tried so hard to live.

"I have that same T-shirt," Cassie said quietly, at my shoulder. "Penney's kids' department." I had seen it on her before, but I knew she wouldn't wear it again. Violated, that innocence was too vast and final to allow any tongue-in-cheek claim of kinship.

"Here's what I wanted to show you," said Sophie briskly. She doesn't approve of either sentimentality or graveyard humor at crime scenes. She says they waste time that should be spent working on the damn case, but the implication is that coping strategies are for wimps. She pointed to the edge of the stone. "Want gloves?"

"I won't touch anything," I said, and crouched in the grass. From this angle I could see that one of the girl's eyes was a slit open, as if she was only pretending to be asleep, waiting for her moment to jump up and yell, *Boo! Fooled you!* A shiny black beetle ticked a methodical path over her forearm.

A groove about a finger wide had been carved around the top of the stone, an inch or two from the edge. Time and weather had worn it smooth, almost glossy, but in one place the maker's handmade chisel had slipped, gouging a chunk out of the side of the groove and leaving a tiny, jagged overhang. A smear of something dark, almost black, clung to the underside.

"Helen here spotted it," Sophie said. The girl tech glanced up and gave me a shy proud smile. "We've swabbed, and it's blood—I'll let you know if it's human. I doubt it has anything to do with our body; her blood had dried by the time she was brought here, and anyway I'd bet this is years old. It could be animal, or it could be from some teenage scrap or whatever, but still, it's interesting."

I thought of the delicate hollow by Jamie's wrist bone, the brown back of Peter's neck bordered by white after a haircut. I could feel Cassie not looking at me. "I don't see how it could be connected," I said. I stood up—it was getting hard to balance on my heels without touching the table—and felt a quick head-rush.

Before we left the site I stood on the little ridge above the girl's body and turned full circle, imprinting an overview of the scene on my mind: trenches, houses, fields, access and angles and alignments. Along the estate wall, a thin rim of trees had been left untouched, presumably to shield the residents' aesthetic sensibilities from the uncompromisingly archaeological view. One had a broken piece of blue plastic rope heavily knotted around a high branch, a couple of feet dangling. It was frayed and mildewed and implied sinister Gothic history—lynch mobs, midnight suicides—but I knew what it was. It was the remnant of a tire swing.

Though I had come to think of Knocknaree as though it had happened to another and unknown person, some part of me had been here all along. While I doodled in Templemore or sprawled on Cassie's futon, that relentless child had never stopped spinning in crazy circles on a tire swing, scrambling over a wall after Peter's bright head, vanishing into the wood in a flash of brown legs and laughter.

There was a time when I believed, with the police and the media and my stunned parents, that I was the redeemed one, the boy borne safely home on the ebb of whatever freak tide carried Peter and Jamie away. Not any more. In ways too dark and crucial to be called metaphorical, I never left that wood.

from

Nudge

Improving Decisions About
Health, Wealth, and Happiness

by

Richard H. Thaler *and*
Cass R. Sunstein

"One of the few books I've read recently that fundamentally changes the way I think about the world. . . . Academics aren't supposed to be able to write this well."
—Steven D. Levitt, coauthor of *Freakonomics*

Nudge *is about choices—how we make them and how we're led to make better ones. Authors Richard H. Thaler and Cass R. Sunstein offer a new perspective on how to prevent the countless bad mistakes we make in our lives—including ill-advised personal investments, consumption of unhealthy foods, neglect of our natural resources, and other numerous bad decisions regarding health care, our families, and education. Citing decades of cutting-edge behavioral science research, they demonstrate that sensible "choice architecture" can successfully nudge people toward the best decision without restricting their freedom of choice. Terrifically straightforward, informative, and often very entertaining, this book is a must-read for anyone with an interest in our individual and collective well-being.*

The Cafeteria

A friend of yours, Carolyn, is the director of food services for a large city school system. She is in charge of hundreds of schools, and hundreds of thousands of kids eat in her cafeterias every day. Carolyn has formal training in nutrition (a master's degree from the state university), and she is a creative type who likes to think about things in nontraditional ways.

One evening, over a good bottle of wine, she and her friend Adam, a statistically oriented management consultant who has worked with supermarket chains, hatched an interesting idea. Without changing any menus, they would run some experiments in her schools to determine whether the way the food is displayed and arranged might influence the choices kids make. Carolyn gave the directors of dozens of school cafeterias specific instructions on how to display the food choices. In some schools the desserts were placed first, in others last, in still others in a separate line. The location of various food items was varied from one school to another. In some schools the French fries, but in others the carrot sticks, were at eye level.

From his experience in designing supermarket floor plans, Adam suspected that the results would be dramatic. He was right. Simply by rearranging the cafeteria, Carolyn was able to increase or decrease the consumption of many food items by as much as 25 percent. Carolyn learned a big lesson: school children, like adults, can be greatly influenced by small changes in the context. The influence can be exercised for better or for worse. For example, Carolyn knows that she can increase consumption of healthy foods and decrease consumption of unhealthy ones.

With hundreds of schools to work with, and a team of graduate student volunteers recruited to collect and analyze the data, Carolyn believes that she now has considerable power to influence what kids eat. Carolyn is pondering what to do with her newfound power. Here are some suggestions she has received from her usually sincere but occasionally mischievous friends and coworkers:

1. Arrange the food to make the students best off, all things considered.
2. Choose the food order at random.
3. Try to arrange the food to get the kids to pick the same foods they would choose on their own.
4. Maximize the sales of the items from the suppliers that are willing to offer the largest bribes.
5. Maximize profits, period.

Option 1 has obvious appeal, yet it does seem a bit intrusive, even paternalistic. But the alternatives are worse! Option 2, arranging the food at random, could be considered fair-minded and principled, and it is in one sense neutral. But if the orders are randomized across schools, then the children at some schools will have less healthy diets than those at other schools. Is this desirable? Should Carolyn choose that kind of neutrality, if she can easily make most students better off, in part by improving their health?

Option 3 might seem to be an honorable attempt to avoid intrusion: try to mimic what the children would choose for themselves. Maybe that is really the neutral choice, and maybe Carolyn should neutrally follow people's wishes (at least where she is dealing with older students). But a little thought reveals that this is a difficult option to implement. Adam's experiment proves that what kids choose depends on the order in which the items are displayed. What, then, are the true preferences of the children? What does it mean to say that Carolyn should try to figure out what the students would choose "on their own"? In a cafeteria, it is impossible to avoid some way of organizing food.

Option 4 might appeal to a corrupt person in Carolyn's job, and manipulating the order of the food items would put yet another weapon in the arsenal of available methods to exploit power. But Carolyn is honorable and honest, so she does not give this option any thought. Like Options 2 and 3, Option 5 has some appeal, especially if Carolyn thinks that the best cafeteria is the one that makes the most money. But should Carolyn really try to maximize profits if the result is to make children less healthy, especially since she works for the school district?

Carolyn is what we will be calling a *choice architect*. A choice architect has the responsibility for organizing the context in which people make decisions. Although Carolyn is a figment of our imagination, many real people turn out to be choice architects, most without realizing it. If you design the ballot voters use to choose candidates, you are a choice architect. If you are a doctor and must describe the alternative treatments available to a patient, you are a choice architect. If you design the form that new employees fill out to enroll in the company health care plan, you are a choice architect. If you are a parent, describing possible educational options to your son or daughter, you are a choice architect. If you are a salesperson, you are a choice architect (but you already knew that).

There are many parallels between choice architecture and more traditional forms of architecture. A crucial parallel is that there is no such thing as a "neutral" design. Consider the job of designing a new academic building. The architect is given some requirements. There must be room for 120 offices, 8 classrooms, 12 student meeting rooms, and so forth. The building must sit on a specified site. Hundreds of other constraints will be imposed—some legal, some aesthetic, some practical. In the end, the architect must come up with an actual building with doors, stairs, windows, and hallways. As good architects know, seemingly arbitrary decisions, such as where to locate the bathrooms, will have subtle influences on how the people who use the building interact. Every trip to the bathroom creates an opportunity to run into colleagues (for better or for worse). A good building is not merely attractive; it also "works."

As we shall see, small and apparently insignificant details can have major impacts on people's behavior. A good rule of thumb is to assume that "everything matters." In many cases, the power of these small details comes from focusing the attention of users in a particular direction. A wonderful example of this principle comes from, of all places, the men's rooms at Schiphol Airport in Amsterdam. There the authorities have etched the image of a black housefly into each urinal. It seems that men usually do not pay much attention to where they aim, which can create a bit of a mess, but if they see a target, attention and therefore accuracy are much increased. According to the man who came up with the idea, it works wonders. "It improves the aim," says Aad Kieboom. "If a man sees a fly, he aims at it." Kieboom, an economist, directs Schiphol's building expansion. His staff conducted fly-in-urinal trials and found that etchings reduce spillage by 80 percent.[1]

The insight that "everything matters" can be both paralyzing and empowering. Good architects realize that although they can't build the perfect building, they can make some design choices that will have beneficial effects. Open stairwells, for example, may produce more workplace interaction and more walking, and both of these are probably desirable. And just as a building architect must eventually build some particular building, a choice architect like Carolyn must choose a particular arrangement of the food options at lunch, and by so doing she can influence what people eat. She can nudge.*

Libertarian Paternalism

If, all things considered, you think that Carolyn should take the opportunity to nudge the kids toward food that is better for them, Option

---

*Please do not confuse *nudge* with *noodge*. As William Safire has explained in his "On Language" column in the *New York Times Magazine* (October 8, 2000), the "Yiddishism *noodge*" is "a noun meaning 'pest, annoying nag, persistent complainer.' . . . To *nudge* is 'to push mildly or poke gently in the ribs, especially with the elbow.' One who *nudges* in that manner—'to alert, remind, or mildly warn another'—is a far *geshrei* from a *noodge* with his incessant, bothersome whining." *Nudge* rhymes with *judge*, while the *oo* sound in *noodge* is pronounced as in *book*.

While we are all down here, a small note about the reading architecture of this book when it comes to footnotes and references. Footnotes such as this one that we deem worth reading are keyed with a symbol and placed at the bottom of the page, so that they are easy to find. We have aimed to keep these to a minimum. Numbered endnotes contain information about source material. These can be skipped by all but the most scholarly of readers. When the authors of cited material are mentioned in the text, we sometimes add a date in parentheses—Smith (1982), for example—to enable readers to go directly to the bibliography without having first to find the endnote.

1, then we welcome you to our new movement: *libertarian paternalism*. We are keenly aware that this term is not one that readers will find immediately endearing. Both words are somewhat off-putting, weighted down by stereotypes from popular culture and politics that make them unappealing to many. Even worse, the concepts seem to be contradictory. Why combine two reviled and contradictory concepts? We argue that if the terms are properly understood, both concepts reflect common sense—and they are far more attractive together than alone. The problem with the terms is that they have been captured by dogmatists.

The libertarian aspect of our strategies lies in the straightforward insistence that, in general, people should be free to do what they like—and to opt out of undesirable arrangements if they want to do so. To borrow a phrase from the late Milton Friedman, libertarian paternalists urge that people should be "free to choose."[2] We strive to design policies that maintain or increase freedom of choice. When we use the term *libertarian* to modify the word *paternalism,* we simply mean liberty-preserving. And when we say liberty-preserving, we really mean it. Libertarian paternalists want to make it easy for people to go their own way; they do not want to burden those who want to exercise their freedom.

The paternalistic aspect lies in the claim that it is legitimate for choice architects to try to influence people's behavior in order to make their lives longer, healthier, and better. In other words, we argue for self-conscious efforts, by institutions in the private sector and also by government, to steer people's choices in directions that will improve their lives. In our understanding, a policy is "paternalistic" if it tries to influence choices in a way that will make choosers better off, *as judged by themselves.*[3] Drawing on some well-established findings in social science, we show that in many cases, individuals make pretty bad decisions—decisions they would not have made if they had paid full attention and possessed complete information, unlimited cognitive abilities, and complete self-control.

Libertarian paternalism is a relatively weak, soft, and nonintrusive type of paternalism because choices are not blocked, fenced off, or significantly burdened. If people want to smoke cigarettes, to eat a lot of candy, to choose an unsuitable health care plan, or to fail to save for retirement, libertarian paternalists will not force them to do otherwise—or even make things hard for them. Still, the approach we recommend does count as paternalistic, because private and public choice architects are not merely trying to track or to implement people's anticipated choices. Rather, they are self-consciously attempting to move people in directions that will make their lives better. They nudge.

A nudge, as we will use the term, is any aspect of the choice architecture that alters people's behavior in a predictable way without forbidding any options or significantly changing their economic incentives. To count as a mere nudge, the intervention must be easy and cheap to avoid. Nudges are not mandates. Putting the fruit at eye level counts as a nudge. Banning junk food does not.

Many of the policies we recommend can and have been implemented by the private sector (with or without a nudge from the government). Employers, for example, are important choice architects in many of the examples we discuss in this book. In areas involving health care and retirement plans, we think that employers can give employees some helpful nudges. Private companies that want to make money, and to do good, can even benefit from environmental nudges, helping to reduce air pollution (and the emission of greenhouse gases). But as we shall show, the same points that justify libertarian paternalism on the part of private institutions apply to government as well.

Humans and Econs: Why Nudges Can Help

Those who reject paternalism often claim that human beings do a terrific job of making choices, and if not terrific, certainly better than anyone else would do (especially if that someone else works for the government). Whether or not they have ever studied economics, many people seem at least implicitly committed to the idea of *homo economicus,* or economic man—the notion that each of us thinks and chooses unfailingly well, and thus fits within the textbook picture of human beings offered by economists.

If you look at economics textbooks, you will learn that homo economicus can think like Albert Einstein, store as much memory as IBM's Big Blue, and exercise the willpower of Mahatma Gandhi. Really. But the folks that we know are not like that. Real people have trouble with long division if they don't have a calculator, sometimes forget their spouse's birthday, and have a hangover on New Year's Day. They are not homo economicus; they are homo sapiens. To keep our Latin usage to a minimum we will hereafter refer to these imaginary and real species as Econs and Humans.

Consider the issue of obesity. Rates of obesity in the United States are now approaching 20 percent, and more than 60 percent of Americans are considered either obese or overweight. There is overwhelming evidence that obesity increases risks of heart disease and diabetes, frequently leading to premature death. It would be quite fantastic to suggest that everyone is choosing the right diet, or a diet that is preferable to what might be produced with a few nudges.

Of course, sensible people care about the taste of food, not simply about health, and eating is a source of pleasure in and of itself. We do not claim that everyone who is overweight is necessarily failing to act rationally, but we do reject the claim that all or almost all Americans are choosing their diet optimally. What is true for diets is true for other risk-related behavior, including smoking and drinking, which produce more than five hundred thousand premature deaths each year. With respect to diet, smoking, and drinking, people's current choices cannot reasonably be claimed to be the best means of promoting their well-being. Indeed, many smokers, drinkers, and overeaters are willing to pay third parties to help them make better decisions.

But our basic source of information here is the emerging science of choice, consisting of careful research by social scientists over the past four decades. That research has raised serious questions about the rationality of many judgments and decisions that people make. To qualify as Econs, people are not required to make perfect forecasts (that would require omniscience), but they are required to make unbiased forecasts. That is, the forecasts can be wrong, but they can't be systematically wrong in a predictable direction. Unlike Econs, Humans predictably err. Take, for example, the "planning fallacy"—the systematic tendency toward unrealistic optimism about the time it takes to complete projects. It will come as no surprise to anyone who has ever hired a contractor to learn that everything takes longer than you think, even if you know about the planning fallacy.

Hundreds of studies confirm that human forecasts are flawed and biased. Human decision making is not so great either. Again to take just one example, consider what is called the "status quo bias," a fancy name for inertia. For a host of reasons, which we shall explore, people have a strong tendency to go along with the status quo or default option.

When you get a new cell phone, for example, you have a series of choices to make. The fancier the phone, the more of these choices you face, from the background to the ring sound to the number of times the phone rings before the caller is sent to voice mail. The manufacturer has picked one option as the default for each of these choices. Research shows that whatever the default choices are, many people stick with them, even when the stakes are much higher than choosing the noise your phone makes when it rings.

Two important lessons can be drawn from this research. First, never underestimate the power of inertia. Second, that power can be harnessed. If private companies or public officials think that one policy produces better outcomes, they can greatly influence the outcome by choosing it as the default. As we will show, setting default options, and other similar seemingly trivial menu-changing strategies, can have huge effects on outcomes, from increasing savings to improving health care to providing organs for lifesaving transplant operations.

The effects of well-chosen default options provide just one illustration of the gentle power of nudges. In accordance with our definition, a nudge is any factor that significantly alters the behavior of Humans, even though it would be ignored by Econs. Econs respond primarily to incentives. If the government taxes candy, they will buy less candy, but they are not influenced by such "irrelevant" factors as the order in which options are displayed. Humans respond to incentives too, but they are also influenced by nudges.* By properly deploying both incentives and nudges, we can improve our ability to improve people's lives, and help solve many of society's major problems. And we can do so while still insisting on everyone's freedom to choose.

---

*Alert readers will notice that incentives can come in different forms. If steps are taken to increase people's cognitive effort—as by placing fruit at eye level and candy in a more obscure place—it might be said that the "cost" of choosing candy is increased. Some of our nudges do, in a sense, impose cognitive (rather than material) costs, and in that sense alter incentives. Nudges count as such, and qualify as libertarian paternalism, only if any costs are low.

A False Assumption and Two Misconceptions

Many people who favor freedom of choice reject any kind of paternalism. They want the government to let citizens choose for themselves. The standard policy advice that stems from this way of thinking is to give people as many choices as possible, and then let them choose the one they like best (with as little government intervention or nudging as possible). The beauty of this way of thinking is that it offers a simple solution to many complex problems: Just Maximize (the number and variety of) Choices—full stop! The policy has been pushed in many domains, from education to prescription drug insurance plans. In some circles, Just Maximize Choices has become a policy mantra. Sometimes the only alternative to this mantra is thought to be a government mandate which is derided as "One Size Fits All." Those who favor Just Maximize Choices don't realize there is plenty of room between their policy and a single mandate. They oppose paternalism, or think they do, and they are skeptical about nudges. We believe that their skepticism is based on a false assumption and two misconceptions.

The false assumption is that almost all people, almost all of the time, make choices that are in their best interest or at the very least are better than the choices that would be made by someone else. We claim that this assumption is false—indeed, obviously false. In fact, we do not think that anyone believes it on reflection.

Suppose that a chess novice were to play against an experienced player. Predictably, the novice would lose precisely because he made inferior choices—choices that could easily be improved by some helpful hints. In many areas, ordinary consumers are novices, interacting in a world inhabited by experienced professionals trying to sell them things. More generally, how well people choose is an empirical question, one whose answer is likely to vary across domains. It seems reasonable to say that people make good choices in contexts in which they have experience, good information, and prompt feedback—say, choosing among ice cream flavors. People know whether they like chocolate, vanilla, coffee, licorice, or something else. They do less well in contexts in which they are inexperienced and poorly informed, and in which feedback is slow or infrequent—say, in choosing between fruit and ice cream (where the long-term effects are slow and feedback is poor) or in choosing among medical treatments or investment options. If you are given fifty prescription drug plans, with multiple and varying features, you might benefit from a little help. So long as people are not choosing perfectly, some changes in the choice architecture could make their lives go better (as judged by their own preferences, not those of some bureaucrat). As we will try to show, it is not only possible to design choice architecture to make people better off; in many cases it is easy to do so.

The first misconception is that it is possible to avoid influencing people's choices. In many situations, some organization or agent *must* make a choice that will affect the behavior of some other people. There is, in those situations, no way of avoiding nudging in some direction, and whether intended or not, these nudges will affect what people choose. As illustrated by the example of Carolyn's cafeterias, people's choices are pervasively influenced by the design elements selected by choice architects. It is true, of course, that some nudges are unintentional; employers may decide (say) whether to pay employees monthly or biweekly without intending to create any kind of nudge, but they might be surprised to discover that people save more if they get paid biweekly because twice a year they get three pay checks in one month. It is also true that private and public institutions can strive for one or another kind of neutrality—as, for example, by choosing randomly, or by trying to figure out what most people want. But unintentional nudges can have major effects, and in some contexts, these forms of neutrality are unattractive; we shall encounter many examples.

Some people will happily accept this point for private institutions but strenuously object to government efforts to influence choice with the goal of improving people's lives. They worry that governments cannot be trusted to be competent or benign. They fear that elected officials and bureaucrats will place their own interests first, or pay attention to the narrow goals of self-interested private groups. We share these concerns. In particular, we emphatically agree that for government, the risks of mistake, bias, and overreaching are real and sometimes serious. We favor nudges over commands, requirements, and prohibitions in part for that reason. But governments, no less than cafeterias (which governments frequently run), have to provide starting points of one or another kind. This is not avoidable. As we shall emphasize, they do so every day through the rules they set, in ways that inevitably affect some choices and outcomes. In this respect, the antinudge position is unhelpful—a literal nonstarter.

The second misconception is that paternalism always involves coercion. In the cafeteria example, the choice of the order in which to present food items does not force a particular diet on anyone, yet Carolyn, and others in her position, might select some arrangement of food on grounds that are paternalistic in the sense that we use the term. Would anyone object to putting the fruit and salad before the desserts at an elementary school cafeteria if the result were to induce kids to eat more apples and fewer Twinkies? Is this question fundamentally different if the customers are teenagers, or even adults? Since no coercion is involved, we think that some types of paternalism should be acceptable even to those who most embrace freedom of choice.

In domains as varied as savings, organ donations, marriage, and health care, we will offer specific suggestions in keeping with our general approach. And by insisting that choices remain unrestricted, we think that the risks of inept or even corrupt designs are reduced. Freedom to choose is the best safeguard against bad choice architecture.

Choice Architecture in Action

Choice architects can make major improvements to the lives of others by designing user-friendly environments. Many of the most successful companies have helped people, or succeeded in the marketplace, for exactly that reason. Sometimes the choice architecture is highly visible, and consumers and employers are much pleased by it. (The iPod and the iPhone are good examples because not only are they elegantly styled, but it is also easy for the user to get the devices to do what they want.) Sometimes the architecture is taken for granted and could benefit from some careful attention.

Consider an illustration from our own employer, the University of Chicago. The university, like many large employers, has an "open enrollment" period every November, when employees are allowed to revise the selections they have made about such benefits as health insurance and retirement savings. Employees are required to make their choices online. (Public computers are available for those who would otherwise not have

Internet access.) Employees receive, by mail, a package of materials explaining the choices they have and instructions on how to log on to make these choices. Employees also receive both paper and email reminders.

Because employees are human, some neglect to log on, so it is crucial to decide what the default options are for these busy and absent-minded employees. To simplify, suppose there are two alternatives to consider: those who make no active choice can be given the same choice they made the previous year, or their choice can be set back to "zero." Suppose that last year an employee, Janet, contributed one thousand dollars to her retirement plan. If Janet makes no active choice for the new year, one alternative would be to default her to a one thousand–dollar contribution; another would be to default her to zero contribution. Call these the "status quo" and "back to zero" options. How should the choice architect choose between these defaults?

Libertarian paternalists would like to set the default by asking what reflective employees in Janet's position would actually want. Although this principle may not always lead to a clear choice, it is certainly better than choosing the default at random, or making either "status quo" or "back to zero" the default for everything. For example, it is a good guess that most employees would not want to cancel their heavily subsidized health insurance. So for health insurance the status quo default (same plan as last year) seems strongly preferred to the back to zero default (which would mean going without health insurance).

Compare this to the employee's "flexible spending account," in which an employee sets aside money each month that can be used to pay for certain expenditures (such as uninsured medical or child care expenses). Money put into this account has to be spent each year or it is lost, and the predicted expenditures might vary greatly from one year to the next (for example, child care expenses go down when a child enters school). In this case, the zero default probably makes more sense than the status quo.

This problem is not merely hypothetical. We once had a meeting with three of the top administrative officers of the university to discuss similar issues, and the meeting happened to take place on the final day of the employees' open enrollment period. We mentioned this and asked whether the administrators had remembered to meet the deadline. One said that he was planning on doing it later that day and was glad for the reminder. Another admitted to having forgotten, and the third said that he was hoping that his wife had remembered to do it! The group then turned to the question of what the default should be for a supplementary salary reduction program (a tax-sheltered savings program). To that point, the default had been the "back to zero" option. But since contributions to this program could be stopped at any time, the group unanimously agreed that it would be better to switch to the status quo "same as last year" default. We are confident that many absent-minded professors will have more comfortable retirements as a result.

This example illustrates some basic principles of good choice architecture. Choosers are human, so designers should make life as easy as possible. Send reminders, and then try to minimize the costs imposed on those who, despite your (and their) best efforts, space out. As we will see, these principles (and many more) can be applied in both the private and public sectors, and there is much room for going beyond what is now being done.

A New Path

We shall have a great deal to say about private nudges. But many of the most important applications of libertarian paternalism are for government, and we will offer a number of recommendations for public policy and law. Our hope is that that those recommendations might appeal to both sides of the political divide. Indeed, we believe that the policies suggested by libertarian paternalism can be embraced by Republicans and Democrats alike. A central reason is that many of those policies cost little or nothing; they impose no burden on taxpayers at all.

Many Republicans are now seeking to go beyond simple opposition to government action. As the experience with Hurricane Katrina showed, government is often required to act, for it is the only means by which the necessary resources can be mustered, organized, and deployed. Republicans want to make people's lives better; they are simply skeptical, and legitimately so, about eliminating people's options.

For their part, many Democrats are willing to abandon their enthusiasm for aggressive government planning. Sensible Democrats certainly hope that public institutions can improve people's lives. But in many domains, Democrats have come to agree that freedom of choice is a good and even indispensable foundation for public policy. There is a real basis here for crossing partisan divides.

Libertarian paternalism, we think, is a promising foundation for bipartisanship. In many domains, including environmental protection, family law, and school choice, we will be arguing that better governance requires less in the way of government coercion and constraint, and more in the way of freedom to choose. If incentives and nudges replace requirements and bans, government will be both smaller and more modest. So, to be clear: *we are not for bigger government, just for better governance.*

Actually we have evidence that our optimism (which we admit may be a bias) is more than just rosy thinking. Libertarian paternalism with respect to savings, discussed in Chapter 6, has received enthusiastic and widespread bipartisan support in Congress, including from current and former conservative Republican senators such as Robert Bennett (Utah) and Rick Santorum (Pa.) and liberal Democrats such as Rahm Emanuel of Illinois. In 2006 some of the key ideas were quietly enacted into law. The new law will help many Americans have more comfortable retirements but costs essentially nothing in taxpayer dollars.

In short, libertarian paternalism is neither left nor right, neither Democratic nor Republican. In many areas, the most thoughtful Democrats are going beyond their enthusiasm for choice-eliminating programs. In many areas, the most thoughtful Republicans are abandoning their knee-jerk opposition to constructive governmental initiatives. For all their differences, we hope that both sides might be willing to converge in support of some gentle nudges.

from

People of the Book

by

Geraldine Brooks

**"[A] marvelously intertwined narrative, with one strand
tied to the contemporary world and the other leading us
back into European history, into wars and inquisitions
and family tragedies, all of this making up a vividly
narrated, powerfully emotional quest."**
—*The Dallas Morning News*

*Hanna Heath, an Australian rare book expert, has been
offered the job of a lifetime: analysis and conservation of
the famed Sarajevo Haggadah, rescued from Serb shelling
during the Bosnian war. Priceless and beautiful, the book is
one of the earliest Jewish volumes ever to be illuminated with
images. When Hanna discovers a series of tiny artifacts in
its ancient binding—an insect wing fragment, wine stains,
salt crystals, a white hair—she begins to unlock the book's
mysteries, ushering in its exquisite and atmospheric past,
from its salvation back to its creation through centuries of
exile and war.*

Inspired by a true story, People of the Book *is a novel
of sweeping historical grandeur and intimate emotional
intensity—an acclaimed and ambitious work from a
Pulitzer Prize-winning author.*

I

I MIGHT AS WELL SAY, right from the jump: it wasn't my usual kind of job.

I like to work alone, in my own clean, silent, well-lit laboratory, where the climate is controlled and everything I need is right at hand. It's true that I have developed a reputation as someone who can work effectively out of the lab, when I have to, when the museums don't want to pay the travel insurance on a piece, or when private collectors don't want anyone to know exactly what it is that they own. It's also true that I've flown halfway around the world, to do an interesting job. But never to a place like this: the boardroom of a bank in the middle of a city where they just stopped shooting at each other five minutes ago.

For one thing, there are no guards hovering over me at my lab at home. I mean, the museum has a few quiet security professionals cruising around, but none of them would ever dream of intruding on my work space. Not like the crew here. Six of them. Two were bank security guards, two were Bosnian police, here to keep an eye on the bank security, and the other two were United Nations peace-keepers, here to keep an eye on the Bosnian police. All having loud conversations in Bosnian or Danish over their crackly radio handsets. As if that wasn't enough of a crowd, there was also the official UN observer, Hamish Sajjan. My first Scottish Sikh, very dapper in Harris tweed and an indigo turban. Only in the UN. I'd had to ask him to point out to the Bosnians that smoking wasn't going to be happening in a room that would shortly contain a fifteenth-century manuscript. Since then, they'd been even more fidgety.

I was starting to get fidgety myself. We'd been waiting for almost two hours. I'd filled the time as best I could. The guards had helped me reposition the big conference table nearer to the window, to take advantage of the light. I'd assembled the stereo microscope and laid out my tools: documentation cameras, probes, and scalpels. The beaker of gelatin was softening on its warming pad, and the wheat paste, linen threads, gold leaf were laid out ready, along with some glassine envelopes in case I was lucky enough to find any debris in the binding—it's amazing what you can learn about a book by studying the chemistry of a bread crumb. There were samples of various calfskins, rolls of handmade papers in different tones and textures, and foam forms positioned in a cradle, ready to receive the book. If they ever brought the book.

"Any idea how much longer we're going to have to wait?" I asked Sajjan. He shrugged.

"I think there is a delay with the representative from the National Museum. Since the book is the property of the museum, the bank cannot remove it from the vault unless he is present."

Restless, I walked to the windows. We were on the top floor of the bank, an Austro-Hungarian wedding cake of a building whose stuccoed facade was speckled with mortar pockmarks just like every other structure in the city. When I put my hand on the glass, the cold seeped through. It was supposed to be spring; down in the small garden by the bank's entrance, the crocuses were blooming. But it had snowed earlier that morning, and the bowl of each small flower brimmed with a foam of snowflakes, like tiny cups of cappuccino. At least the snow made the light in the room even and bright. Perfect working light, if only I could get to work.

Simply to be doing something, I unrolled some of my papers—French-milled linen. I ran a metal ruler over each sheet, working it flat. The sound of the metal edge traveling across the large sheet was like the sound of the surf I can hear from my flat at home in Sydney.

I noticed that my hands were shaking. Not a good thing in my line of work.

My hands are not what you'd call one of my better features. Chapped, wattled across the back, they don't look like they belong on my wrists, which I am happy to report are slender and smooth like the rest of me. Charwoman's hands, my mother called them, the last time we argued. After that, when I had to meet her at the Cosmopolitan for coffee—brief, correct, the pair of us brittle as icicles—I wore a pair of gloves from the Salvos as a sort of piss-take. Of course, the Cosmopolitan is probably the only place in Sydney where someone might miss the irony in that gesture. My mother did. She said something about getting me a hat to match.

In the bright snow light, my hands looked even worse than usual, all ruddy and peeling from scouring the fat off cow gut with a pumice stone. When you live in Sydney, it's not the simplest thing in the world to get a meter of calf's intestine. Ever since they moved the abattoir out of Homebush and started to spruce the place up for the 2000 Olympics, you have to drive, basically, to woop woop, and then when you finally get there, there's so much security in place because of the animal libbers you can barely get in the gate. It's not that I blame them for thinking I was a bit sketchy. It's hard to grasp right off the bat why someone might *need* a meter of calf's appendix. But if you are going to work with five-hundred-year-old materials, you have to know how they were made five hundred years ago. That's what my teacher, Werner Heinrich, believed. He said you could read about grinding pigments and mixing gesso all you like, but the only way to understand is to actually do it. If I wanted to know what words like *cutch* and *schoder* really described, I had to make gold leaf myself: beat it and fold it and beat it again, on something it won't stick to, like the soft ground of scoured calf intestine. Eventually, you'll have a little packet of leaves each less than a thousandth of a millimeter thick. And you'll also have horrible-looking hands.

I made a fist, trying to smooth out the old-lady wattle skin. Also to see if I could stop the trembling. I'd been nervous ever since I

changed planes in Vienna the day before. I travel a lot; you basically
have to, if you live in Australia and want a piece of the most interesting projects in my field, which is the conservation of medieval manuscripts. But I don't generally go to places that are datelines in war
correspondents' dispatches. I know there are people who go in for
that sort of thing and write great books about it, and I suppose they
have some kind of "It can't happen to me" optimism that makes it
possible for them. Me, I'm a complete pessimist. If there's a sniper
somewhere in the country I'm visiting, I fully expect to be the one in
his crosshairs.

Even before the plane landed, you could see the war. As we broke
through the gray swag of cloud that seems to be the permanent condition of the European sky, the little russet-tiled houses hugging the
Adriatic looked familiar at first, just like the view I'm used to, down
over the red rooftops of Sydney to the deep blue arc of Bondi Beach.
But in this view, half the houses weren't there anymore. They were
just jagged bits of masonry, sticking up in ragged rows like rotting
teeth.

There was turbulence as we went over the mountains. I couldn't
bring myself to look as we crossed into Bosnia so I pulled down the
window shade. The young bloke next to me—aid worker, I guessed,
from the Cambodian scarf and the gaunt malarial look of him—
obviously wanted to look out, but I ignored his body language and
tried to distract him with a question.

"So, what brings you here?"

"Mine clearance."

I was tempted to say something really borderline like, "Business
booming?" but managed, uncharacteristically, to restrain myself.
And then we landed, and he was up, with every single other person
in the plane, jostling in the aisle, ferreting around in the overhead
bins. He shouldered an immense rucksack and then proceeded to
almost break the nose of the man crowding the aisle behind him.
The lethal backpacker ninety-degree turn. You see it on the bus at
Bondi all the time.

The cabin door finally opened, and the passengers oozed forward as if they were glued together. I was the only one still seated. I felt as if I'd swallowed a stone that was pinning me to my spot.

"Dr. Heath?" The flight attendant was hovering in the emptied aisle.

I was about to say, "No, that's my mother," when I realized she meant me. In Australia only prats flaunt their PhDs. I certainly hadn't checked in as anything other than Ms.

"Your United Nations escort is waiting on the tarmac." That explained it. I'd already noticed, in the run-up to accepting this gig, that the UN liked to give everyone the flashiest possible handle.

"Escort?" I repeated stupidly. "Tarmac?" They'd said I'd be met, but I thought that meant a bored taxi driver holding a sign with my name misspelled. The flight attendant gave me one of those big, perfect, German smiles. She leaned across me and flung up the drawn shade. I looked out. Three huge, armor-plated, tinted-window vans, the kind they drive the American president around in, stood idling by the plane's wingtip. What should have been a reassuring sight only made the stone in my gut a ton heavier. Beyond them, in long grass posted with mine-warning signs in various languages, I could see the rusting hulk of a huge cargo plane that must have missed the runway during some earlier unpleasantness. I looked back at Fräulein Smiley-Face.

"I thought the cease-fire was being observed," I said.

"It is," she said brightly. "Most days. Do you need any assistance with your hand luggage?"

I shook my head, and bent to tug out the heavy case wedged tightly under the seat in front of me. Generally, airlines don't like collections of sharp metal things on board, but the Germans are great respecters of trades, and the check-in clerk understood when I explained how I hate to check my tools in case they end up touring Europe without me while I sit on my rear end unable to do my work.

I love my work. That's the thing. That's why, despite being a world-class coward, I agreed to take this job. To be honest, it never occurred to me not to take it. You don't say no to the chance to work on one of the rarest and most mysterious volumes in the world.

The call had come at 2:00 a.m., as so many calls do when you live in Sydney. It drives me spare sometimes, the way the smartest people— museum directors who run internationally renowned institutions or CEOs who can tell you to the cent what the Hang Seng was at on any given day—can't retain the simple fact that Sydney is generally nine hours ahead of London and fourteen hours ahead of New York. Amitai Yomtov is a brilliant man. Probably the most brilliant in the field. But could he figure the time difference between Jerusalem and Sydney?

"Shalom, Channa," he said, his thick sabra accent putting a guttural *ch* sound into my name as usual. "I'm not waking you?"

"No, Amitai," I said. "I'm always up at two a.m.; best part of the day."

"Ah, well, sorry, but I think you might be interested to know that the Sarajevo Haggadah has turned up."

"No!" I said, suddenly wide awake. "That's, um, great news." And it was, but it was great news I could easily have read in an e-mail at a civilized hour. I couldn't imagine why Amitai had felt it necessary to call me.

Amitai, like most sabras, was a pretty contained character, but this news had made him ebullient. "I always knew that book was a survivor. I knew it would outlast the bombs."

The Sarajevo Haggadah, created in medieval Spain, was a famous rarity, a lavishly illuminated Hebrew manuscript made at a time when Jewish belief was firmly against illustrations of any kind. It was thought that the commandment in Exodus "Thou shalt not make unto thee any graven image or likeness of any thing" had suppressed figurative art by medieval Jews. When the book came to light in Sarajevo in 1894, its pages of painted miniatures had turned this idea on its head and caused art history texts to be rewritten.

At the beginning of the Sarajevo siege in 1992, when the museums and libraries became targets in the fighting, the codex had gone missing. The Bosnian Muslim government had sold it to buy arms, one rumor said. No, Mossad agents had smuggled it out through a tunnel under the Sarajevo airport. I never believed either scenario. I thought that the beautiful book had probably been part of the blizzard of burning pages—Ottoman land deeds, ancient Korans, Slavic scrolls—that had fallen in a warm snow upon the city after the flames of phosphorous bombs.

"But, Amitai, where's it been the past four years? How did it turn up?"

"You know it's Pesach, right?"

As a matter of fact I did; I was still nursing the ragged end of a red wine hangover from the raucous and highly unorthodox Passover picnic that one of my mates had hosted on the beach. The name for the ritual meal in Hebrew is *seder*, which means order; this had been one of the more *dis*orderly nights in my recent history.

"Well, last night the Jewish community in Sarajevo had their seder, and in the middle of it—very dramatic—they brought out the haggadah. The head of the community made a speech saying that the survival of the book was a symbol of the survival of Sarajevo's multiethnic ideal. And do you know who saved it? His name is Ozren Karaman, head of the museum library. Went in under intense shelling." Amitai's voice suddenly seemed a bit husky. "Can you imagine, Channa? A Muslim, risking his neck to save a Jewish book."

It wasn't like Amitai to be impressed by tales of derring-do. An indiscreet colleague had once let drop that Amitai's compulsory army service had been in a commando squad so supersecret that Israelis refer to it only as "the unit." Even though that was long in his past when I first met him, I'd been struck by his physique, and by his manner. He had the dense muscle of a weight lifter and a kind of hypervigilance. He'd look right at you when he was talking to you, but the rest of the time his eyes seemed to be scanning the surroundings, aware of everything. He'd seemed genuinely pissed off when

I'd asked him about the unit. "I never confirmed this to you," he'd snapped. But I thought it was pretty amazing. You certainly don't meet that many ex-commandos in book conservation.

"So what did this old bloke do with the book once he had it?" I asked.

"He put it in a safe-deposit box in the vault of the central bank. You can imagine what that's done to the parchment. . . . No one in Sarajevo's had any heat through at least the last two winters . . . and some metal cash box . . . metal, of all things . . . it's back there now. . . . I can't bear to think about it. Anyway, the UN wants someone to inspect its condition. They're going to pay for any necessary stabilization work—they want to exhibit it as soon as possible, to raise the city's morale, you know. So I saw your name on the program for next month's conference at the Tate, and I thought that, while you are coming to this side of the world, maybe you could fit this job in?"

"Me?" My voice actually squeaked. I don't go in for false modesty: I'm great at what I do. But for a job like this, a once-in-a-lifetime career maker, there were at least a dozen people with more years on the clock and better connections in Europe. "Why not you?" I asked.

Amitai knew more about the Sarajevo Haggadah than anybody alive; he'd written monographs on it. I knew he would have loved this chance to handle the actual codex. He gave a deep sigh. "The Serbs have spent the past three years insisting that the Bosnians are fanatical Muslims, and finally, maybe, a few Bosnians have started to believe them. Seems the Saudis are big donors there now, and there was opposition to giving the job to an Israeli."

"Oh, Amitai, I'm sorry. . . ."

"It's all right, Channa. I'm in good company. They didn't want a German either. Of course, I suggested Werner first—no offense. . . ." Since Herr Doktor Doktor Werner Maria Heinrich was not only my teacher, but also, after Amitai himself, the leading Hebrew manuscripts specialist in the world, I was hardly likely to take any. But

Amitai explained that the Bosnians were still carrying a grudge against Germany for setting off the war in the first place, by recognizing Slovenia and Croatia. "And the UN doesn't want an American because the U.S. Congress is always bad-mouthing UNESCO. So I thought you would be good, because who has any strong opinions about Australians? Also I told them that your technical skills are not bad."

"Thanks for that ringing endorsement," I said. And then, more sincerely, "Amitai, I'll never forget this. Thank you, really."

"You can repay me by making good documentation of the book, so at least we can print a beautiful facsimile. You'll send me the pictures you make, yes, and a draft of your report, as soon as you can?"

His voice sounded so wistful I felt guilty about my own elation. But there was one question I had to ask him.

"Amitai, are there any issues of authenticity? You know the rumors, during the war . . ."

"No, we have no concerns there. The librarian Karaman and his boss, the director of the museum, have authenticated it beyond doubt. Your job is merely technical at this point."

Technical. We'll see about that, I thought to myself. A lot of what I do *is* technical; science and craftsmanship that anyone with decent intelligence and good fine-motor skills can be taught to do. But there is something else, too. It has to do with an intuition about the past. By linking research and imagination, sometimes I can think myself into the heads of the people who made the book. I can figure out who they were, or how they worked. That's how I add my few grains to the sandbox of human knowledge. It's what I love best about what I do. And there were so many questions about the Sarajevo Haggadah. If I could answer just one of them . . .

I couldn't get back to sleep, so I threw on my sweats and went out, through the nighttime streets still faintly sour with the mingled stink of spewed beer and deep-fryer fat, down to the beach, where the air blows, clean and briny, over half a planet's worth of uninterrupted ocean. Because it was autumn, and a midweek night, there

139

was hardly anyone around. Just a few drunks, slumped by the wall of the surf club, and a pair of lovers, entwined on a beach towel. No one to notice me. I started walking along the edge of the foam, luminous against the lacquered darkness of the sand. Before I knew it, I was running and skipping, dodging the breakers like a child.

That was a week ago. In the days following, that feeling of exhilaration had been gradually buried under visa applications, reissued airline tickets, UN red tape, and a thick dollop of nerves. As I staggered down the stairs from the plane to the tarmac under the weight of my case, I had to keep reminding myself that this was exactly the kind of assignment I lived for.

I had barely a second to take in the mountains, rising all around us like the rim of a giant bowl, and then a blue-helmeted soldier—tall and Scandinavian-looking—leaped from the middle vehicle and seized my bag, hurling it into the rear of the van.

"Steady!" I said. "There's delicate equipment in there!" The soldier's only reply was to grab me by the arm and propel me into the backseat, slamming the door and jumping in front alongside the driver. The automatic locks clicked down with a definitive *thunk,* and the driver gunned the engine.

"Well, this is a first for me," I said, trying for some wan levity. "Book conservators don't usually have much call to travel in armored cars." There was no response from the soldier or the thin, drawn civilian hunched over the wheel of the immense vehicle, his head pulled into his shoulders like a tortoise. Through the tinted glass the devastated city passed in a blur of shrapnel-splashed buildings. The vans drove fast, swerving around cavernous potholes made by mortar shells and bumping over bitumen shredded by the tracks of armored vehicles. There wasn't much traffic. Most people were on foot; gaunt, exhausted-looking people, coats pulled tight against the chill of a spring that hadn't quite arrived. We passed an apartment block that looked like the dollhouse I'd had as a girl, where the entire front wall lifted off to reveal the rooms within. In this block, the wall had been peeled away by an explosion. But like my dollhouse, the exposed rooms were furnished. As we sped by, I realized that people were somehow still living there, their only protection a few sheets of plastic billowing in the wind. But they'd done their laundry. It flapped from lines strung between the twisted spikes of reinforcing bars that protruded from the shattered concrete.

I thought they'd take me straight to see the book. Instead, the day was consumed by endless, tedious meetings, first with every UN official who'd ever had a thought about a cultural matter, then with the director of the Bosnian museum, then with a bunch of government officials. I doubt I'd have gotten much sleep anyway, given the anticipation of starting work, but the dozen or so cups of strong Turkish coffee I'd been served in the course of the day hadn't helped. Maybe that's why my hands were still shaking.

There was a burst of static from the police radios. Suddenly all the people were up on their feet: the police, the guards, Sajjan. The bank official shot the door bolts and a whole lot more guards entered in a sort of flying wedge. At the center was a thin young man in faded blue jeans. The slacker from the museum, probably, who'd kept us all waiting. But I didn't have time to be irritated with him, because he was cradling a metal box. When he set it down on the bench I saw it was sealed in several places with stamped wax and adhesive papers. I passed him my scalpel. He broke the seals and eased open the lid. He unwrapped several sheets of silk paper. And then he handed me the book.

II

AS MANY TIMES as I've worked on rare, beautiful things, that first touch is always a strange and powerful sensation. It's a combination between brushing a live wire and stroking the back of a newborn baby's head.

No conservator had handled this manuscript for a century. I had the forms positioned, ready. I hesitated for just a second—a Hebrew book, therefore spine to the right—and laid it in the cradling foam.

Until you opened it, the book was nothing that an untrained eye would look twice at. It was small, for one thing, convenient for use at the Passover dinner table. Its binding was of an ordinary nineteenth-century style, soiled and scuffed. A codex as gorgeously illustrated as this one would originally have had an elaborate binding. You don't make filet mignon then serve it on a paper plate. The binder might have used gold leaf or silver tooling, maybe inlays of ivory or pearl shell. But this book had probably been rebound many times in its long life. The only one we knew about for sure, because it had been documented, was the last time, in Vienna in the 1890s. Unfortunately, the book had been terribly mishandled in that instance. The Austrian binder had cropped the parchment heavily and discarded the old binding—something no one, especially not a professional working for a major museum—would ever do anymore. It was impossible to say what information might have been lost at that time. He had re-bound the parchments in simple cardboard covers with an inappro-priate Turkish printed floral paper decoration, now faded and discolored. Only the corners and spine were calfskin, and this was dark brown and flaking away, exposing the edge of the gray board beneath.

I ran my middle finger lightly along the cracked corners. These I would consolidate over the coming days. As my finger followed the edges of the board, I noticed something unexpected. The binder had made a pair of channels and a set of small holes in the board edge to accept a pair of clasps. It was usual for books of parchment to have clasps, to hold the pages flat. Yet there were no clasps on this binding. I made a note to myself to investigate this.

Moving the forms to support the spine, I opened the cover and leaned close to examine the torn endpapers. I would mend these with wheat paste and shreds of matching linen paper. I could see at once that the linen cords the Viennese binder had used were frayed, barely holding. That meant I would have to take the quires apart and restitch them. Then I breathed deeply and turned the page to the parchment of the manuscript itself. This was what mattered; this was what would disclose what four hard years had done to a survivor of five centuries.

The snow light flared on brightness. Blue: intense as a midsummer sky, obtained from grinding precious lapis lazuli carried by camel caravan all the way from the mountains of Afghanistan. White: pure, creamy, opaque. Less glamorous, more complicated than the blue. At that time it would still have been made according to the method discovered by ancient Egyptians. You cover lead bars with the dregs of old wine and seal them up in a shed full of animal dung. I'd done it once, in my mother's greenhouse in Bellevue Hill. She'd had a load of manure delivered, and I couldn't resist. The acid in the vinegary wine converts lead to its acetate, which in turn combines with the carbon dioxide released by the dung to make basic white lead carbonate, $PbCO_3$. My mother pitched a fit about it, of course. Said she couldn't stand to go near her bloody prize orchids for weeks.

I turned a page. More dazzle. The illuminations were beautiful, but I didn't allow myself to look at them as art. Not yet. First I had to understand them as chemicals. There was yellow, made of saffron. That beautiful autumn flower, *Crocus sativus Linnaeus*, each with just three tiny precious stigmas, had been a prized luxury then and remained one, still. Even if we now know that the rich color comes from a carotene, crocin, with a molecular structure of 44 carbon, 64 hydrogen, and 24 oxygen, we still haven't synthesized a substitute as complex and as beautiful. There was malachite green, and red; the intense red known as worm scarlet—*tola'at shani* in Hebrew—extracted from tree-dwelling insects, crushed up and boiled in lye. Later, when alchemists learned how to make a similar red from sulfur and mercury, they still named the color "little worm"—*vermiculum*. Some things don't change: we call it vermilion even today.

Change. That's the enemy. Books do best when temperature, humidity, the whole environment, stay the same. You could hardly get more dramatic changes than this book had been through: moved under extreme difficulties and without preparation or precaution, exposed to wild swings of temperature. I'd been worried that the parchment might have shrunk, the pigments cracked and lifted. But the colors had held fast, as pure and as vivid as the day the paint was applied. Unlike the leaf on the spine, which had flaked away, the burnished gold of the illuminations was fresh and blazing. The gilder of five hundred years ago had definitely had a better grasp of his trade than the more modern Viennese bookbinder. There was silver leaf also. This had oxidized and turned dark gray, as you would expect.

"Will you be replacing that?" It was the thin young man from the museum. He was pointing at a distinct area of tarnish. He was standing too close. Because parchment is flesh, human bacteria can degrade it. I moved my shoulder so that he had to withdraw his hand and take a step backward.

"No," I said. "Absolutely not." I did not look up.

"But you're a restorer; I thought . . ."

"Conservator," I corrected. The last thing I wanted right then was a long discussion on the philosophy of book conservation. "Look," I said, "you're here; I'm instructed that you have to be here, but I'd appreciate it if you didn't interrupt my work."

"I understand," he said, his voice gentle after my abrasiveness. "But you must also understand: I am the *kustos*, the book is in my care."

Kustos. It took a minute to sink in. I turned then, and stared at him. "*You* can't be Ozren Karaman? The one who saved the book?"

The UN rep, Sajjan, sprang up, all apologies. "I am sorry, I should have made the introduction. But you were so anxious to get to work. I— Dr. Hanna Heath, please may I present Dr. Ozren Karaman, chief librarian of the National Museum and professor of librarianship at the National University of Bosnia."

"I— Sorry, that was rude of me," I said. "I expected that you'd be much older, to be chief curator of such a major collection." I also didn't expect a person in that position to look quite so disheveled. He was wearing a scuffed leather jacket over a crumpled white T-shirt.

His jeans were frayed. His hair—wild, curly, neither combed nor cut—flopped over a pair of glasses that were mended in the middle with a bit of duct tape.

He raised an eyebrow. "You yourself, of course, being so very advanced in years, would have every reason to think that." He kept a perfectly straight face as he said this. I guessed he was about thirty, like me. "But I would be very pleased, Dr. Heath, if you could spare a moment to say what you have in mind to do." He shot Sajjan a glance as he said this, and in it I could read a volume. The UN thought it was doing Bosnia a favor, funding the work so that the haggadah could be properly displayed. But when it comes to national treasures, no one wants outsiders calling the shots. Ozren Karaman clearly felt he'd been sidelined. The last thing I wanted was to get involved in any of that. I was here to care for a book, not some librarian's bruised ego. Still, he had a right to know why the UN had chosen someone like me.

"I can't say exactly the extent of my work till I've thoroughly inspected the manuscript, but here's the thing: no one hires me looking for chemical cleanups or heavy restorations. I've written too many papers knocking that approach. To restore a book to the way it was when it was made is to lack respect for its history. I think you have to accept a book as you receive it from past generations, and to a certain extent damage and wear reflect that history. The way I see it, my job is to make it stable enough to allow safe handling and study, repairing only where absolutely necessary. This, here," I said, pointing to a page where a russet stain bloomed over the fiery Hebrew calligraphy, "I can take a microscopic sample of those fibers, and we can analyze them, and maybe learn what made that stain— wine would be my first guess. But a full analysis might provide clues as to where the book was at the time it happened. And if we can't tell now, then in fifty, a hundred years, when lab techniques have advanced, my counterpart in the future will be able to. But if I chemically erased that stain—that so-called damage—we'd lose the chance at that knowledge forever." I took a deep breath.

Ozren Karaman was looking at me with a bemused expression. I suddenly felt embarrassed. "Sorry, you know all that, of course. But it's a bit of an obsession with me, and once I get started . . ." I was only digging a deeper hole, so I stopped. "The thing is, they've given me only a week's access to the book, so I really need every minute. I'd like to get started. . . . I'll have it till six this evening, yes?"

"No, not quite. I'll need to take it about ten minutes before the hour, to get it secured before the bank guards change shifts."

"All right," I said, drawing my chair in close. I inclined my head to the other end of the long table where the security detachment sat. "Any chance we could get rid of a few of them?"

He shook his uncombed head. "I'm afraid we'll all be staying."

I couldn't help the sigh that escaped me. My work has to do with objects, not people. I like matter, fiber, the nature of the varied stuffs that go to make a book. I know the flesh and fabrics of pages, the bright earths and lethal toxins of ancient pigments. Wheat paste—I can bore the pants off anyone about wheat paste. I spent six months in Japan, learning how to mix it for just the necessary amount of tension.

Parchment, especially, I love. So durable it can last for centuries, so fragile it can be destroyed in a careless instant. One of the reasons, I'm sure, that I got this job was because I have written so many journal articles on parchment. I could tell, just from the size and scatter of the pore holes, that the parchments in front of me had been made from the skin of a now-extinct breed of thick-haired Spanish mountain sheep. You can date manuscripts from the kingdoms of Aragon and Castile to within a hundred years or so if you know when that particular breed was all the go with the local parchment makers.

Parchment is leather, essentially, but it looks and feels different because the dermal fibers in the skin have been reorganized by stretching. Wet it, and the fibers revert to their original, three-dimensional network. I had worried about condensation within the metal box, or exposure to the elements during transport. But there was very little sign of either. There were some pages that showed signs of older water damage, but under the microscope I saw a rime of cube-shaped crystals that I recognized: NaCl, also known as plain old table salt. The water that had damaged this book was probably the saltwater used at the seder table to represent the tears of the slaves in Egypt.

Of course, a book is more than the sum of its materials. It is an artifact of the human mind and hand. The gold beaters, the stone grinders, the scribes, the binders, those are the people I feel most comfortable with. Sometimes, in the quiet, these people speak to me. They let me see what their intentions were, and it helps me do my work. I worried that the *kustos,* with his well-meaning scrutiny, or the cops, with the low chatter of their radios, would keep my friendly ghosts at bay. And I needed their help. There were so many questions.

For a start, most books like this, rich in such expensive pigments, had been made for palaces or cathedrals. But a haggadah is used only at home. The word is from the Hebrew root *ngd,* "to tell," and it comes from the biblical command that instructs parents to tell their children the story of the Exodus. This "telling" varies widely, and over the centuries each Jewish community has developed its own variations on this home-based celebration.

But no one knew why this haggadah was illustrated with numerous miniature paintings, at a time when most Jews considered figurative art a violation of the commandments. It was unlikely that a Jew would have been in a position to learn the skilled painting techniques evinced here. The style was not unlike the work of Christian illuminators. And yet, most of the miniatures illustrated biblical scenes as interpreted in the Midrash, or Jewish biblical exegesis.

I turned the parchment and suddenly found myself gazing at the illustration that had provoked more scholarly speculation than all the others. It was a domestic scene. A family of Jews—Spanish, by their dress—sits at a Passover meal. We see the ritual foods, the matzoh to commemorate the unleavened bread that the Hebrews baked in haste on the night before they fled Egypt, a shank bone to remember the lamb's blood on the doorposts that had caused the angel of death to "pass over" Jewish homes. The father, reclining as per custom, to show that he is a free man and not a slave, sips wine from a golden goblet as his small son, beside him, raises a cup. The mother sits serenely in the fine gown and jeweled headdress of the day. Probably the scene is a portrait of the family who commissioned this particular haggadah. But there is another woman at the table, ebony-skinned and saffron-robed, holding a piece of matzoh. Too finely dressed to be a servant, and fully participating in the Jewish rite, the identity of that African woman in saffron has perplexed the book's scholars for a century.

Slowly, deliberately, I examined and made notes on the condition of each page. Each time I turned a parchment, I checked and adjusted the position of the supporting forms. Never stress the book—the conservator's chief commandment. But the people who had owned this book had known unbearable stress: pogrom, Inquisition, exile, genocide, war.

As I reached the end of the Hebrew text, I came to a line of script in another language, another hand. *Revisto per mi. Gio. Domenico Vistorini, 1609.* The Latin, written in the Venetian style, translated as "Surveyed by me." Were it not for those three words, placed there by an official censor of the pope's Inquisition, this book might have been destroyed that year in Venice, and would never have crossed the Adriatic to the Balkans.

"Why did you save it, Giovanni?"

I looked up, frowning. It was Dr. Karaman, the librarian. He gave a tiny, apologetic shrug. Probably he thought I was irritated at the interruption, but actually I was surprised that he had voiced the very question in my mind. No one knew the answer; any more than they knew how or why—or even when—the book had come to this city. A bill of sale from 1894 stated that someone named Kohen had sold it to the library. But no one had thought to question the seller. And since World War II, when two-thirds of the Jews in Sarajevo were slaughtered and the city's Jewish quarter ransacked, there had been no Kohens left in the city to ask. A Muslim librarian had saved the book from the Nazis then, too, but the details of how he'd done it were sparse and conflicting.

When I had completed the notes on my initial examination, I set up an eight-by-ten camera and worked through again from the beginning, photographing every page so as to make an accurate record of the book's condition before any conservation work was attempted. When I was done with the conservation work and before I re-bound the pages, I would photograph each page again. I would send the negatives to Amitai in Jerusalem. He would direct the making of a set of high-grade prints for the world's museums and the printing of a facsimile edition that ordinary people everywhere would be able to enjoy. Normally, a specialist would do those photos, but the UN didn't want to jump through the hoops of finding another expert that passed muster with all the city's constituencies, so I'd agreed to do it.

I flexed my shoulders and reached for my scalpel. Then I sat, my chin resting on one hand, the other poised over the binding. Always a moment of self-doubt, at the instant before you begin. The light glinted on the bright steel, and made me think of my mother. If she hesitated like this, the patient would bleed out on the table. But my mother, the first woman to chair a department of neurosurgery in the history of Australia, was a stranger to self-doubt. She hadn't doubted her right to flout every convention of her era, bearing a child without troubling to take a husband, or even naming a father. To this day, I have no idea who he was. Someone she loved? Someone she used? The latter, more likely. She thought she was going to raise me in her own image. What a joke. She's fair and perpetually tennis-tanned; I'm dark and pale as a Goth. She has champagne tastes. I prefer beer straight out of the tinnie.

I realized a long time ago that she would never respect me for choosing to be a repairer of books rather than bodies. For her, my double-honors degrees in chemistry and ancient Near Eastern languages might as well have been used Kleenex. A masters in chemistry and a PhD in fine art conservation didn't cut it, either.

"Kindergarten work," she calls it, my papers and pigments and pastes. "You'd be through your internship by now," she said when I got back from Japan. "At your age I was chief resident" was all I got when I came home from Harvard.

Sometimes, I feel like a figure in one of the Persian miniatures I conserve, a tiny person forever watched by immobile faces, staring down from high galleries or spying from behind lattice screens. But in my case, the faces are always just that one face, my mother's, with her pursed mouth and disapproving glare.

And here I am, thirty years old, and still she can get between me and my work. That feeling, of her impatient, disapproving scrutiny, finally stirred me. I slipped the scalpel under the thread, and the codex eased apart into its precious folios. I lifted the first one. A tiny speck of something fluttered from the binding. Carefully, with a sable brush, I moved it onto a slide and passed it under the microscope. Eureka. It was a tiny fragment of insect wing, translucent, veined. We live in a world of arthropods, and maybe the wing came from a common insect and wouldn't tell us anything. But maybe it was a rarity, with a limited geographic range. Or maybe it was from a species now extinct. Either would add knowledge to the history of the book. I placed it in a glassine envelope and labeled it with a note of its position.

A few years ago, a tiny sliver of quill paring I'd found in a binding had caused a complete uproar. The work was a very beautiful little set of suffrages, short prayers to individual saints, supposedly part of a lost Book of Hours. It was owned by an influential French collector who had charmed the Getty into considering paying an absolute fortune for it. The collector had provenance documents going way back, attributing it to the Bedford Master who had painted in Paris around 1425. But something about it didn't sit just right with me.

Generally, a quill paring won't tell you much. You don't need an exotic feather to make a quill. Any good strong flight feather from any robust bird can be made into a serviceable pen. It always makes me laugh when I see actors in period movies scribbling away with flamboyant ostrich feathers. For one thing, there weren't a whole lot of ostriches marching around in medieval Europe. And for another, scribes always trimmed the feather down to something that looked pretty much like a stick, so the fluffy bits didn't get in their way while they were working. But I insisted on checking out the paring with an ornithologist, and what do you know? The paring came from a Muscovy duck feather. Muscovys are common everywhere these days, but in the 1400s they were still pretty much confined to Mexico and Brazil. They weren't introduced to Europe until the early 1600s. Turned out the French "collector" had been faking manuscripts for years.

As I gently lifted off the haggadah's second folio, I drew out the frayed thread holding it, and noticed that a fine white hair, about a centimeter long, had become trapped in the thread fiber. Checking under magnification, I could see that the hair had left a very slight indentation near the binding, on the page that depicted the Spanish family seder. Gently, with surgical tweezers, I disentangled it and placed it in its own envelope.

I needn't have worried about the people in the room being a distraction. I didn't even notice they were there. People came and went, and I didn't raise my head. It was only when the light began to fade that I realized I'd worked right through the day without a break. I suddenly felt stiff from tension, and ravenously hungry. I stood, and Karaman was immediately there, his dreadful metal box ready. I laid the book with its separated folios carefully inside.

"We absolutely have to change this right away," I said. "Metal is the worst thing for transmitting variations in heat and cold." I placed a sheet of glass on top and weighed it with little velvet sandbags to keep the parchments flat. Ozren fiddled with his wax, stamps, and strings while I cleaned and organized my tools. "How do you find our treasure?" he said, inclining his head toward the book.

"Remarkable for its age," I said. "There's no apparent recent damage from inappropriate handling. I'm going to do some tests on a few microscopic samples to see what they'll tell us. Otherwise, it's just a matter of stabilization, and repair of the binding. As you know, it's a late-nineteenth-century binding, and about as physically and mechanically tired as you'd expect."

Karaman leaned down hard on the box, pressing the library's stamp into the wax. Then he stood aside while a bank official did the same with the bank's stamp. The elaborate weave of strings and wax seals meant that any unauthorized access to the contents of the box would be instantly apparent.

"I'd heard that you are Australian," Karaman said. I suppressed a sigh. I was still transported by my day's work and not in the mood for small talk. "It seems a strange occupation for a person from such a young country, looking after other people's ancient treasures." I didn't say anything. Then he added: "I suppose you were hungry for some culture, growing up there?"

Because I had been rude before, I made an effort now. A slight effort. That young country–cultural desert stuff gets very old. Australia happens to have the longest continuous artistic tradition in the world—Aboriginal people were making sophisticated art on the walls of their dwellings thirty thousand years before the people in Lascaux chewed the end off their first paintbrush. But I decided to spare him the full lecture. "Well," I said, "you should consider that immigration has made us the most ethnically diverse country in the world. Australians' roots run very deep and wide. That gives us a stake in all the world's cultural heritage. Even yours." I didn't add that when I was growing up, the Yugoslavs were famous as the only migrant group who'd managed to import their Old World grievances. Everyone else soon succumbed to a kind of sunstruck apathy, but Serbs and Croats were forever going at it, bombing each other's soccer clubs, stoushing with each other even in end-of-the-earth outback shitholes like Coober Pedy.

He received the barb with good grace, smiling at me over the box. He had a very nice smile, I have to say. His mouth sort of turned down and up at the same time, like a Charles Schulz drawing.

The guards stood to escort Karaman and the book. I followed

down the long, ornate corridors until they descended the marble staircase to the vaults. I was waiting for someone to unlock the main doors when Karaman turned back and called after me.

"Perhaps I could invite you to dinner? I know a place in the Old City. It just reopened last month. To be quite frank and sincere, I cannot guarantee the food, but at least it will be Bosnian."

I was about to say no. It's just a reflex with me. And then I thought, why not? Better than some bland, room-service mystery meat in my bleak little hotel room. I told myself that it was legitimate research. Ozren Karaman's rescue had made him part of the history of the book, and I wanted to know more about that.

I waited for him at the top of the stairs, listening to the pneumatic swish of the vault and then the clang of the metal bars that enclosed it. The sound was final and reassuring. The book, at least, would be safe for the night.

from

Rooftops of Tehran

by

Mahbod Seraji

"*Rooftops of Tehran* is a richly rendered first novel about courage, sacrifice, and the bonds of friendship and love. In clear, vivid details, Mahbod Seraji opens the door to the fascinating world of Iran and provides a revealing glimpse into the life and customs of a country on the verge of a revolution. A captivating read."

—Gail Tsukiyama, author of *The Street of a Thousand Blossoms* and *The Samurai's Garden*

An unforgettable debut novel of young love and coming of age in an Iran headed toward revolution.

In a middle-class neighborhood of Iran's sprawling capital city, 17-year-old Pasha Shahed spends the summer of 1973 on his rooftop with his best friend Ahmed, joking around one minute and asking burning questions about life the next. He also hides a secret love for his beautiful neighbor Zari, who has been betrothed since birth to another man. But the bliss of Pasha and Zari's stolen time together is shattered when Pasha unwittingly acts as a beacon for the Shah's secret police. The violent consequences awaken him to the reality of living under a powerful despot, and lead Zari to make a shocking choice . . .

Winter of 1974
Roozbeh Psychiatric Hospital, Tehran

I hear someone's voice chanting, and the repetitive verses lap like water at the edge of my consciousness.

If I had a book, I would read it.
If I had a song, I would sing it.

I look around until I see an old man standing a few meters away chanting in a steady, empty tone. The place does not look familiar to me. The blue robe that covers my body, the wheelchair I am sitting in, the sunlight creeping between the shades that warms me—all feel strange.

If I knew a dance, I would dance it.
If I knew a rhyme, I would chant it.
If I had a life, I would risk it.
If I could be free, I would chance it.

Outside in the yard, men of all shapes and ages shuffle around in blue robes. There is something peculiar about each of them. They look lost.

Suddenly a surge of emotions fills my chest and rushes into my throat. A little nurse with a kind, full face that resembles an apple runs up to me and plants her hands on my shoulders and screams, "Help me out here, help me out!" A man in a white uniform runs over and tries to hold me down.

"Stay in your chair, honey. Stay in your chair," Apple Face shouts, which means I must be moving. I focus on sitting still, and look toward the old man on the far side of the room. He is gazing at me as he frantically repeats his mantra:

If I had a horse, I would ride it.
If I had a horse, I would ride it.
If I had a horse . . .

I am taken to a room with a bed, and Apple Face says, "I'm going to give you a sedative to make you feel better, darling."

I feel a pinch in my arm, and suddenly my head and arms become unbearably heavy and my eyes slide shut.

1

Summer of 1973
Tehran

My Friends, My Family, and My Alley

Sleeping on the roof in the summer is customary in Tehran. The dry heat of the day cools after midnight, and those of us who sleep on the rooftops wake with the early sun on our faces and fresh air in our lungs. My mother is strictly against it, and reminds me each evening, "Hundreds of people fall off the roofs every year." My best friend, Ahmed, and I trade hidden smiles with each warning, then climb the stairs to spend our nights under stars that seem close enough to touch. The alley below settles into a patchwork of streetlight, shadow, and sound. A car hums slowly down the deserted street, cautious not to wake anyone, as a stray dog in the distance releases a string of officious barks.

"I hear your mother calling," Ahmed mumbles in the dark. I smile, aiming a good-natured kick that he easily rolls away from.

Our house is the tallest in the neighborhood, which makes our roof an ideal spot for stargazing. In fact, naming stars for our friends and the people we love is one of our favorite pastimes.

"Does everyone have a star?" Ahmed asks.

"Only good people."

"And the better you are the bigger your star, right?"

"Bigger and brighter," I say, as I do every time he asks the same question.

"And your star guides you when you're in trouble, right?"

"Your star and the stars of the people you love."

Ahmed closes one eye and lifts his thumb to block out one of the brighter stars. "I'm tired of looking at your big fat face."

"Shut up and go to sleep then," I say, laughing, letting my gaze relax into the velvety emptiness between each pinprick of light. My eyes travel down the sky until they rest on the familiar rise and fall of the Alborz Mountains, which serpentine between the desert and the blue-green Caspian Sea. I get distracted for a moment trying to decide if the darkness is black or so deeply blue that it just appears inky in comparison.

"I wonder why people are so unabashedly afraid of the dark," I ponder, and Ahmed chuckles. I know without asking that he is amused by my eccentric vocabulary, the product of a lifetime of heavy reading. My father pulled Ahmed and me aside one day and asked me, in front of family friends and relatives, what I thought life was about. I promptly said that life was a random series of beautifully composed vignettes, loosely tied together by a string of characters and time. My father's friends actually applauded, much to my embarrassment. Ahmed leaned over and whispered that I would soon be inaugurated as the oldest seventeen-year-old in the world, especially if I kept saying things like "unabashedly" and "beautifully composed vignettes."

Ahmed and I have just finished the eleventh grade and will be entering our last year of high school in the fall. I look forward to the end of preparatory school as much as the next seventeen-year-old, but this lively anticipation is tempered by my father's plans to send me to the United States to study civil engineering. Long ago, my father worked as a ranger, protecting the nationalized forests from poachers who cut down the trees illegally for personal profit. He now works in an office, managing an entire region with an army of rangers reporting to him.

"Iran is in dire need of engineers," Dad reminds me whenever he gets the chance. "We're on the verge of transforming ourselves from a traditional agricultural country to an industrial one. A person with an engineering degree from an American university secures a great future for himself and his family, in addition to enjoying the prestige of being called 'Mr. Engineer' for the rest of his life." I love my father, and I would never disobey him, but I hate math, I hate the idea of becoming an engineer, and I would hate being called Mr. Engineer. In my dreams I major in literature and study the philosophy of the ancient Greeks, evolution, Marxism, psychoanalysis, Erfan, and Buddhism. Or, I major in film and become a writer or a director, someone who has something worthwhile to say.

For now I live with my parents in a middle-class neighborhood. We have a typical Iranian house with a modest yard, a large guest room, and a *hose*—a small pool in the front yard. In our neighborhood, just like any other in Tehran, tall walls separate houses that have been built connected to each other. Our home has two full levels, and my room occupies a small section of the third floor, where a huge terrace is connected to the roof by a bulky mass of steel steps. Ours is the tallest house in the neighborhood, and has a southern exposure.

"I wouldn't live in a home with a northern exposure if it were given to me for free," my mother states repeatedly. "They never get any sun. They're a breeding ground for germs." My mother never finished high school, yet she speaks about health issues with the authority of a Harvard graduate. She has a remedy for every ailment: herbal tea to cure depression, liquidated camel thorns to smash kidney stones, powdered flowers to annihilate sinus infections, dried leaves that destroy acne, and pills for growing as tall as a tree—despite the fact that she stands an impressive five feet tall in stocking feet.

The peace of each summer night fades with the noises of families starting their day, and our alley bustles with kids of all ages. Boys shout and scuffle as they chase cheap plastic soccer balls, while girls go from house to house, doing what girls do together. Women congregate in different parts of the alley, making it easy to tell who likes whom by the way they assemble. Ahmed has divided these gatherings into three groups: the east, west, and central gossip committees.

Ahmed is a tall skinny kid with dark features and a brilliant smile. His strong but slender body, bold, broad jaw, and bright hazel eyes make him the picture of health, according to my mother's expert opinion. He's well liked in the neighborhood, and funny. I tell him he could become a great comedian if he took his God-given talent more seriously.

"Yes, more seriously," he replies. "I can become the most serious clown in the country!"

I've known Ahmed since I was twelve years old, when my family first moved to the neighborhood. We met for the first time at school when three bullies were beating me up. All the other kids stood by and watched, but Ahmed rushed to my aid. The boys were tall, big, and ugly, and despite our heroic attempts we both took a beating.

"I'm Pasha," I introduced myself after the fight.

Ahmed smiled and reached over for a handshake. "What was the fight about?" he asked.

I laughed. "You didn't know? Why did you help me?"

"Three to one! I have a problem with that. Of course, I knew they'd still take us, but at least it wasn't as unfair as three guys thrashing one."

I knew right then that Ahmed was going to be my best friend forever. His gallantry and upbeat attitude won me over instantly. The experience bound us together and prompted my father, an ex–heavyweight boxing champion, to start teaching us how to box—much to my mother's dismay.

"You're going to make them violent," she would complain to my unsympathetic father. To make things right, every night after dinner she would hold out a glass of amber liquid that smelled like horse urine on a hot summer day. "This will reverse what your father is doing to your temper," she assured me, while forcing me to drink the nauseating brew.

I loved boxing, but my mother's remedy nearly drove me to quit.

After a few months of training, as our punches became crisp—short and quick, but heavy when they needed to be—I began to ache for a rematch with the three bullies at school. My father overheard our plans for revenge and intervened.

"Sit down, Mr. Pasha," he said one day after practice. Then he pointed to Ahmed. "Would you join us, please?"

"Of course, Mr. Shahed," Ahmed responded, and as he was sitting next to me, he whispered, "I think we're in trouble, Mr. Pasha!"

"When one learns how to box," Dad started thoughtfully, "he joins the fraternity of athletes who never raise a hand against people weaker than themselves."

My mother stopped what she had been doing and walked up to stand sternly next to my father.

"But, Dad, if we don't beat up people weaker than ourselves, who do we beat up?" I asked, stunned. "And wouldn't it be dumb to pick on people stronger than ourselves anyway?"

Dad was doing his best not to look at Mom, who was staring at him like a tiger checking out a deer right before the final, fateful dash.

"I taught you how to box so you could defend yourself," he mumbled. "I don't want you to go looking for a fight."

Ahmed and I couldn't believe what we were hearing.

"I want you to promise me that you will always respect the code of our fraternity," my father insisted.

We must have been slow to react.

"I want you to promise," he repeated, his voice rising.

And so Ahmed and I grudgingly joined the fraternity of athletes who never beat up bullies who break the faces of kids weaker than themselves. At the time, of course, we had no idea that such a fraternity never existed.

"Iraj is lucky your dad made us promise," Ahmed says later, making us both laugh.

Iraj is a small, scruffy kid with a long pointed nose whose sunburned features make him look Indian. He's smart, has the best grades in our school, and loves physics and mathematics, the two subjects I hate most.

I am convinced Iraj likes Ahmed's oldest sister, because he can't keep his eyes off her when she is in the alley. Everyone knows you don't fancy a friend's sister, as if she were a girl from another neighborhood. If I were Ahmed and caught Iraj checking out my sister, I'd kick the shit out of him. But I'm not Ahmed. "Hey," he'll shout, trying hard not to smile when he startles Iraj, "stop looking at her or I'll break my pledge to the sacred brotherhood of the boxing fraternity."

"Sacred brotherhood of the boxing fraternity?" I whisper under my breath with a smile. "Brotherhood and fraternity mean the same thing. You shouldn't use them in the same sentence."

"Oh, you shut up." Ahmed laughs.

Iraj is the chess champion of our neighborhood. He is so good that no one is willing to play against him anymore. When we play soccer in the alley, Iraj plays chess against himself.

"Who's winning?" Ahmed asks with a smirk. Iraj ignores him. "Have you ever beaten yourself?" Ahmed asks. "You could, you know—if you weren't so fucking preoccupied with my sister."

"I'm not preoccupied with your sister," Iraj mumbles, rolling his eyes.

"Right," Ahmed replies, nodding. "If you have any trouble beating yourself, let me know and I'll be happy to do it for you."

"You know," I tease, "I used to get mad at him for looking at your sister, but it might not be so bad to have a chess champion as a brother-in-law."

"Bite your tongue," Ahmed growls, "or I'll raid your mother's pantry to mix you a special brew that will grow hair on your tongue."

The threat has some weight, considering the way my mother has applied her unique brand of knowledge and listened to her gut to diagnose me as an extreme introvert.

"Do you know what happens to people who keep everything to themselves?" she asks, not waiting for my answer. "They get sick." When I object that I'm not an introvert, she reminds me of the time I was four years old and fell down the steps. My two aunts, two uncles, and grandparents were visiting us that day, and my mother estimated that watching me tumble down two flights of stairs nearly caused two heart attacks, three strokes, and a handful of small ulcers.

"You broke your shin in three places!" she chides. "The doctor said he'd seen grown men cry after a break like that, but not you. Do you know what that kind of stress does to your body?"

"No," I say.

"It causes cancer."

Then she spits three times to atone for the thought.

In order to cure my introversion, she insists I drink a dusky concoction that looks and smells like used motor oil. I complain that her remedy tastes horrible, and she tells me to be quiet and stop whining.

"I thought this potion was to bring me out of my shell," I remind her.

"Hush," she orders, "whining doesn't count. If you want to be successful in life you must force yourself to be an extrovert," she explains. "Introverts end up as lonely poets or destitute writers."

"So," Ahmed ponders one day, "the engine oil makes you an extrovert, and the horse urine helps you crawl back into your shell." He shakes his head in empathy. "You are going to be one fucked-up person by the time your mother gets done with you."

2

Faheemeh's Tears and Zari's Wet Hair

Our summer nights on the roof are spent basking in the wide-open safety of our bird's-eye view. There are no walls around what we say, or fears shaping what we think. I spend hours listening to stories of Ahmed's silent encounters with Faheemeh, the girl he loves. His voice softens and his face quiets as he describes how she threw back her long black hair while looking at him—and how that must mean she loves him. Why else would she strain her neck to communicate with him? My father says that Persians believe in silent communication; a look or a gesture imparts far more than a book full of words. My father is a great silent communicator. When I behave badly, he just gives me a dirty look that hurts more than a thousand slaps in the face.

I listen while Ahmed's voice chatters on about Faheemeh, but my gaze usually wanders into our neighbors' yard, where a girl named Zari lives with her parents and her little brother, Keivan. I've never seen Faheemeh up close, so when Ahmed talks about her I picture Zari in my mind: her delicate cheekbones, her smiling eyes, and her pale, soft skin. Most summer evenings Zari sits at the edge of her family's little *hose* under a cherry tree, dangling her shapely feet in the cool water as she reads. I'm careful not to let my eyes linger too long because she is engaged to my friend and mentor, Ramin Sobhi, a third-year political science major at the University of Tehran whom everyone, including his parents, calls Doctor. It's low to fancy a friend's girl, and I shove all thoughts of Zari from my head every time I think of Doctor, but Ahmed's lovesick ramblings make it hard for me to keep my mind clear.

Every day Ahmed bikes ten minutes to Faheemeh's neighborhood in the hope of getting a glimpse of her. He says she has two older brothers who protect her like hawks, and that everyone in the neighborhood knows that messing with their sister means getting a broken nose, a dislocated jaw, and a big black eggplant under at least one eye. Ahmed says that if Faheemeh's brothers learned that he fancied their sister, they'd make his ears the biggest parts of his body—meaning that they would cut him into little pieces.

Not one to be thwarted, Ahmed picks a day when Faheemeh's brothers are in the alley and intentionally rides his bike into a wall. He moans and groans with pain, and Faheemeh's brothers take him inside their home and give him a couple of aspirin, then immobilize his injured wrist by wrapping a piece of fabric around it. Faheemeh is only a few steps away, and knows full well what the handsome stranger is up to.

Ahmed now rides his bike to Faheemeh's alley without a worry in the world, spending hours with Faheemeh's brothers and talking about everything from the members of this year's Iranian national soccer team to next year's potential honorees. He says he doesn't mind that her brothers bore him to death as long as he is close to her. They play soccer all afternoon in the alley and Ahmed insists on playing goalie, even though he stinks in that position. While the other kids chase the ball in the scorching heat of Tehran's afternoons, Ahmed stands still. Supposedly he's defending his team's goal, but really he's watching Faheemeh, who watches him from the roof of her house.

After only a few games, Ahmed is forced to abdicate his post as the goalie. He is so preoccupied with Faheemeh that he is never prepared for the opponent's attackers and his team always loses by at least five or six points. When Ahmed begins to play forward his team starts to win again, but now he has to run after the ball, which means he can no longer exchange silent looks with Faheemeh.

So Ahmed comes to me with a plan. I am to accompany him to Faheemeh's alley the next day. He will introduce me to his new friends and will make sure that I end up on the opposite team. I will aim at his knee during a crucial play and he'll fake a bad fall and a serious injury. Then he will have no choice but to play as goalie again. He will be a goalie in agony, playing despite his pain, and that will undoubtedly impress Faheemeh.

I agree to go along but worry deep down about what Faheemeh might think of me after I knock Ahmed down. I feel better when I imagine the day we tell her the whole thing was a setup to get Ahmed back in the goalie position.

"Don't hurt me for real, now," Ahmed warns with a smile on his face.

"Make sure the orthopedic surgeon is on call, pal," I respond, getting into the spirit.

"Oh, come on. You know I have fragile bones. Just touch me lightly and I'll do the rest."

The plan is carried out masterfully. Ahmed deserves an Oscar for his portrayal of a boy in pain, and a gold medal for playing goalie after his dreadful injury. Looking at his face, which glows with the knowledge that Faheemeh is watching, I worry that he might really hurt himself with his courageous dives to the left, to the right, and under the feet of our attackers—all of this on asphalt. We can't score on him. He scrapes his hands and elbows, and tears his pants at the knees. Each time he stops us he grimaces with pain, releases the ball,

and looks up toward the roof where Faheemeh is watching atten-
tively. I even see her smile at him once.

One of Faheemeh's brothers notices that I'm looking toward the
roof, and I know from that moment on he doesn't like me anymore, just
as I don't like Iraj for staring at Ahmed's sister. He doesn't shake my
hand when I say good-bye to everyone. I size him up surreptitiously.
He's taller and bigger than I am. I leave with the comfort of knowing
that I would not be letting down the sacred brotherhood of the boxing
fraternity if he ever decided to be an asshole to me or to Ahmed.

A couple of weeks pass, and I'm sitting on our roof in the dark, my
ears and eyes filled with the rush and sway of the light wind that bends
the treetops, when I hear the door to Zari's yard open, then shut.

Don't look, I think resolutely, but my body resorts to quick, shallow breaths as soon as it recognizes the sound. *It could just be Keivan,*
I reason. I decide to close my eyes, but my heart races as I realize that
doing so has only sharpened my hearing. Bare feet pad across the yard,
then the water in the *hose* begins to murmur with the slow churning of
her legs as the pages of her book turn with the soft, rhythmic hiss so
familiar from my own hours spent reading. She's read four pages by
the time Ahmed arrives on my roof. He sits silently on the short wall
that runs between our rooftops and lights a cigarette with shaking
hands. The momentary illumination from the match reveals tears in
his eyes.

"Is something wrong?" I ask, my chest growing tight at the expression on his face.

He shakes his head no, but I don't believe him. We Persians as a
people are too deeply immersed in misery to resist despair when it
knocks on our door.

"Are you sure?" I insist, and he nods his head yes.

I decide to leave him alone because that's what I wish people
would do for me when I don't feel like talking.

He sits as still as stone for a few minutes as the cigarette's glowing coal creeps toward his fingers, then whispers, "She has a suitor."

"Who has a suitor?" I ask, glancing below at Zari; her ivory feet stir the moon's reflection on the water's surface so that it shimmers like liquid gold.

"Faheemeh. A guy who lives a couple of doors down from them is sending his parents to her house tomorrow night."

It feels like someone knocked the wind out of me. I don't know what to say. People who insist on sticking their noses into other people's business seldom know what to say or do. I wonder why they ask in the first place. I pretend to study the blinking city lights that sprawl across the shadowy distance.

"When did you find out?" I finally ask.

"After you left this afternoon, her brothers and I went into her yard to get some cool water and that's when they told me."

"Was she around?"

"Yes," he says, looking up hard at the sky to keep the tears from falling down his face. "She was pouring water from a pitcher into my glass when they told me." He remembers his cigarette and takes a big puff. "I was sitting in a chair and she was standing over me, actually bending over me. She looked at my eyes the whole time, never blinked." Ahmed shakes his head as his lips twist into the ghost of a smile. "She was so close I could feel her breath on my face, and her skin smelled clean—like soap, but sweeter. One of her brothers asked if I was going to congratulate their little sister, but I couldn't make my voice come out of my throat." Ahmed lets his face and his tears fall as he drops the spent cigarette and steps on it.

"She's too young," I whisper. "For crying out loud, how old is she, seventeen? How can they marry off a seventeen-year-old kid?"

Ahmed shakes his head again, mute.

"Maybe her parents will reject him," I say, to plant hope in his heart.

"Her family loves him," he says with a short bitter laugh as he pulls another cigarette from the pack. "He's a twenty-six-year-old college graduate who works for the Agriculture Ministry, owns a car, and will soon be buying his own home in Tehran Pars. They won't say no to him." He lights the cigarette, then holds the pack out in my direction. I picture my father appearing unexpectedly and pinning me down with one of his dirty looks, the ones that hurt more than a thousand slaps in the face. I shake my head no.

I look at Ahmed's sad face and wish I could do something to help him out. This is a historic night for both of us. We're experiencing the first major personal crisis of our young lives. It's sad, but I must admit, on some level it's also exciting. It makes me feel grown-up.

"Do you know how bad this feels?" Ahmed asks between puffs.

"Well," I begin, wanting desperately to carry his pain, "I've only read about it in books," I confess, somewhat embarrassed. Then I look toward Zari's yard, and add, "But I think I can imagine."

Late the next afternoon, Ahmed asks me to go to Faheemeh's alley with him. I do, despite my apprehension about seeing Faheemeh's brothers again, especially the one who hates me for being like Iraj. The sun has just set, and the lights in the alley are springing on one by one. Some people have just watered their trees and hosed their sidewalks, as is customary in Tehran, and the scent of wet dust makes the dry heat of the evening feel more tolerable. A group of kids is playing soccer and making a lot of noise. I figure it must be the final game of the evening. The ladies stand close to each other trading talk while the younger girls run arm in arm, giggling.

I have never seen Ahmed so consumed by grief. We walk up and down the alley, and he slows every time we reach Faheemeh's house. "I can feel her on the other side of these walls," he says, resting his forehead against the stone and closing his eyes. "She knows I'm here," he whispers. "We're breathing the same air." Some kids walk by and recognize Ahmed. They want to chat, but neither Ahmed nor I is in a mood to talk, and we continue to pace. When we reach Faheemeh's house again he stops and presses both fists to the stone, like a tired warrior at the base of a fortress.

Inside, a bunch of adults are discussing a lifetime's commitment between two young people. The mother of the bride-to-be is usually happy and proud, unless the suitor is a real loser. The mother of the groom-to-be is civilized and calm; she makes mental notes to use later if a deal cannot be consummated, details that will stay fixed in her mind until the couple is happily married off. Who knows what will happen between two strangers? Good information can always tilt the balance in her favor if the union should fail. Everything is fair game, from the color of the wallpaper in the living room to the size of the future mother-in-law's bottom. The fathers are agreeable and more concerned about drinking, eating, and bragging about the stuff fathers brag about: people they know in high places, the bargain they got on a prime piece of land by the Caspian Sea. Then there is the cast of aunts and uncles, best friends and family members, all happy to be there because they have nothing better to do with their time.

Most of the discussions will focus on money. What does the groom have? Does he own a house? Does he drive a car? What model and year is it? Hopefully it's an American car, a Buick or a Ford. How much is the dowry? How much does the family of the groom pay the family of the bride for this auspicious occasion? What would be the alimony if there were a divorce in the future?

The bride- and groom-to-be normally sit far apart and don't speak. They even avoid looking at each other. I know Ahmed is wondering what Faheemeh is thinking, sitting quietly in that crowded room. That's what I would be worried about if, for example, I loved Zari and she were being married off to someone other than Doctor. I would wonder if Zari were thinking of me. I would wonder if she had made herself pretty, and if she had, I would be questioning why. Doesn't she want my rival to think that she is ugly, and not worthy of marriage? I would be so jealous of the man who would be looking into her beautiful blue eyes, thinking of embracing her, touching her face, feeling her warm body against his. *God, I'm so glad I don't love Zari; poor Ahmed must be going through hell.*

We wait until ten o'clock, but no one comes out of Faheemeh's house. We ride our bikes back to our neighborhood, have a quick dinner, then retreat to the roof. Hours crawl by in heavy silence. The outline of Mount Alborz, usually uplifting, seems to huddle in the growing dark like a lonesome dog. The heat has been unusually persistent all day, and we sit and sweat without speaking for what feels like days. What do you say to a seventeen-year-old boy who has fallen in love with a seventeen-year-old girl who is about to be auctioned off for a few thousand Persian toomans of dowry and the dubious promise of happiness?

"I think you should tell her that you love her," I blurt, suddenly.

Ahmed exhales with a derisive snort. "What good will that do? Besides, don't you think she already knows?"

"*Maybe* she knows . . . *maybe* she thinks that *maybe* you love her—but she doesn't know for sure, does she? You haven't told her how you feel, and you certainly haven't done anything to show her."

"I communicate in silence with her every day," he mumbles.

His answer makes me smile. "Ahmed, she's the only one who can stop this wedding. Her parents may still force her to marry him, so there's no guarantee that your actions would change anything, but you have to give her a reason to fight."

"You think she might?" Ahmed asks, genuine wonder trembling in his voice.

"I think she might if you intervened, and if she doesn't, what have you lost?"

The light above Zari's door blinks on, and she comes into her yard and kneels gracefully at the edge of the *hose*. The night has been slow to cool, and she leans down and to the side to wet her hair, dipping it in the water, then twisting it artfully and pinning it to her head so that the water slides in drops down her neck and back. I'm not sure how long I've been looking into Zari's yard when I feel Ahmed staring at me.

"So," he says, scratching the top of his head thoughtfully, "you think if someone walked up to Zari and told her he loved her, she would reconsider marrying Doctor?"

"That's not . . . that's different," I stutter. "Zari wants to marry Doctor, so that's not a fair question, and this is not about Zari and me. I mean, this is about you and Faheemeh."

Ahmed bites his lower lip to mask his smile, then asks, "You think she would go against her parents' wishes?"

"I said Zari's situation is different!" I bark back.

"I didn't mean Zari. I was talking about Faheemeh." This time Ahmed doesn't bother to hide his smile. "So you think she would go against her parents' wishes?" he repeats.

I shake my head slightly to dislodge any more thoughts of Zari, then fix my friend with a confident stare and answer, "People do amazing things for love. Books are full of wonderful stories about this kind of stuff, and stories aren't just fantasies, you know. They're so much a part of the people who write them that they practically teach their readers invaluable lessons about life."

Ahmed notes the gleam in my eye, shakes his head and chuckles. "I know, I should read more."

I wake the next day alone, squinting at the hot sun hanging dead center in the sky, and realize I must have slept late. My waking fog clears sharply as I notice that Ahmed is already gone. I run downstairs, pull my shoes on, and mumble a hello to my mother, who is heading up the hallway with a large glass of her special engine oil for me. I grimace, then sprint past her into the yard to my bike.

My mother yells, "Where're you going? You haven't eaten breakfast!"

"No time!" I shout as I'm jumping on my bike, and hear the familiar muttering of my mother cursing under her breath.

I pedal as fast as I can to Faheemeh's alley, and my heart sinks as I round the corner. A bunch of kids are holding back Faheemeh's two brothers, and Ahmed's face is covered with blood. There's lots of screaming and yelling, and Faheemeh's oldest brother is telling Ahmed to get lost. Ahmed is standing quietly, with no one holding him back. I jump off my bike and run up to him.

"What's going on?" I ask, anxiously. When Ahmed doesn't speak, I assume the worst and whirl to face our attackers. I will my body to become loose and ready, bouncing lightly on the balls of my feet and shaking my hands briefly to warm them before I curl them into fists.

Ahmed smiles gently and grabs my arm. "I followed your advice. I was trying to tell Faheemeh I love her," he explains, pointing up to the weeping girl on the roof, "but I think the whole world heard."

Faheemeh is watching us, knowing full well that a seventeen-year-old boy has taken his first step toward becoming a man, and in the process has made her feel more like a woman than all the aunts, uncles, and formalities of the night before. If she must marry a man her parents have chosen for her, at least she knows that she is loved by someone with enough courage to defy tradition.

I can only hope that she will summon her own courage to defy her parents, for Ahmed's sake.

A few nights later, at dinner, my mother mentions a rumor she's heard about a sweet young girl in a nearby neighborhood who is being forced to marry a man she doesn't love. "I don't know her," Mom says, "but I feel horrible for her." I listen hard, but keep my face still. "I hear that she has locked herself in a room and refuses to come out, eat, or speak to anyone," Mom reports.

My father shakes his head. "It's time for the parents in this country to learn that the souls of their children are more important than tradition," he says. "You young people need to assume responsibility for your own futures," he tells me. "If someone's old enough to be married off, then they're sure as hell old enough to decide who they should marry." My mother nods in agreement.

Sitting out on the roof after dinner that night, I smell Ahmed's cigarette and hear his steps on the stairs long before he settles down beside me.

"Do I have a star up there?" he asks. I know he isn't expecting an answer, so I remain silent. "I see yours," he claims, pointing at a brilliant star far from the horizon. "It's blinding!"

"That's not me," I argue, my face warming imperceptibly. "Too bright. Must be Faheemeh. The light is stronger because she's thinking of you."

Ahmed sighs as he stretches out on his back and closes his eyes. I follow suit, knowing that the hushed symphony of night noises won't be nearly loud enough to rescue us from our worries. I breathe in the scent of wet asphalt, enjoying the way the night breeze brushes my closed eyes.

from

The Shadow of the Wind

by

Carlos Ruiz Zafón

"Anyone who enjoys novels that are scary, erotic, touching, tragic and thrilling should rush right out to the nearest bookstore and pick up *The Shadow of the Wind*. Really, you should."
—Michael Dirda, *The Washington Post*

Barcelona, 1945: A city slowly heals from its war wounds, and Daniel, an antiquarian book dealer's son who mourns the loss of his mother, finds solace in a mysterious book entitled The Shadow of the Wind, *by one Julián Carax. But when he sets out to find the author's other works, he makes a shocking discovery: someone has been systematically destroying every copy of every book Carax has written. In fact, Daniel may have the last of Carax's books in existence. Soon Daniel's seemingly innocent quest opens a door into one of Barcelona's darkest secrets—an epic story of murder, madness, and doomed love.*

The

Cemetery of

Forgotten Books

I STILL REMEMBER THE DAY MY FATHER TOOK ME TO THE CEMETERY OF Forgotten Books for the first time. It was the early summer of 1945, and we walked through the streets of a Barcelona trapped beneath ashen skies as dawn poured over Rambla de Santa Mónica in a wreath of liquid copper.

"Daniel, you mustn't tell anyone what you're about to see today," my father warned. "Not even your friend Tomás. No one."

"Not even Mommy?"

My father sighed, hiding behind the sad smile that followed him like a shadow through life.

"Of course you can tell her," he answered, heavyhearted. "We keep no secrets from her. You can tell her everything."

Shortly after the Civil War, an outbreak of cholera had taken my mother away. We buried her in Montjuïc on my fourth birthday. I can only recall that it rained all day and all night, and that when I asked my father whether heaven was crying, he couldn't bring himself to reply. Six years later my mother's absence remained in the air around us, a deafening silence that I had not yet learned to stifle with words. My father and I lived in a modest apartment on Calle Santa Ana, a stone's throw from the church square. The apartment was directly above the bookshop, a legacy from my grandfather that specialized in rare collectors' editions and secondhand books—an enchanted bazaar, which my father hoped would one day be mine. I was raised among books, making invisible friends in pages that seemed cast from dust and whose smell I carry on my hands to this day. As a child I learned to fall asleep talking to my mother in the darkness of my bedroom, telling her about the day's events, my adventures at school, and the things I had been taught. I couldn't hear her voice or feel her touch, but her radiance and her warmth haunted every corner of our home, and I believed, with the innocence of those who can still count their age on their ten fingers, that if I closed my eyes and spoke to her, she would be able to hear me wherever she was. Sometimes my father would listen to me from the dining room, crying in silence.

On that June morning, I woke up screaming at first light. My heart was pounding in my chest as if it feared that my soul wanted to carve its way out and run off down the stairs. My father hurried into my room and held me in his arms, trying to calm me.

"I can't remember her face. I can't remember Mommy's face," I muttered, breathless.

My father held me tight.

"Don't worry, Daniel. I'll remember for both of us."

We looked at each other in the half-light, searching for words that didn't exist. For the first time, I realized my father was growing old. He stood up and drew the curtains to let in the pale glint of dawn.

"Come, Daniel, get dressed. I want to show you something," he said.

"Now? At five o'clock in the morning?"

"Some things can only be seen in the shadows," my father said, flashing a mysterious smile probably borrowed from the pages of one of his worn Alexandre Dumas romances.

Night watchmen still lingered in the misty streets when we stepped out of the front door. The lamps along the Ramblas sketched an avenue of vapor that faded as the city began to awake. When we reached Calle Arco del Teatro, we continued through its arch toward the Raval quarter, entering a vault of blue haze. I followed my father through that narrow lane, more of a scar than a street, until the gleam of the Ramblas faded behind us. The brightness of dawn filtered down from balconies and cornices in streaks of slanting light that dissolved before touching the ground. At last my father stopped in front of a large door of carved wood, blackened by time and humidity. Before us loomed what to my eyes seemed the carcass of a palace, a place of echoes and shadows.

"Daniel, you mustn't tell anyone what you're about to see today. Not even your friend Tomás. No one."

A smallish man with vulturine features framed by thick gray hair opened the door. His impenetrable aquiline gaze rested on mine.

"Good morning, Isaac. This is my son, Daniel," my father announced. "Soon he'll be eleven, and one day the shop will be his. It's time he knew this place."

The man called Isaac nodded and invited us in. A blue-tinted gloom obscured the sinuous contours of a marble staircase and a gallery of frescoes peopled with angels and fabulous creatures. We followed our host through a palatial corridor and arrived at a sprawling round hall, a virtual basilica of shadows spiraling up under a high glass dome, its dimness pierced by shafts of light that stabbed from above. A labyrinth of passageways and crammed bookshelves rose from base to pinnacle like a beehive woven with tunnels, steps, platforms, and bridges that presaged an immense library of seemingly impossible geometry. I looked at my father, stunned. He smiled at me and winked.

"Welcome to the Cemetery of Forgotten Books, Daniel."

I could make out about a dozen human figures scattered among the library's corridors and platforms. Some of them turned to greet me from afar, and I recognized the faces of various colleagues of my father's, fellows of the secondhand-booksellers' guild. To my ten-year-old eyes, they looked like a brotherhood of alchemists in furtive study. My father knelt next to me and, with his eyes fixed on mine, addressed me in the hushed voice he reserved for promises and secrets.

"This is a place of mystery, Daniel, a sanctuary. Every book, every volume you see here, has a soul. The soul of the person who wrote it and of those who read it and lived and dreamed with it. Every time a book changes hands, every time someone runs his eyes down its pages, its spirit grows and strengthens. This place was already ancient when my father brought me here for the first time, many years ago. Perhaps as old as the city itself. Nobody knows for certain how long it has existed, or who created it. I will tell you what my father told me, though. When a library disappears, or a bookshop closes down, when a book is consigned to oblivion, those of us who know this place, its guardians, make sure that it gets here. In this place, books no longer remembered by anyone, books that are lost in time, live forever, waiting for the day when they will reach a new reader's hands. In the shop we buy and sell them, but in truth books have no owner. Every book you see here has been somebody's best friend. Now they have only us, Daniel. Do you think you'll be able to keep such a secret?"

My gaze was lost in the immensity of the place and its sorcery of light. I nodded, and my father smiled.

"And do you know the best thing about it?" he asked.

I shook my head.

"According to tradition, the first time someone visits this place, he must choose a book, whichever he wants, and adopt it, making sure that it will never disappear, that it will always stay alive. It's a very important promise. For life," explained my father. "Today it's your turn."

For almost half an hour, I wandered within the winding labyrinth, breathing in the smell of old paper and dust. I let my hand brush across the avenues of exposed spines, musing over what my choice would be. Among the titles faded by age, I distinguished words in familiar languages and others I couldn't identify. I roamed through galleries filled with hundreds, thousands of volumes. After a while it occurred to me that between the covers of each of those books lay a boundless universe waiting to be discovered, while beyond those walls, in the outside world, people allowed life to pass by in afternoons of football and radio soaps, content to do little more than gaze at their navels. It might have been that notion, or just chance, or its more flamboyant relative, destiny, but at that precise moment I knew I had already chosen the book I was going to adopt, or that was going to adopt me. It stood out timidly on one corner of a shelf, bound in wine-colored

dome above. I drew near and caressed them with the tips of my fingers, reading to myself.

The Shadow of the Wind
Julián Carax

I had never heard of the title or the author, but I didn't care. The decision had been taken. I pulled the volume down with great care and leafed through the pages, letting them flutter. Once liberated from its prison on the shelf, the book shed a cloud of golden dust. Pleased with my choice, I tucked it under my arm and retraced my steps through the labyrinth with a smile on my lips. Perhaps the bewitching atmosphere of the place had got the better of me, but I felt sure that *The Shadow of the Wind* had been waiting for me there for years, probably since before I was born.

That afternoon, back in the apartment on Calle Santa Ana, I barricaded myself in my room to read the first few lines. Before I knew what was happening, I had fallen right into it. The novel told the story of a man in search of his real father, whom he never knew and whose existence was only revealed to him by his mother on her deathbed. The story of that quest became a ghostly odyssey in which the protagonist struggled to recover his lost youth, and in which the shadow of a cursed love slowly surfaced to haunt him until his last breath. As it unfolded, the structure of the story began to remind me of one of those Russian dolls that contain innumerable ever-smaller dolls within. Step by step the narrative split into a thousand stories, as if it had entered a gallery of mirrors, its identity fragmented into endless reflections. The minutes and hours glided by as in a dream. When the cathedral bells tolled midnight, I barely heard them. Under the warm light cast by the reading lamp, I was plunged into a new world of images and sensations, peopled by characters who seemed as real to me as my room. Page after page I let the spell of the story and its world take me over, until the breath of dawn touched my window and my tired eyes slid

and listened to the murmur of the sleeping city. My eyes began to close, but I resisted. I did not want to lose the story's spell or bid farewell to its characters yet.

ONCE, IN MY FATHER'S BOOKSHOP, I HEARD A REGULAR CUSTOMER SAY that few things leave a deeper mark on a reader than the first book that finds its way into his heart. Those first images, the echo of words we think we have left behind, accompany us throughout our lives and sculpt a palace in our memory to which, sooner or later—no matter how many books we read, how many worlds we discover, or how much we learn or forget—we will return. For me those enchanted pages will always be the ones I found among the passageways of the Cemetery of Forgotten Books.

· 1 ·

A SECRET'S WORTH DEPENDS ON THE PEOPLE FROM WHOM IT MUST be kept. My first thought on waking was to tell my best friend about the Cemetery of Forgotten Books. Tomás Aguilar was a classmate who devoted his free time and his talent to the invention of wonderfully ingenious contraptions of dubious practicality, like the aerostatic dart or the dynamo spinning top. I pictured us both, equipped with flashlights and compasses, uncovering the mysteries of those bibliographic catacombs. Who better than Tomás to share my secret? Then, remembering my promise, I decided that circumstances advised me to adopt what in detective novels is termed a different modus operandi. At noon I approached my father to quiz him about the book and about Julián Carax—both world famous, I assumed. My plan was to get my hands on his complete works and read them all by the end of the week. To my surprise, I discovered that my father, a natural-born librarian and a walking lexicon of publishers' catalogs and oddities, had never heard of *The Shadow of the Wind* or Julián Carax. Intrigued, he examined the printing history on the back of the title page for clues.

"It says here that this copy is part of an edition of twenty-five hundred printed in Barcelona by Cabestany Editores, in June 1936."

"Do you know the publishing house?"

"It closed down years ago. But, wait, this is not the original. The first edition came out in November 1935 but was printed in Paris. . . . Published by Galiano & Neuval. Doesn't ring a bell."

"So is this a translation?"

"It doesn't say so. From what I can see, the text must be the original one."

"A book in Spanish, first published in France?"

"It's not that unusual, not in times like these," my father put in. "Perhaps Barceló can help us. . . ."

Gustavo Barceló was an old colleague of my father's who now owned a cavernous establishment on Calle Fernando with a commanding position in the city's secondhand-book trade. Perpetually affixed to his mouth was an unlit pipe that impregnated his person with the aroma of a Persian market. He liked to describe himself as the last romantic, and he was not above claiming that a remote line in his ancestry led directly to Lord Byron himself. As if to prove this connection, Barceló fashioned his wardrobe in the style of a nineteenth-century dandy. His casual attire consisted of a cravat, white patent leather shoes, and a plain glass monocle that, according to malicious gossip, he did not remove even in the intimacy of the lavatory. Flights of fancy aside, the most significant relative in his lineage was his begetter, an industrialist who had become fabulously wealthy by questionable means at the end of the nineteenth century. According to my father, Gustavo Barceló was, technically speaking, loaded, and his palatial bookshop was more of a passion than a business. He loved books unreservedly, and—although he denied this categorically—if someone stepped into his bookshop and fell in love with a tome he could not afford, Barceló would lower its price, or even give it away, if he felt that the buyer was a serious reader and not an accidental browser. Barceló also boasted an elephantine memory allied to a pedantry that matched his demeanor and the sonority of his voice. If anyone knew about odd books, it was he. That afternoon, after closing the shop, my father suggested that we stroll along to the Els Quatre Gats, a café on Calle Montsió, where Barceló and his bibliophile knights of the round table gathered to discuss the finer points of decadent poets, dead languages, and neglected, moth-ridden master-pieces.

Els Quatre Gats was just a five-minute walk from our house and one of my favorite haunts. My parents had met there in 1932, and I attributed my one-way ticket into this world in part to the old café's charms. Stone dragons guarded a lamplit façade anchored in shadows. Inside, voices seemed shaded by the echoes of other times. Accountants, dreamers, and would-be geniuses shared tables with the specters of Pablo Picasso, Isaac Albéniz, Federico García Lorca, and Salvador Dalí. There any poor devil could pass for a historical figure for the price of a small coffee.

"Sempere, old man," proclaimed Barceló when he saw my father come in. "Hail the prodigal son. To what do we owe the honor?"

"You owe the honor to my son, Daniel, Don Gustavo. He's just made a discovery."

"Well, then, pray come and sit down with us, for we must celebrate this ephemeral event," he announced.

"Ephemeral?" I whispered to my father.

"Barceló can express himself only in frilly words," my father whispered back. "Don't say anything, or he'll get carried away."

The lesser members of the coterie made room for us in their circle, and Barceló, who enjoyed flaunting his generosity in public, insisted on treating us.

"How old is the lad?" inquired Barceló, inspecting me out of the corner of his eye.

"Almost eleven," I announced.

Barceló flashed a sly smile.

"In other words, ten. Don't add on any years, you rascal. Life will see to that without your help."

A few of his chums grumbled in assent. Barceló signaled to a waiter of such remarkable decrepitude that he looked as if he should be declared a national landmark.

"A cognac for my friend Sempere, from the good bottle, and a cinnamon milk shake for the young one—he's a growing boy. Ah, and bring us some bits of ham, but spare us the delicacies you brought us earlier, eh? If we fancy rubber, we'll call for Pirelli tires."

The waiter nodded and left, dragging his feet.

"I hate to bring up the subject," Barceló said, "but how can there be jobs? In this country nobody ever retires, not even after they're dead. Just look at El Cid. I tell you, we're a hopeless case."

He sucked on his cold pipe, eyes already scanning the book in my hands. Despite his pretentious façade and his verbosity, Barceló could smell good prey the way a wolf scents blood.

"Let me see," he said, feigning disinterest. "What have we here?"

I glanced at my father. He nodded approvingly. Without further ado, I handed Barceló the book. The bookseller greeted it with expert hands. His pianist's fingers quickly explored its texture, consistency, and condition. He located the page with the publication and printer's notices and studied it with Holmesian flair. The rest watched in silence, as if awaiting a miracle, or permission to breathe again.

"Carax. Interesting," he murmured in an inscrutable tone.

I held out my hand to recover the book. Barceló arched his eyebrows but gave it back with an icy smile.

"Where did you find it, young man?"

"It's a secret," I answered, knowing that my father would be smiling to himself. Barceló frowned and looked at my father. "Sempere, my dearest old friend, because it's you and because of the high esteem I hold you in, and in honor of the long and profound friendship that unites us like brothers, let's call it at forty duros, end of story."

"You'll have to discuss that with my son," my father pointed out. "The book is his."

Barceló granted me a wolfish smile. "What do you say, laddie? Forty duros isn't bad for a first sale. . . . Sempere, this boy of yours will make a name for himself in the business."

The choir cheered his remark. Barceló gave me a triumphant look and pulled out his leather wallet. He ceremoniously counted out two hundred pesetas, which in those days was quite a fortune, and handed them to me. But I just shook my head. Barceló scowled.

"Dear boy, greed is most certainly an ugly, not to say mortal, sin. Be sensible. Call me crazy, but I'll raise that to sixty duros, and you can open a retirement fund. At your age you must start thinking of the future."

I shook my head again. Barceló shot a poisonous look at my father through his monocle.

"Don't look at me," said my father. "I'm only here as an escort."

Barceló sighed and peered at me closely.

"Let's see, junior. *What* is it you want?"

"What I want is to know who Julián Carax is and where I can find other books he's written."

Barceló chuckled and pocketed his wallet, reconsidering his adversary.

"Goodness, a scholar. Sempere, what do you feed the boy?"

The bookseller leaned toward me confidentially, and for a second I thought he betrayed a look of respect that had not been there a few moments earlier.

"We'll make a deal," he said. "Tomorrow, Sunday, in the afternoon, drop by the Ateneo library and ask for me. Bring your precious find with you so that I can examine it properly, and I'll tell you what I know about Julián Carax. Quid pro quo."

"Quid pro what?"

"Latin, young man. There's no such thing as dead languages, only dormant minds. Paraphrasing, it means that you can't get something for nothing, but since I like you, I'm going to do you a favor."

The man's oratory could kill flies in midair, but I suspected that if I wanted to find out anything about Julián Carax, I'd be well advised to stay on good terms with him. I proffered my most saintly smile in delight at his Latin outpourings.

"Remember, tomorrow, in the Ateneo," pronounced the bookseller. "But bring the book, or there's no deal."

"Fine."

Our conversation slowly merged into the murmuring of the other members of the coffee set. The discussion turned to some documents found in the basement of El Escorial that hinted at the possibility that Don Miguel de Cervantes had in fact been the nom de plume of a large, hairy lady of letters from Toledo. Barceló seemed distracted, not tempted to claim a share in the debate. He remained quiet, observing me from his fake monocle with a masked smile. Or perhaps he was only looking at the book I held in my hands.

· 2 ·

THAT SUNDAY, CLOUDS SPILLED DOWN FROM THE SKY AND swamped the streets with a hot mist that made the thermometers on the walls perspire. Halfway through the afternoon, the temperature was already grazing the nineties as I set off toward Calle Canuda for my appointment with Barceló, carrying my book under my arm, beads of sweat on my forehead. The Ateneo was—and remains—one of the many places in Barcelona where the nineteenth century has not yet been served its eviction notice. A grand stone staircase led up from a palatial courtyard to a ghostly network of passageways and reading rooms. There, inventions such as the telephone, the wristwatch, and haste seemed futuristic anachronisms. The porter, or perhaps it was a statue in uniform, barely noticed my arrival. I glided up to the first floor, blessing the blades of a fan that swirled above the sleepy readers, melting like ice cubes over their books.

Don Gustavo's profile was outlined against the windows of a gallery that overlooked the building's interior garden. Despite the almost tropical atmosphere, he sported his customary foppish attire, his monocle shining in the dark like a coin at the bottom of a well. Next to him was a figure swathed in a white alpaca dress who looked to me like an angel.

When Barceló heard my footsteps, he half closed his eyes and signaled for me to come nearer. "Daniel, isn't it?" asked the bookseller. "Did you bring the book?"

I nodded on both counts and accepted the chair Barceló offered me next to him and his mysterious companion. For a while the bookseller only smiled placidly, taking no notice of my presence. I soon abandoned all hope of being introduced to the lady in white, whoever she might be. Barceló behaved as if she wasn't there and neither of us could see her. I cast a sidelong glance at her, afraid of meeting her eyes, which stared vacantly into the distance. The skin on her face and arms was pale, almost translucent. Her features were sharp, sketched with firm strokes and framed by a black head of hair that shone like damp stone. I figured she must be, at most, twenty, but there was something about her manner that made me think she could be ageless. She seemed trapped in that state of perpetual youth reserved for mannequins in shop windows. I was trying to catch any sign of a pulse under her swan's neck when I realized that Barceló was staring at me.

"So are you going to tell me where you found the book?" he asked.

"I would, but I promised my father I would keep the secret," I explained.

"I see. Sempere and his mysteries," said Barceló. "I think I can guess where. You've hit the jackpot, son. That's what I call finding a needle in a field of lilies. May I have a look?"

I handed him the book, and Barceló took it with infinite care. "You've read it, I suppose."

"Yes, sir."

"I envy you. I've always thought that the best time to read Carax is when one still has a young heart and a blank soul. Did you know this was the last novel he wrote?"

I shook my head.

"Do you know how many copies like this one there are in the market, Daniel?"

"Thousands, I suppose."

"None," Barceló specified. "Only yours. The rest were burned."

"Burned?"

For an answer Barceló only smiled enigmatically while he leafed through turned slowly. Her lips formed a timid and trembling smile. Her eyes groped the void, pupils white as marble. I gulped. She was blind.

"You don't know my niece Clara, do you?" asked Barceló.

I could only shake my head, unable to take my eyes off the woman with the china doll's complexion and white eyes, the saddest eyes I have ever seen.

"Actually, the expert on Julián Carax is Clara, which is why I brought her along," said Barceló. "Come to think of it, I'll retire to another room, if you don't mind, to inspect this tome while you get to know each other. Is that all right?"

I looked at him aghast. The scoundrel gave me a little pat on the back and left with my book under his arm.

"You've impressed him, you know," said the voice behind me.

I turned to discover the faint smile of the bookseller's niece. Her voice was pure crystal, transparent and so fragile I feared that her words would break if I interrupted them.

"My uncle said he offered you a good sum of money for the Carax book, but you refused it," Clara added. "You have earned his respect."

"All evidence to the contrary." I sighed.

I noticed that when she smiled, Clara leaned her head slightly to one side and her fingers played with a ring that looked like a wreath of sapphires.

"How old are you?" she asked.

"Almost eleven," I replied. "How old are you, Miss Clara?"

Clara laughed at my cheeky innocence.

"Almost twice your age, but even so, there's no need to call me Miss Clara."

"You seem younger, miss," I remarked, hoping that this would prove a good way out of my indiscretion.

"I'll trust you, then, because I don't know what I look like," she answered. "But if I seem younger to you, all the more reason to drop the 'miss.'"

"Whatever you say, Miss Clara."

I observed her hands spread like wings on her lap, the suggestion of her paleness of her neck, the line of her lips, which I would have given my soul to stroke with the tips of my fingers. Never before had I had a chance to examine a woman so closely and with such precision, yet without the danger of meeting her eyes.

"What are you looking at?" asked Clara, not without a pinch of malice.

"Your uncle says you're an expert on Julián Carax, miss," I improvised. My mouth felt dry.

"My uncle would say anything if that bought him a few minutes alone with a book that fascinates him," explained Clara. "But you must be wondering how someone who is blind can be a book expert."

"The thought had not crossed my mind."

"For someone who is almost eleven, you're not a bad liar. Be careful, or you'll end up like my uncle."

Fearful of making yet another faux pas, I decided to remain silent. I just sat gawking at her, imbibing her presence.

"Here, come, get closer," Clara said.

"Pardon me?"

"Come closer, don't be afraid. I won't bite you."

I left my chair and went over to where she was sitting. The bookseller's niece raised her right hand, trying to find me. Without quite knowing what to do, I, too, stretched out my hand, toward hers. She took it in her left hand and, without saying anything, offered me her right hand. Instinctively I understood what she was asking me to do, and guided her to my face. Her touch was both firm and delicate. Her fingers ran over my cheeks and cheekbones. I stood there motionless, hardly daring to breathe, while Clara read my features with her hands. While she did, she smiled to herself, and I noticed a slight movement of her lips, like a voiceless murmuring. I felt the brush of her hands on my forehead, on my hair and eyelids. She paused on my lips, following their shape with her forefinger and ring finger. Her fingers smelled of cinnamon. I swallowed, feeling my pulse race, and gave silent thanks there were no eyewitnesses to my blushing, which could have set a cigar alight a foot away.

from

The Wednesday Letters

by

Jason F. Wright

"A lovely story: heartening, wholesome, humorous, suspenseful, and redemptive. It resonates with the true meaning of family and the life-healing power of forgiveness all wrapped up in a satisfying ending."
—*Publishers Weekly*

After thirty-nine years of marriage, Jack and Laurel Cooper died in each other's arms. For every week they were married, Jack wrote Laurel a love letter. When their grown children return to the family B&B to arrange the funeral, they discover the thousands of letters left behind.

The loss is not the only burden the children bear. Matthew, the eldest, has a strained marriage, Samantha is a single mother, and Malcolm, the youngest and the black sheep of the family, is returning home after a two-year absence. The letters they read tell of surprising joys and sorrows. They also hint at a shocking family secret—and ultimately force the children to confront a life-changing moment of truth.

CHAPTER 1

April 13, 1988

Wednesday Evening

Shortly after 11:00 P.M., Laurel slid under the maroon comforter and into bed next to her husband, Jack. She wrapped her strong arms around him from behind and worried at how easily she could feel his ribs. She remembered the many years when he'd weighed considerably more than she had.

Assuming Jack was already asleep, she began her nightly routine. Laurel breathed in deeply, expanding and filling every corner of her lungs. With her full lips closed tightly, she let the air slowly escape through her nose. It calmed her.

She closed her eyes; she prayed for each of her children—Matthew, Malcolm, Samantha—and for her only granddaughter, Angela, and for her only sibling, Allyson. Then she pleaded with God for more time and cursed herself for not being stronger. She ended her silent prayer with her first and last tears of the day.

"Hi." Jack's voice startled her.

"Hey you, I thought you were asleep." Laurel dabbed her eyes on her navy blue cotton pillowcase.

"Not quite. You feeling better?"

"I'm fine, but I'm leaving the dishes for Rain to get when she comes in tomorrow morning. I've got some heartburn still. Is it possible I'm too old for my own quesadillas?" She ran her right hand through a single, thinning patch of his grayish, silver hair and with her left hand rubbed her chest. "How 'bout you? Dizzy?"

"Nope, peachy."

"You're a horrible liar, Jack Cooper." Laurel slid her hand from his hair to his forehead.

"You're right. I blame the lump in my head." For eighteen months Laurel's seventy-one-year-old husband had fought an aggressive, inoperable brain tumor that, when discovered, was the size of a perfect shooter marble, but now resembled a Ping-Pong ball. The headaches were inconsistent; he could sometimes go two or three days without suffering. But when they returned, they brought pain, nausea, and vertigo that rendered him, for all practical purposes, tied to his bed. A bucket was never far away.

Though his doctors assured him that new drugs and therapies were rapidly being approved and readied for the market, Jack knew that nothing short of the hand of God would save him. And surely, he thought, God had better things to do than heal a small-town bed-and-breakfast owner. "Like bringing peace to the Middle East or getting my Chicago Cubs back to the World Series," he liked to tell Laurel. She'd heard the joke, and at least fifty variations of it, after every doctor's appointment since his initial diagnosis.

Their Inn, dubbed by the previous owners as *Domus Jefferson—The Home of Jefferson*—rested in the heart of the Shenandoah Valley, squarely between the Allegheny and Blue Ridge Mountains. Jack often said that if he survived judgment day and his Maker granted a choice between heaven and that hillside, the inner debate would be short.

On this spring Wednesday night, their beloved B&B was nearly empty. The only guest was Anna Belle Prestwich, wealthy heiress to a pet food manufacturing fortune. She was no doubt still awake, reading a romance novel in the $190 room for which she insisted on paying $300 a night. The room, decorated with expensive, handmade replica furniture from Thomas Jefferson's home at Monticello, overlooked the four acres of meadow sweeping from the back of the seven-bedroom Inn to the narrow creek at the forest line. When she finished three or four chapters, she'd escape outside with her husband's flashlight to walk her cat, Castro. She knew most people didn't walk cats, but most people weren't Anna Belle. And most cats didn't have weight problems.

Anna Belle had become a regular guest in the last several years, usually staying once or twice a month, though she'd been known to stay for up to ten days at a time. Her own home, a gorgeous, cavernous Southern mansion with four guesthouses—rumored by the chatty townsfolk to be worth anywhere from half a million to one hundred ten million dollars—was less than a mile away. On clear winter mornings, long after the trees had thrown their leaves to the ground, the tall silo of one of her unused barns and the roof of the white main house could be seen through the trees to the east.

The short, rotund, middle-aged Floridian met her husband, Alan Prestwich, on Miami Beach while the two were walking the shore very early one fall morning. He was collecting seashells for his secretary's daughter. Anna Belle was teaching Castro not to fear water.

Their encounter that morning led to an unlikely marriage, the first for both. Her new husband said he loved Anna Belle for being genuine, for having large, bold hips with personalities of their own, for her milky-white and buttery-smooth skin. But mostly he loved her dark red, almost maroon, and now gracefully graying hair. "The women I date," he had told her as they walked the boardwalk that first morning together, "wouldn't dare leave the house without dyeing their hair. But you, Anna Belle—you're a different fish in a sea of sameness."

"If I'm so wonderful," she answered as their first date ended, "how have all the good men eluded me?"

"They haven't. There just haven't been any good enough for you yet."

Six weeks later they were married.

During their third blissful year, Alan, the six-foot-two-inch

classic American entrepreneur and freshman pilot with adventur-
ous eyes, crashed his brand-new Ultralight into the Everglades. All
they recovered was his seventeen-inch Maglite, shining in three
feet of murky water two hundred yards from the plane's impact
crater. Since then Anna Belle carried the flashlight everywhere,
convinced it was a sign that someday she'd need it to find Castro
in the woods after a donut binge, to fend off a black bear, or to use
in some other noble effort.

Anna Belle had always been just north of overweight. When
she took a job at the local A&P stocking groceries, a gaggle of cruel
high school classmates began calling her just that: *A&P.* Just to
spite them she happily adopted the nickname. It stuck and she
never let it bother her. *Nicknames mean you matter,* she told herself.
Now A&P wondered what they'd call her if they knew she'd inherited most of her husband's fortune. She was a millionaire many
times over.

Not long after her husband's crash, Anna Belle picked Woodstock, Virginia, as her new home after seeing the town's name
circled in ballpoint pen on a Civil War Reenactment Association
brochure she found in one of her husband's filing cabinets. She
was a resident less than a month later. Jack and Laurel quickly be-
friended their quirky new neighbor. They privately speculated that
her purpose in life was to spend every penny of her wealth at their
B&B.

"Guess how much A&P tipped me for her evening milk," Laurel whispered.

"A hundred."

"Higher."

"Two-fifty?"

"Higher," Laurel repeated.

"Five hundred dollars?" Jack's voice rose.

"Five hundred and nineteen dollars and fifty-two cents. Everything she had in her purse."

"That's good money for finding milk in the fridge and pouring it in a glass." He sighed and fluffed his pillow. "The woman is incorrigible."

"She's harmless."

Jack rolled over and faced his wife, looking into her experienced brown eyes. His own once-lively eyes now appeared sunken in his head an extra quarter-inch and were guarded beneath by heavy half-moon circles. He'd inherited the raccoon eyes, as Laurel teasingly called them, from his father, but in the last year the dark circles had become even darker and appeared almost separated from his cheeks. His nose almost touched hers. "One of these days we have to tell her, you know."

Ever since A&P's first visit to *Domus Jefferson,* she'd left obscenely generous tips for the most mundane services, and there was no apparent system to her generosity either. If Jack carried a bag for her, she pulled a hundred-dollar bill from her purse. If Laurel left a mint on her pillow after turning down her bed, A&P slipped several twenties into her hand at breakfast. Once, when Laurel's doctors discovered an irregular heartbeat and tracked the defect back two generations, A&P stubbornly urged her to accept money for the medical bills, even though their health insurance paid ninety percent.

Another time, when Jack's twin brother, Joseph, was arrested on misdemeanor drug charges for the third time, A&P insisted on driving to Virginia Beach, bailing him out, and hosting him in her home because all the rooms in the B&B were booked. He stayed with her until he found work and a place of his own. Jack had been grateful to A&P and suspected the drive from Virginia Beach to Woodstock had been the longest of Joe's life.

The Coopers learned early in their relationship with A&P not to refuse her money. Their favorite guest was stubborn to a fault and would simply up the ante until they relented. Of course she had no idea they were simply giving the money to a children's shelter in southeast Washington, D.C. Without knowing it, in recent years the benevolent Anna Belle Prestwich had funded improvements to the shelter's kitchen, repaired a section of the dilapidated roof, and contributed the majority share to a new basketball court and adjoining playground with high, safe fences. There was even talk of creating a mini-library bearing her name.

"Sure, we'll tell her . . . Someday . . ." Laurel answered, but before Jack could respond, her eyes opened wide and she rolled from her side to her back, both hands grasping at her chest.

"Sweetheart!" Jack lifted his head. "What is it? Laurel? Sit up."

She struggled halfway up but fell back against the wooden headboard. "I've . . . no . . . breath . . . my chest . . . call . . ." The words were bursts of air.

Jack turned to the open window and called for A&P. "Mrs. Prestwich, come! Come quick! *Please!*"

But A&P was already on her evening walk, strolling along the creek's edge, counting stars in the reflection of the slow-moving water and chatting astrology with Castro as she tugged his leash.

"Oh, Lord, *help us!*" Jack cried out as Laurel's breathing became more pained and her eyes screamed. He looked toward the cordless phone cradle on Laurel's nightstand.

It was empty.

"My arm, Jack!" Laurel's eyes appeared to follow the pain from her chest down her left arm, past her hip, and to her foot. "Jack." She somehow made the single word sound like an apology.

"Dear Lord!" he called again.

Jack fought to sit up. He screamed into her face, "Laurel!" But neither her mouth nor her eyes responded. He swung his legs over the edge of the bed and put his feet on the floor. He could take only two steps before losing his balance and falling forward. The room spun around him and he careened into a brass floor lamp. As he tried to steady himself, the lamp gave way and he crashed on top of it, crushing the glass lampshade beneath his weight on the hardwood floor.

"Oh, Lord! Help us, Lord!" Jack lay on his back, hands flat against

the floor as he looked up at the ceiling. His head ached. Heavy tears pooled in his eyes. Turning his head to the side, his eyes found Laurel's old Tennessee license plate mounted on the far wall.

Gradually the room calmed and Jack pulled himself back onto their high, log-frame bed. Laurel's position was unchanged but her eyes were now closed. Her arms rested at her side.

"Laurel?" He put a hand on her cheek. "Sweetheart?" He placed his other hand on her quiet chest. "My sweetheart." Jack wrapped his arms around her and pulled her toward him. "My sweetheart," he said again. Carefully he rocked her listless body back and forth.

Moments later Jack tenderly placed his wife's head on her pillow.

Then from the top drawer of his nightstand, he pulled a pen, an envelope already containing several letters, and a piece of clean *Domus Jefferson* stationery. Using his King James Bible as a writing surface, he wrote:

April 13, 1988
My Dearest Laurel,

Ten minutes later Jack finished the letter, sealed it in the envelope along with the others, wrote a short note on the outside, and buried the entire stack somewhere in the New Testament. He returned the book to the nightstand, and he slid back toward his wife. Once again he carefully wedged an arm beneath her and pulled her to him. He gently brushed her soft, light-brown hair off her neck and whispered something in her still-warm ear. He kissed the corner of her forehead.

Then he thought of his son Malcolm and prayed he would survive the days ahead.

Finally, Jack gave in to his very last headache. And he slept.

It was 9:04 the next morning when a worried A&P and Castro finally pushed open the Cooper's master bedroom door. They found Jack and Laurel at peace in one another's cold arms.

CHAPTER 11

At 1:30 A.M. on Saturday morning, Matthew, Samantha, and A&P were sifting through boxes of paperwork at the dining room table when they heard a noise in the driveway and saw two sets of headlights illuminating the foyer. Samantha jumped from her seat and ran to the front door.

"You better stay," Matthew said to A&P as he stood to follow. "This will be ugly."

"Say no more. Castro and I will mind the store." After Matthew vanished down the hall, A&P picked the cat up from the floor and placed him on the table next to a pile of papers from a box. "Your hearing still good?"

Castro blinked twice.

Samantha charged down the porch stairs just as an officer opened the rear door of Samantha's cruiser.

Malcolm stepped out, handcuffed and angry. "Can you believe this, Sammie? They cuffed me!"

"Sorry, Malcolm," Keith said. "Your sister's orders."

"You don't have to apologize, Keith," Samantha said. "Malcolm, handcuffs are the least of your concerns right now. What were you thinking?"

She gestured at the cuffs and Keith quickly removed them.

"I'm a victim here, Sammie. It's police brutality! Everyone knows I bruise easily!"

"Shut it!" Samantha shrieked loud enough that back inside the Inn, A&P raised her eyebrows while Castro jumped off the table and scurried to safety underneath A&P's chair.

Samantha turned to the two officers. "So how bad is it? Where did you find him?"

"He was sitting outside the movie theater on Main."

"That's it?"

"Yeah," Malcolm answered for them. "I wanted to be first in line for *The Princess Bride.* I have a lot of movies to catch up on. Where's the crime in that?"

"The crime's the stolen car."

"Technicality."

She glared at Malcolm. Not pulling her eyes from him, she said to the officers, "I'm sorry, guys. This will *not* happen again."

"Don't worry," Keith smiled and tossed Samantha her keys.

"I appreciate that. And thanks for bringing my wheels back."

"Sure. 'Night, Sam. 'Night, Malcolm," Barry said, and then noticed Matthew standing on the porch. "Oh, hey, Matt."

"Hey, guys."

"Sorry about your folks."

"Thanks," Matthew said. "And thanks for bringing my kid brother back."

The two officers climbed into the second police car and drove away, free to laugh once they'd pulled onto Route 11. They did.

"Thanks, Sis. I was worried you'd be mad."

"Oh, I'm mad. I'm *more* than mad. I'm so ticked I could kick your butt from here back to Brazil."

"You know, that Keith guy is a real cat. I think he's sweet on you." Malcolm lowered his voice to sound extra sultry. "I could hear things in the car."

Matthew laughed from the front porch.

"Something funny, Matt?" she snapped over her shoulder, though her eyes remained trained on Malcolm.

"Hey y'all," A&P called through the screen door. "Come see what I found."

"We'll finish this later," Samantha said as Malcolm moved toward the steps and followed Matthew into the house. She held the door open and as Malcolm passed through, she smacked him hard on the back of the head with the hand that held her keys.

They gathered around the table. Malcolm gave A&P a hug, kissed her on the cheek and whispered, "Thank you, *for everything*" in her ear. She kissed him back.

"What'd you find, Anna Belle?" Samantha asked, still flustered.

"So I finished that last box, and I went back to the basement looking for the other boxes that had tax documents, the ones you asked for, Matthew, and I found this one." She pulled a box from the floor that was labeled *LC '48-'55*. "They're letters. From your dad to your mom. At least that's all I see in this box."

"I always thought those boxes were tax returns or something," said Samantha.

Matthew was puzzled. "I don't think I've ever seen them before. Are there more?"

"Don't know. I opened this one downstairs and brought it right up. Look in the back, boys, past the food storage, against the wall. The writing faces away so they look like regular boxes, nothing special."

For fifteen minutes Samantha and A&P read while the brothers made trips to the basement, retrieving boxes and stacking them around the dining room table.

After a while, A&P gathered her purse and her cat, kissed each of the Coopers good-bye and walked toward the back door. "Look around that table, kids," she said, turning to pull the door shut behind her. "You're all you've got." She wanted to say more, but didn't. Instead she talked to Castro all the way home.

Some letters they read quietly to themselves and solemnly returned to their envelopes like bodies to their caskets. Others they shared with the group. Many of the letters were uninteresting recaps of weeks spent together and apart. Many had stamps with postmarks from Richmond, Charlottesville, Norfolk, New York, and Memphis. Some had never been mailed and the children imagined they'd been slid under Laurel's pillows or into her latest book. They thought a select few seemed too personal to be finished and were silently mixed back into the high stacks.

Jack's letters appeared on photocopy paper, lined notebook paper, tattered spiral notebook paper, and hotel stationery. Several were even scribbled on napkins. Matthew found one stapled to a dollar bill and another written on the back of a flier announcing celebrity appearances at a special advance screening in Washington, D.C., of *Star Trek: The Motion Picture.*

November 14, 1979
Laurel,

It's Wednesday, but just barely! I'm sitting in the parking lot of the theater and all I've got to write on is a flier from tonight. I'm watching Joe tell jokes to some women across the street.

But time for the news of the night. You better be sitting. I MET WILLIAM SHATNER!

Did you hear that? I MET WILLIAM SHATNER!

I was sure when they said there would be cast members from the show at the theater tonight they meant George Takei or some extra whose name you never knew. But as Joe and I were standing around the lobby, he just walked in. What a sight! He's just as nice in person as I thought he'd be. Some think he's a windbag and maybe he is. I think he's always in character. And really, who isn't?

I wish I'd thought to have him sign something. I was so nervous when he shook my hand that all I could say was, "Live long and prosper." He looked at me and just smiled. He didn't say I was the most pitiful sixty-two-year-old man he'd ever met, but I had to be. Probably had no idea what to say to me. Who cares? I MET WILLIAM SHATNER!

By the way, the movie was amazing! I can't wait to take the boys on opening night. You'll come with us, right?

You know what? Joe was really grateful for the night out, Laurel. He wanted me to thank you. And thanks from me, too, for being so great about it. He needed it.

By the time you read this I will have told you all this already, probably more than once, knowing me. Who cares? I love you.

And are you still sitting down? I love you more than Star Trek.

Jack (Kirk)

November 3, 1948
Laurel,

I don't have long. It's lunch and all the boys can talk about is the election. Someone said one of the papers even had a headline that said *"Dewey Defeats Truman!"* I would love to get my hands on that for the collection.

I wonder what would have happened if the Republicans had let MacArthur run instead. I would have been more excited about voting, for sure. Still, I thought Dewey had it won. That silly train tour or whistle tour or whatever President Truman called it must have worked.

So here it comes. Brace yourself. YOU WERE RIGHT! And now we all get to suffer through four more years of a Democrat. I hope you're happy, Laurel Cooper. You win!

No matter. I still love you. Be you a Democrat, Republican— even Dixiecrat. (By the way, Joe told me he was voting for Strom Thurmond, even if he was the only one. Maybe if he'd stuck with Dewey, I wouldn't be wearing black today.)

Love you,

Jack

P.S. I'm a man of my word. Here's your $1. I guess the buck stops here after all.

April 22, 1970
To my *"exquisite bride,"*

What a trip! More than any letter I've written so far, I am writing this one as if years from now, when I am dead and gone, you will find this and need it to remember the details of this amazing week. And because you'll be old and tired and ready to meet me in heaven, you'll rely on these letters to fill in the holes from our years together. Maybe me leaving before you will cause you to lose your mind? To go crazy? Wishful thinking? I thought so.

I can count on one hand the number of experiences I've ever had that will live in my mind until they drag me from this earth. If I'm lucky, I'll get to take this one with me.

Last night, against all odds, we visited Graceland! No, we didn't just "visit" Graceland, did we, dear? Last night was our second in Memphis. You'd been begging me for years to visit and, at last, we had dinner on Beale Street. It's a trip I wouldn't have dreamt of even a few months ago. But when the stars align, you don't argue with them.

So tell me, Laurel Cooper, how and when did you become so convincing an actress? You had the King eating out of your hand! Who could have guessed it would go so well? Better than we planned?

I'll admit I'm still a little sore we didn't get a photo, but I understand their reasons. Can you imagine what would happen if we broke our promise and began telling people we got in to Graceland? That we met Elvis and Priscilla Presley? You were amazing. And, by the way, Elvis Presley made a pinkie promise with us. I bet that doesn't happen everyday.

It started at the security gate. You were divine. If I hadn't known you were fibbing, I would have broken into tears myself! You looked at that guard with such conviction and said you were thirty-six hours from certain death. "From what?" He laughed.

How did you keep a straight face when you told him you suffered from Asian Stone Lung Disorder? And your cough—your cough was brilliant! It sounded like you had marbles in your chest. I don't want to know when you found time to perfect that.

So he called into the house and got Priscilla on the phone. A miracle by itself, eh? When she asked him to escort us to the east entrance I thought I'd wet my pants. You took his hand and thanked him, and then while his mouth hung open, you kissed the back of his hand like it was the last thing you'd ever do in this life.

I bet you $1 that after he returned to his guard shack, he soaked his hand in rubbing alcohol for an hour.

Priscilla was so kind. So beautiful. She was also more gentle than I thought she'd be. What a true lady.

The tour was a bonus; I never imagined we'd see so much of the house. I would have liked to see upstairs, but I'm not sure my heart could have handled that much excitement.

After fifteen minutes, maybe a few more, as we stood at the door waiting for the guard to retrieve us, three cars pulled up. It couldn't have been more obvious who was in them if there had been a giant sign on top of the hood.

When the King got out and sauntered past us to kiss his wife, I swear you almost melted. She introduced us, explained why we were there and how close you were to death. His voice is still ringing—no singing—inside my head.

"You drove all the way to Memphis to meet us right as you're readyin' to meet your God?"

They should have handed you the Academy Award right then.

"It's always been my dream, Sir, to meet you and your"—cough, cough—"exquisite bride."

And Samantha thinks she's the best actress in the family?

"Bless you, woman. God bless your soul." He hugged you and kissed your cheek and you about buckled again. I wonder what he would have done if I'd popped him in the chin.

While the guard came up to escort us back off the property, Elvis asked one of his boys to remove the license plate from one of his cars. He did, and he brought it over to us. Upon the King's request, the same man pulled a pen from his coat pocket and both the King and Priscilla signed the back.

What a trip!

I don't remember much else about the last few days in Tennessee. What's to remember besides our fifteen minutes with the King of Rock and Roll and his "exquisite bride"?

I can't wait for the kids to hear this story. I suppose one day when we're gone, they'll find this letter and suddenly realize why there's a Tennessee license plate on our bedroom wall.

<blockquote>

I love you,

Jack Cooper,

husband of the only known

survivor of the Asian Stone

Lung Disorder

</blockquote>

92

P.S. I think when we get home and the license plate is in a safe place we should send a letter and apologize. What do you think?

Before Samantha finished the P.S., Malcolm and Matthew pushed their chairs from the table and raced one another from the room and up the stairs, jostling for position and shoving one another into the walls. As they neared the door to the master bedroom, Matthew slowed down enough to let Malcolm sneak by and through the doorway. Then from behind Matthew shoved his brother onto the master bed and lunged for the Tennessee license plate hanging on the wall.

"I can't believe it!"

"What's it say?" Malcolm asked, rolling off the side of the bed, regaining his balance, and snatching the plate from his brother.

"'To Laurel and Jack,'" Malcolm read. "'Enjoy your last days. Elvis and Priscilla, 1970.'"

"Mom and Dad said this was a souvenir from their trip, not an autograph. I can't believe we didn't ever see this!"

"What a trip," Malcolm said, shaking his head. "What a trip."

The boys returned to the dining room to find Samantha crying.

"Sis, what's wrong? What'd you find?" Matthew asked.

She held up a letter. "Dad was asking Mom what she thought would happen to the Inn when he was gone."

Matthew and Malcolm sat.

"When was it written?" Matthew asked.

She looked at the date. "Last year, June."

"Think he knew?" Malcolm asked.

Samantha didn't answer.

"Dad and I actually talked about this over the holidays," Matthew said. "He told me Alex Palmer—"

"Who?" Malcolm interrupted.

"Dad's attorney. He's in Front Royal. Dad said Alex helped him update his will last year, I imagine after things got really bad for him. He and Mom have some money hidden away in a couple of accounts. Not a lot. Most of it went into this place. Dad had an insurance policy so Mom would be all right when he died." Matthew hesitated. "Anyway, there's some work to be done. I'll get with the attorney."

"Dad couldn't have imagined they'd be leaving us at the same time," Samantha mused.

No one spoke.

"And the Inn?" Malcolm eventually asked.

"We're supposed to split everything three ways, including the Inn. It will take a while to sell, though, they usually do. Unless . . ." Matthew looked at his sister across the table. "Unless one of us wants to run it. Dad made it clear that was his first choice."

Samantha and Malcolm stared at their brother.

"You know I can't," Matthew answered their looks. "I can't leave New York. I've got clients, interests. And you know Monica's not going to live in Woodstock."

Samantha and Malcolm both nodded.

"I could. I guess." Samantha tried to smile.

"You're a cop," Malcolm said. "Your heart isn't in running a bed-and-breakfast."

Samantha knew he was right.

"What about keeping it anyway?" Malcolm asked. "Rain could run it."

"Maybe for a little while, Mal, but she'll be gone soon. No way Nathan stays in Woodstock for very long." Samantha regretted saying what they already knew. "Sorry." She rubbed Malcolm's forearm.

He smiled. "Forget it." He squeezed her hand. "Let's read."

from

The Well and the Mine

by

Gin Phillips

In a small Alabama coal-mining town during the summer of 1931, nine-year-old Tess Moore sits on her back porch and watches a woman toss a baby into her family's well without a word. This shocking act of violence sets in motion a chain of events that forces Tess and her older sister Virgie to look beyond their own door and learn the value of kindness and lending a helping hand. As Tess and Virgie try to solve the mystery of the well, an accident puts their seven-year-old brother's life in danger, causing the Moore family to see their community in all its complexity, and learn a fuller definition of compassion.

1 Water Calling

Tess   AFTER SHE THREW THE BABY IN, NOBODY BELIEVED me for the longest time. But I kept hearing that splash.

The back porch comes right off our kitchen, with wide gray-brown boards you can lose a penny between if you're not careful. The boards were warm with heat from the August air, but breathing was less trouble than it was during daytime. Everybody else was on the front porch after supper, so I could sit by myself, nothing but night and trees around me, a thin moon punched out of the sky. The garden smelled stronger than the leftover fried cornbread and field peas with onions. And the breeze tiptoed across the porch, carrying those smells of meals done and still to come, along with a whiff of Papa's cigarette and snatches of talk from out front. It was the best time of the day to sit with the well, its wooden box taking up one corner of the porch and me taking up another.

I loved the well then.

I leaned against the kitchen door and looked through the wood posts of the railing, even though I couldn't see anything but black. There weren't clouds covering that slice of moon or the blinking stars, but they still didn't throw enough light. The light from the kitchen door let me see to the edge of the porch. But the woman she didn't see me, I guess. Sometimes the Hudsons down below got their drinking water here—they didn't have their own well—and I thought it was Mrs. Hudson at first. But she was like a bird, and this was a big, solid woman, with shoulders like a man. She climbed the stairs two at a time. Then she hefted that heavy cover off the well, like a man would, with no trouble.

I couldn't see the baby at first 'cause it was underneath her coat. But she took it out, a still, little, bean-shaped bundle wrapped up like it was January.

I could have reached her in five or six steps. If I'd moved.

She held the bundle like a baby for a minute, tucked under her chin like she was patting it to sleep, whispering. The blanket fell back from its head, and I saw a flash of skin. Then she tossed it in. Just like that. Not long after the splash—just a quiet, small sound—she lifted the square cover again and fit it back into its cut-out space, settling it in with careful little touches. Even with all that weight, the porch boards didn't creak when she left.

The splash wasn't so much the sound of the baby hitting the water as it was the yelp my well made; it sounded shocked and upset knowing something inside it was awful. Wanting my help.

I felt my teeth dig into my bottom lip, maybe drawing blood, but I was quiet as a mouse and stiller than one. Mice scatter like marbles.

After I don't know how long, Virgie pushed at the door. I knew the sound of her feet on the floorboards. I scooted up, and she poked her head out.

Virgie wore cicada shells, pinned like brooches at her collar. We used to wear them all the time, rows of them like buttons down our shirts during summer, but since she'd be going to the high school next year, she wouldn't wear them to school no more. She'd gotten too old.

"We're all out front—why're you hidin' back here?" She looked down at me, then up at the well. "I swear, you'd marry that well if it'd give you a ring."

Beyond it was pitch. The kind of black you think you'd smash into like a wall if you were to run into it. The woman was gone.

"Some lady threw a baby down it," I said.

Virgie looked at me some more. "Down the well?"

I nodded.

She laughed, and I knew without looking at her she was rolling her eyes. "Hush up and go inside."

"She did!" My mouth was still the only part of me I could make work—it felt like I'd taken root in the floorboards.

"Nobody's been near our well. Quit tellin' stories."

She knew I didn't tell stories. I swallowed hard, and it loosened my feet. I pushed myself up and took a step toward the well. "She was, too! A big woman with a baby in her arms. And she threw her baby in without sayin' a thing."

"Why would she do it with you watchin' her?" She said it like she was grown-up, not just fourteen and only five years older than me.

"She didn't see me." My voice was high, and my chest ached with wanting her to believe. At the well, I tried to slide the cover back, but it was too heavy. "Look in here."

"You don't have a lick of sense."

"Virgie . . ." I was begging.

She looked a little bit sorry, and came over to stroke my hair like Mama did when I got upset. "Were you daydreamin'? Maybe you saw somebody walk by the porch and you imagined it."

"No. We have to look in the well."

"How do you know it was a baby?"

"It was."

"Was it cryin'?"

"No."

Finally she looked worried, looking out at the night instead of looking at me. "Somebody mighta thrown some garbage or somethin' in there outta spite. But who'd do it?"

"It wasn't garbage. It was a baby. And I'm gone tell Papa."

I turned and marched off toward the front porch, going back through the house with Virgie right behind me. That last week in August, the nighttime wind was enough to cool your face but not enough to carry off a day's worth of sunshine. The sun was twice its normal size at the tail end of summer. We'd all stay outside until it was about time to go to bed. Papa and Mama were in their rockers, with Mama shelling peas and Papa smoking a cigarette. They were lit from the lights in the den—Papa was still smudged, even though he'd washed and washed his face and hands. He was bluish instead of black.

Virgie announced it before I could. "Tess says she saw somebody throw somethin' in the well."

Papa caught my arm and pulled me over to him. He curled one arm around my waist and set me on his lap. I reached down and felt the leather of his hand, snuggled closer to him.

"What did you see, Tessie?"

"It was a woman, Papa. And she had a baby in her arms, wrapped up, and she threw it in the well." I spoke slowly and carefully.

Papa used his knuckle to nudge my chin up. "It's awful dark out back. Maybe you just saw some shadows."

I shook my head until a curl popped loose from my ribbon. They were always coming loose. (Virgie had gotten her blond angel hair bobbed to her shoulders and she curled it like in magazines at the newsstand.)

"I saw her. I did. I was sittin' by the door, and I was gettin' too chilled so I was gone come in, but then I saw her walkin' up the back road. I didn't know her, but she was comin' right straight here, so I sat and waited and nearly said hello to her when she got to the steps, but then she didn't walk towards the door at all. She stopped at the well. She looked around, moved the cover, and tossed a baby in. And then she left."

"I think maybe somebody tossed an old sack of trash or maybe a dead squirrel or somethin' in there just for meanness," Virgie said.

I looked straight at Papa. "I swear, it was a baby."

"Don't ever swear, Tess," he said with a little shake of his head, looking back toward the dark. Two lightning bugs went off at the same time.

Mama looked puzzled, the lines in her forehead deeper than usual. "Why would she throw it in our well?"

Virgie looked mad at me. "Now you've upset Mama."

Albert I DIDN'T BELIEVE HER WHEN SHE TOLD ME. EVEN though her face was white as chalk and her eyes big as silver dollars. They've all got Leta's eyes, wet-earth eyes. Rich like good soil.

She was always a dreamer, but the girl never made up tales. Didn't look for attention. Some girls her age did that, though. And it didn't make no sense what she was saying. Land's sake, no woman'd toss her baby in a well.

But Tessie kept on about it, nagging me. Not like her one bit. There was a sweetness about Tess. She liked to please, didn't like to upset nobody. Not to say she lacked spirit. She'd bend, but that girl wouldn't ever break.

The night she was so wrought up, I lifted the cover off and looked down in there, but she just said, no, I couldn't see proper without any light. I ain't never home during good daylight when I'm on the day shift, so I told her the next night I'd shine a lamp down there and we'd have a good look.

If there's one thing I'm good at, it's shining a light in the dark. I know the dark. I'm stained with it. It's caked permanent in the creases of my elbows, in the lines on my hands, under my fingernails. I can taste it deep down my throat and I cough it up in the middle of the night. Up in the daylight, men sort and clean the coal we bring up, picking out slate while they squint in the sun and crisp their skin, and I am no part of them. I wasn't that much older than Tess when I started tending to the mules, getting used to hours without the sun, headed down and down and down, my boots clomping along next to the hooves. I got used to the heft of an axe and the smell of burned powder and the burn of dirt falling in my eyes and every bit of it was in pitch black with the fuzzy weak lamps on our heads and on the walls making just the slightest dent in that pitch. So you would think this one thing my baby girl asked of me, this one time she wanted me to shine my light in the dark for her, I could have done it as easy as breathing. Wouldn't have cost me nothing but a little time. But I didn't have it for her. Thought there wasn't nothing to it, no reason to give up those few precious minutes of sitting in my chair and letting the day roll off me.

'Course then the next day afore I got home, Leta felt the bucket hit something when she was getting water to boil the corn. Pulled up the bucket, and it had a blanket in it.

Leta   I THOUGHT SURE WE'D GET SICK. CAN'T EVEN THINK about it—the poor little thing. But in the drinking water.

I waited 'til Albert came home from work. When I pulled up the blanket with the morning water, I knew Tess had been telling the truth, and we'd all ought to have known that. She's a good girl. I didn't let the bucket down again, just sat the blanket on the side of the well. I hurried to the store and bought a new tin bucket, too, thinking I wouldn't want to be using that one again if the night passed like I thought it would. When the girls and Jack came home from school, I told 'em we'd be having cornbread and milk for lunch. Couldn't do much else with no water, and I wasn't touching what I'd already drawn.

"You found it, didn't you, Mama?" Tess asked. Her voice was hoarse, and she was chewing on her braid. I didn't get on to her for it.

"Found a blanket. We'll get it all straightened out when your papa comes home."

"You believe me now, don't you?" She seemed concerned, like I might actually still say she was making things up. I knelt down, took the braid from her mouth, and kissed her forehead—dirty already from who knows what.

"I believe you, Tessie. Get washed up for dinner."

I poured fresh milk over dewberries for dessert. None of them complained.

With the last touches of sun in the sky, backs sore from peering in and eyes tired from squinting, we thought we'd have to find some netting. Then, when we'd lost count of how many times we'd tried, Albert pulled it up with a tiny, pale arm hanging over that tall tin bucket. It was naked, and it was a boy.

My mama died when I was four, and I remember her laying there with the blood soaking the sheets and the sweat not even dried off her face. I saw the baby she'd had die two days later, its face blue and its body shrunk like a dried peach. I've seen men carried home from the mines with eyes torn out and arms just about ripped clean off still hanging by pieces of skin. None of it stuck in my head like that little swollen thing that used to be a baby hanging over the side of our water bucket.

Virgie I THOUGHT SHE MADE IT UP AT FIRST. TO FEEL IMPORTANT.

Tess was the hatefulest thing when she was little. Mama would leave me watching her, and she'd wander off and I'd have to drag her back just a'screaming. The white fence around the yard had to be built to keep her in. Then she just learned to un-latch the gate. She wouldn't mind worth a flip. And after Jack came, she didn't ever get tired of tattling on him. But she never told lies.

She couldn't sleep that first night, and I didn't even say a word to her. I thought she was being silly. I lay there mad at her, listening to the sleep sounds coming from the rest of the house. Papa's snores. Mama's restless shifting—even in her sleep, she couldn't be still. Jack murmuring as he rolled over. The train whistle outside. Wind against the glass panes. But no sounds from Tess. She was lying there awake just like I was, and I didn't even say good night.

The next night, the night the baby had laid on top of our well covered in its still-damp blanket and the sheriff had come and carried it off in a basket, Tess didn't say a word to me. I watched her for a while, tucked into a little S with her back to me in bed, and I inched over to her, even though the pins for my curls stuck into my head when I moved.

"Tessie," I whispered. It tickled her ear, and she hitched her shoulder up.

"What?"

"Y'alright?"

She didn't answer me. I poked her with my big toe, aiming for the sole of her foot.

"Stop."

I jabbed at her calf next.

"Stop it, Virgie," she hissed. "You'll draw blood with that toe."

"Roll over."

She did, looking sleepy and put-upon. Her pretty black curls were spread over the pillow, falling into her face, too, so that she kept swatting at it. She kicked at my feet. "Keep your feet on your side."

I slid my hand over, just touching her arm.

"Keep your hand on your side," she whispered.

I flopped over on my back, looked at the ceiling for a while, then met her wide-open eyes. "I'm sorry I didn't believe you."

"I know," she answered, and that was that.

I woke up hours later to her thrashing around, moonlight streaming through the window. She'd pulled the sheet off me and twisted our top quilt, the one with the bluebirds on it, around her like a cocoon. Her legs were flailing, and she was talking nonsense. I couldn't make it out.

I said her name softly. "Tess, Tess, wake up." I touched her shoulder, shook her lightly. "Tess, it's alright. Wake up." A little louder. Still mumbling and tossing. I felt her forehead for fever.

"Shhh. You're having a nightmare."

She rolled to the left suddenly and, *thump*, she was on the floor. I lurched toward her, peering over the bed. Soon a head popped up.

"I fell out of bed," she announced. She shifted and the moon hit her so that I saw the tears streaked down her face. I didn't say anything.

She looked around, looked at me, looked at her empty pillow, and repeated—for no good reason— "I fell out of bed."

My mouth started twitching then, and so did hers, and soon we were sniggering so hard we had tears rolling down our cheeks. She climbed back in bed, and we both struggled for breath.

Finally we settled down, tugging the covers back over us, burrowing down in the feathers, and I felt sleep pulling me down. "I dreamed I was in the well with him," she whispered, but before I could answer, we were asleep.

Albert THE THING WAS, YOU'D HAVE TO WORK TO TAKE THE cover off the well. That cover was a square of wood no bigger across than from my elbow to my fingertips—just big enough to let the bucket go down—but it was wedged tight into its slot. I'd sawed it out of the center of the wooden piece that made the well top, before I nailed the top onto the wooden sides, so the cover always fit snug. Rain blowing on it over the years had warped it, making it mighty hard to pry out, especially on muggy days. Plus it was heavy, thick pine, unwieldy enough to make Leta gasp when she moved it, strong as she is for a woman. You had to grab it just right, wedge your fingers underneath, and lift in one great pull. And I worried that only somebody who'd seen us do it, who knew how it worked, would be able to get it off in one tug. Wouldn't be no spur-of-the-moment thing.

Tess I MISSED MY WELL. THERE WASN'T MUCH SPACE IN the house for five people, even when one of them was as small as Jack. At the front of the house was the sitting room on one side, with a door leading out to the porch; the bedroom where Virgie and I slept was on the other side, with another door to the porch. Our bedroom connected to Mama and Papa's bedroom through a big, open space with no door—from our pillows we could see just their heads, small and still against the big curlicued headboard at night—and off from their bedroom was the dining room connected to the kitchen. Five rooms for five people. The two fireplaces, one in each bedroom, shared a chimney, and we closed the doors during the winter so only the bedrooms stayed warm. No use wastin' heat, Mama would say as she went around tugging doors shut, them scraping against the frames before they clicked, *shiiii-shunk*. Jack got his own bed because he was the boy, but it was just a pallet near the fireplace. Ours was a feather bed like Mama and Papa's. Not from our chickens—Grandpa Tobin made it for Mama when she got married. I felt sorry for those hens, naked and cold and wanting to curl up with us in their stolen clothes.

But, still and all, Jack had his own place. Mama had her rosebushes. Virgie took off for long walks in the woods. Papa had the mines . . . even though he wasn't really alone there and sometimes walls fell in and killed bushels of men. He still had a place that was separate. And I had my well.

The well was really only a planked-in holeful of creek—a part you could keep and watch and have, like a June bug on a string. Underground, a little stream trickled into the well, stayed awhile, and went on its way, but you could pull up a bucket of that stream anytime you wanted. After sunset, the back porch was quiet and closed in by trees; the sounds of frogs and crickets reminded me of when I stayed too late swimming and had to run back for supper. Of course, I couldn't swim in the well water, but sometimes I could draw up a bucket and take a swallow straight from it, even though Mama told me it wasn't right to drink from something that hung where bugs could land and crawl on it. (I saw flies land on the tea pitcher sometimes when we'd forget to lay the cloth back over it, but Mama'd just wipe it off and still pour from it. But that was inside and different somehow.) She always poured the water from the tall, narrow well bucket to the inside bucket, shorter and squatter, and only from there would it splash into our washbowls and pitchers and cooking pots. But I'd take long, cool mouthfuls at night, then dump the rest back into the well's black mouth.

I was the only girl who would swim in the swimming hole, and first all the boys went off for a while, telling me they'd never come back if I was gone be mucking around, but they did. Papa didn't like me swimmin' with them, but I started taking Jack with me, and that made him feel better. Jack'd play with the boys if they were around his age, and I'd stay separate, seeing how deep I could dive, pushing my arms back and forth through the water to make butterfly wings, letting my hair swirl around me and pretending I was a sea witch with seaweed hair.

But you couldn't go to the creek just anytime. The well was always there, waiting. I could smell the water in it, and I knew that at the bottom it was cool with slippery moss like on creek rocks. I used to stare down it and imagine that we might scoop up mermaids or talking fish with the bathwater.

Don't throw the baby out with the bathwater.

After the dead baby, I didn't like to stare down there anymore. I didn't think about talking fish. I thought about the nightmares. They started with me diving down underwater with my eyes open, and then I'd see a baby reaching for me. I was running out of breath, but I couldn't swim up because the baby's hands were in my hair, and I couldn't move him. I couldn't see his face at first, but when he lifted his head, I could see he had black holes where his eyes should be. It was the first nightmare I could ever remember when I woke up. And I'd remember it all day long until I fell asleep the next night.

Virgie PAPA SAID IT WAS AN ABOMINATION WHAT THAT WOMAN did. That God would judge her. But I wondered did that woman think she couldn't scare up enough food for another lunch, and with the others barefoot and winter coming, this would be the better way? Or did he just cry and cry until she thought her head would burst? Was it that she couldn't handle it anymore, that this was the fifth or the sixth or the tenth little one underfoot and it was more than she could stand?

I wondered did Mama ever stand by the well and think how her life could be easier.

Tess NOBODY TALKED MUCH AT SUPPER THAT NIGHT. MAINLY the forks and knifes went *clank, clank.* Then there'd be chewing, tea-swallowing sounds, a little smacking from Jack. Then Mama'd say, "Don't smack your food, Jack." Then *clank, clank.* Good yellow squash and sugar snap peas and some fried ham and biscuits. We hadn't had ham for months and we didn't even have to kill a pig, Mama said. She told us to tell the Hudsons thank you when we saw them.

Finally, Papa wiped his mouth. He was always the first one finished. "Enjoyed it, Leta."

We all echoed him, telling Mama how good it was. She smiled and said "thank you" as fast and soft as she could. Then she looked at my plate and frowned. "You're not eatin' much, Tessie."

"You still upset?" asked Papa.

I didn't know how to answer that. "Just not too hungry."

"You're leavin' your ham on your plate?" asked Jack, sounding like it was the same as taking my head off and leaving it there.

"'Course not," I said. I started to nibble on the ham again. You didn't leave anything on your plate.

"Don't know why a baby in the well's got anything to do with eatin' ham," he muttered.

"You shouldn't talk about the poor thing like that, Jack," said Mama. "It was a child, same as you or Virgie or Tess."

Papa put his hand on mine, the one that wasn't holding my fork. "Tessie, you got every right to be upset. Must've been a shock to you. Still is. It don't matter about the ham."

"I'll eat it," said Jack.

I kicked at him under the table. "Not if I eat it myself, you little pig."

But that kick didn't have much feeling behind it; I only managed it out of habit. I couldn't get worked up over Jack being a bottomless pit. I knew Papa was feeling guilty. Mama, too. Wasn't no reason to—I knew they didn't have space in their heads to be thinking on babies being in the well.

"I'm gettin' better 'bout it," I told Papa.

"I heard you tossin' in your sleep," Mama said. "You were whimperin' like a baby."

I put my fork down. "Just bad dreams," I said.

"Aren't y'all thinking about it?" Virgie asked, looking back and forth from Mama to Papa. "'Bout who did it? Why she'd do it?"

Mama and Papa looked at each other but didn't really answer. I couldn't bring myself to pick up my fork again, even if Jack did get to eat my ham. Mama noticed that I'd wiped my mouth and given up.

"Sure you don't want her ham, Albert?" asked Mama. Papa shook his head and flicked his hand toward Jack. "Go on then, Jack," she said.

"I can't imagine," Virgie said as Jack forked my ham.

"But eat your squash," Mama said to me.